RED FLAG
# BLUE
# MEMBER

# RED FLAG
# BLUE
# MEMBER

*the Colonel*
*saves*
*the Lao People's Democratic Republic*

## ROBERT FOX

**FOCUS BOOKS ASIA**

through

## TRAFFORD

• Canada • UK • Ireland • USA •

Note for Librarians: A cataloguing record for this book is available from Library and Archives Canada at www.collectionscanada.ca/amicus/index-e.html
ISBN 1-4120-7789-3

*Trafford's print shop runs on "green energy" from solar, wind and other environmentally-friendly power sources.*

# TRAFFORD
## PUBLISHING™
*Offices in Canada, USA, Ireland and UK*
This book was published *on-demand* in cooperation with Trafford Publishing. On-demand publishing is a unique process and service of making a book available for retail sale to the public taking advantage of on-demand manufacturing and Internet marketing. On-demand publishing includes promotions, retail sales, manufacturing, order fulfilment, accounting and collecting royalties on behalf of the author.

**Book sales for North America and international:**
Trafford Publishing, 6E–2333 Government St.,
Victoria, BC v8t 4p4 CANADA
phone 250 383 6864 (toll-free 1 888 232 4444)
fax 250 383 6804; email to orders@trafford.com
**Book sales in Europe:**
Trafford Publishing (uk) Limited, 9 Park End Street, 2nd Floor
Oxford, UK oxi 1hh UNITED KINGDOM
phone 44 (0)1865 722 113 (local rate 0845 230 9601)
facsimile 44 (0)1865 722 868; info.uk@trafford.com
**Order online at:**
trafford.com/05-2686

10 9 8 7 6 5 4 3 2

To the President of the Lao People's Democratic Republic, the Prime Minister, all the unprimed Ministers, all the Deputy Prime Ministers, all the Deputy Ministers, all the Minister Equivalents, all the Deputy Minister Equivalents and Acting Deputy Minister Equivalents. To the Politbureau, the Central Committee, the Mass Organizations, the police, the army, the people's militia, the navy (yes, there is one), the air force (ibid), the National Assembly, the broad masses of the Lao multi-ethnic peoples, and above all to the indivisible and indissoluble Party.

Let the party begin.

This is a work of fiction. Unless they exist in a parallel universe, there is no Colonel to save the Lao PDR, or the rest of the world for that matter, there is no Willie Winkle to blow it up, no Souk to betray all that can be betrayed, no Black Princess hiding in the folded wings of history, no Rupert Sweetheart to lead his congregation into death or salvation. Real policemen in the Lao PDR would never dream of behaving like the fictitious Chantavong. And, of course, there is nowhere in the world remotely like Vientiane.

# About the Author

Robert is an Englishman who has lived most of his life in Asia. He speaks Lao, Thai, French, Malay and Indonesian. Awarded a doctorate for his studies among the hill peoples of Laos and Thailand, he lectured in anthropology at the University of Singapore before joining the United Nations High Commissioner for Refugees. Often stationed in remote hardship stations, where he witnessed all too frequently man's inhumanity to man, he escaped from hardships and dangers into the world of writing. He considers 19 years within the hullabaloo of the UN the best apprenticeship for a writer of the absurd and recognizes that while he can take humour to its rococo limits, he can never quite equal the black comedy of the real world.

Taking a very early retirement from the UN, he joined the British Foreign and Commonwealth Office in 2,000 as Head of the British Trade Office in the Lao People's Democratic Republic. He spent a year in northern Viet Nam advising the government on poverty reduction, before returning in 2005 to live and write in Laos and neighbouring Thailand.

Robert, under the name Robert Cooper, has written widely on the region, including the well-known *Culture Shock Thailand* and *Thais Mean Business*. He has also written cultural guide books to Bahrain, Bhutan, Croatia, and Indonesia, and the ethnography *The Hmong*. *Red Flag* is the second in the series chronicling the Colonel's quixotic attempts to right the wrongs of the world. Robert Fox is also author of *Professor Dog*, a comedy set in Singapore.

1

———————

# Memo from *upstairs*

**"Hey, Godfrey. You remember William Winkle, don't you?"**

Nigel spoke with just the faintest trace of a sneer, indeed, not really a sneer at all, more the hanging whisper of imperialism long past, or, as Nigel would have preferred to think of it, an affable lilt on a class-dialect inflection. Only Godfrey would pick up the inflection as a sneer, and even Godfrey had got used to it. Godfrey big-heartedly allowed that Nigel, the silly old sod, was too old a dog to change now. Anyway, it was just as well to have some sort of barrier between them, and the occasional hint of insolence from Nigel gave Godfrey license to be himself, in fact to be a bit more than his real self. Anyway, given their histories and occupation, they got on well enough. Godfrey was, after all, Nigel's assistant, and if there was any insolence in the air, it was Nigel's view that Godfrey put it there.

As he spoke, Nigel lifted his pasty, middle-aged, seriously white face from close scrutiny of a short one-pager in his in-tray, pushed his multi-focals further up his thin, bony nose and pointed his nose across in the direction of Godfrey, his much younger, taller, healthier, more relaxed and indelibly blacker colleague in the Foreign Office. *Sorry*, that should of course read Foreign *and Commonwealth* Office, the italics being mine, the Colonel's chronicler, not those of the British Government.

As Nigel, Godfrey, even the Colonel for that matter, and every right-thinking, left-thinking, lateral-thinking or even non-thinking, person knows, there were very good reasons for changing the FO letter-head to put a C between F and O, and to hell with the expense. The big C stands for the big Commonwealth. But putting in the big C, even if it did take quite a few decades of reflection before it got there, was much more than just an adjustment of company name. The intermediate C obliges Her Majesty's men to pout and round their lips between F and O, a preparation for a multi-racial embrace that proves there is nothing racist or elitist about the Establishment's most prestigious institution, at least not any more. Racial and ethnic harmony in the service of Her Majesty is a fact, and a fact personified by Godfrey who, as it happens, is black, with a IIi from Hull, and Nigel who, as it happens, is white, with a First from Oxford. And although at this time Nigel has a bigger desk than Godfrey, Godfrey will, one day, when he reaches Nigel's maturity of status and time in service, have a desk every bit as big as that of Nigel, in fact, Godfrey was bloody sure, he would have an even bigger desk than Nigel.

"William Winkle?" replied Godfrey. "Whose he when he's at home?" Godfrey pulled back a well-pressed, pink cuff-linked sleeve and looked at his gold Gucci watch. Nearly lunch time, thank God.

"The only Trink bank robber not caught when the four of them escaped twenty-nine plus years ago." Nigel spoke slowly, clearly and concisely, as he always did when speaking to the natives and the immigrants; if only, he thought, they would make the same effort, then everybody might understand each other better. "And he's not at home as it happens, Godfrey. Report here from the Head of our British Trade Office in Laos, says he's in Laos and engaged in nefarious activities, bringing disrepute to the fair name of the United Kingdom."

"Twenty-nine years ago? Do me a favour. *You know full well I was sucking on me mammy's titties* at the time. Why the interest now? Why not just forget the poor bugger? Or is he black? Laos is in Africa, isn't it?"

Nigel gave an almost inaudible sigh and let Godfrey's language pass. "Actually, not, Godfrey. Not black that is. As for Laos, I think you're mixing it up with Lagos. That's in Africa, isn't it? Laos is some tiny landlocked place of absolutely no interest to the UK, east of Burma and north of Thailand."

"Laos? Can't say it dominates me old world view. Absolutely no interest to the UK, eh? Not Commonwealth then?"

"Foreign."

"That's a relief. Let the Embassy there handle it."

"Don't have one. Ambassador covers it from Bangkok – that's in Thailand by the way, also foreign. In Laos, we just have a one-man Trade Office. Chap called Welder runs it. He says in this report that Winkle, that's the bank robber, is boasting that there's only thirty days left under the Statute of Limitations, then he can't be tried even if he takes the first plane back to London. Welder seems to think the FCO or somebody should do something about it."

"Well," said Godfrey and paused. He knew full well that Bangkok was in Thailand, after all he'd been on holiday to Phuket, hadn't he? Was that an edge of sarcasm on Nigel's voice? Godfrey ran gold-ringed fingers through the cropped fuzz of hair on his well-tended head. Time to pull Nigel down a peg. "How come you know this Winkle bloke's a bank robber if he's never been tried?"

"All right," said Nigel, concedingly lifting a hand to hook his black-rimmed specs higher up on the bridge of his nose, exposing an off-white shirt-cuff, slightly frayed and loosely buttoned, "*suspected* bank robber. But the evidence is pretty overwhelming against Winkle, and why's he boasting now that we can't touch him, if he didn't do it? The four Trink robbers, *suspected* robbers, escaped by helicopter while on their way to stand trial. The other three were recaptured and tried and found guilty, and they blamed as much as they could on Winkle – including four murders committed during the robbery, all of them, by the way, of blacks. One black security guard and three black baggage handlers."

Godfrey's eyebrows rose. "Black Commonwealth or black foreign?"

"Welder doesn't say."

"And you can't remember?"

"No. Sorry."

"And so you should be, Nigel."

"Memo came down from upstairs."

"Probably Commonwealth then. Most blacks were then, anyway. Bit of a coincidence 'though, wasn't it Nige? Only blacks being killed. No whites injured?"

"The hoist was at Heathrow," Nigel replied by way of explanation. He had long ago given up trying to get Godfrey to stop referring to him by the diminutive, since it only seemed to encourage him.

"So?" Godfrey's youth clouded his understanding of ethno-history.

"Cleaners. Baggage handlers. Godfrey, we are talking about the 1970s. One black cleaner and three black baggage handlers."

"So, only killed blacks, did he? I suppose that's why nobody has bothered to extradite this Winkle? Racist is he?"

Nigel sighed inwardly. "All this, Godfrey, was in 1975. A bloody civil war was just coming to an end in Laos, it was the height of the Cold War, and the communists had just taken over Laos and two of its neighbours, Viet Nam and Cambodia."

"History," Godfrey, born the year after the 1975 takeover and liberation of Indochina, rejoined with a dismissive tone. "Same thing was happening in Ghana and lots of African countries. But that's all changed now."

"Not quite all. Laos remains one of the few countries in the world still Communist with a C as big as the one in Commonwealth. Under control of the Lao People's Party since 1975. There was no legal system for years after the takeover, and even now there are no real procedures for extradition to the UK. That's presumably why Winkle chose to hide out there. Welder suggests he took a large part of the loot with him. None of it was ever recovered."

"Yer, well, that makes sense. But not worth doing much about it *now*, is it?"

"To tell the truth, Godfrey, there's not a lot we can do. But *upstairs* thinks we should be *seen* trying to do something about it."

If there was one concept that Godfrey fully understood, it was *upstairs*. Being young, gifted and black, and working class of origin would not protect him should he ever be foolish enough to anger *upstairs*. He made a "Hmm…" and stroked his fashion-stubble, thinking out loud. "Why not write one of your nice memo's to this British Ambassador in Bangkok asking him to pop up to Laos and collar this Winkle bastard before he kills any more blacks. Get the Lao police to hand him over, drag him screaming onto a plane – I suppose they have planes? – and bring him back for trial. Offer the Lao some development deal – usual stuff, couple of Land Rovers for Foreign Affairs and the Ministry of Justice."

"Even if the Lao would play ball, the only way to the UK would mean a change of plane in Bangkok or Hanoi. Nobody wants to ask the Vietnamese for a favour and the Thais, informally of course, say no. Seems Winkle used the proceeds of the bank job to set himself up quite nicely in Laos, and with some influential Thai and Lao partners. And a couple of Land Rovers would be a drop in the ocean compared to what Welder says Winkle already hands out."

"So, what you need is some clever little patsy to hop over and kidnap the bastard and get him to some friendly Commonwealth place like Singapore?"

"Yes. Wouldn't use the word kidnap, of course. But that's precisely what we need." Nigel looked over the top of his glasses at Godfrey.

"Well, don't look at me, Nige. What about this Trade Office bloke? Can't he do it?"

"Can't be trusted."

13

"You saying the FCO employs people it can't trust?"

"No, Godfrey. I would never say that. But he's on a local contract and gone native. He's employed as part of the economy drive. Saves giving a proper salary and benefits. Didn't even bother to have him vetted. Point is, I suppose, that in addition to being *called* Welder, Welder actually *was* a welder, and you know what welders are like."

"Can't say I do, Nige. Never met one. You don't mean, do you Nige, that Welder's *working class!?*"

"Now Godfrey, let's not start on that. We are all working class now."

"But some of us are more working class than others, right Nige? Like welders, I suppose. Anyway, the fact is that I have never met a welder, so I don't have a clue what they are like."

"Well, you wouldn't meet them, not now everything's plastic. But they used to be all over the place. And believe me, if you were in the company of a welder, you knew it. Practically had a language of their own, and 95% filth it was too. Anyway, that's a bit beside the point. Thing is there's practically no UK trade with Laos, and our political relations, as far as we have any, are monotone. And the Ambassador in Bangkok just wants to leave things like that – quiet. Last thing he wants is to have to go to Laos and ask for something when he knows the answer will be 'we'll think about it', which means a resounding no."

"How do you know all this? I've never even heard of Laos."

"It says so here. All in one page. Whatever else he is, Welder's a good, concise writer."

"Be no good here then," said Godfrey.

"Well," said Nigel, waving the memo as he sighed, this time audibly, for Godfrey's benefit. Why was it so difficult to get Godfrey involved in even the simplest project? Blowed if Nigel knew. "This might just be one page but there's a *For Action* sticker on it, *both* of our initials at the top of the sticker and the Head's initialed it personally at the bottom *and* scored a line under *Action*. So *somebody* has to do something about it."

"I know what I'm doing about it. Going for lunch. Coming? I mean, we can hardly send in the SAS can we, Nige?"

Nigel slowly took off his glasses, wiped his nose with a hanky that had seen better days and uses, and looked thoughtful. "You know, you may have something there, Godfrey."

"Send in the SAS to a commie country? You joking?"

"Not the SAS exactly. Thing's got to be low-key, so when it flops, no repercussions – especially not back to this room. As you said Godfrey, we need a patsy. Not one of our lot, but somebody a lot higher sounding than the Welder fellow. Somebody who actually thinks he *is* the SAS – or better. And I think I know just the bloke."

"Well, it's your generation stuff," said Godfrey. "Some retired Colonel, I suppose?"

"Bingo," said Nigel, smiling a row of national-health assisted ivories.

"So," continued Godfrey. "We get some nutcase old colonel who thinks he can right the wrongs of the world to go to Laos, cock everything up, and then explain to *upstairs* over a cup of tea why in this case he just happened to fail completely – or, even better, why what might look like failure was in fact a great success, bearing in mind the international situation."

"My goodness, Godfrey. You *do* understand. You know, I was always in favour of opening up to the red-brick universities and pluralism. You've hit the nail right on the head. And, as I said, I know just the man who would jump at the chance of a free trip to Laos and death or glory when he gets there."

"Good," said Godfrey. "Give him a call and invite him for a banana. But after lunch."

# 2

# East of Everest

**And so, before you could say "kukri", our Colonel found himself East of the Himalayas.** A little off his beaten track, although come to think of it, he was rarely on any track he had already beaten. After all, the Colonel was lots of things, but he was not a sadist, and if he had beaten a track once, why go back and beat the poor thing again? The Colonel was approaching his sixth decade of this his twenty-third reincarnation, but the world was still a place of novelty and freshness to our Colonel, and he loved the new as much as the old, and there was always a new track, always a detour worth following. And as long as life continued that way, the Colonel remained as ageless as the world itself.

Of course, Man being the creature he is, black or white, Oxford or Hull, *mauvaise langues* will have absolutely no problem turning a hero into a madman. Such was the shared opinion of those poor desk-bound souls, buried deep in the Foreign and Commonwealth Office who – difficult to believe as this may be – after a two cups of tea and gingerbicky briefing on the Willy Winkle case to the Colonel, doubted the Colonel had really ever been on any track at all. Still, as Nigel and Godfrey readily agreed after wishing the Colonel good speed on his mission and closing the door on his back, a ticket to Laos and reasonable expenses for the Colonel's stay there, let *them* off the hook, posed absolutely no budget problems, and might even be a bit of a laugh.

Even before the Colonel had been escorted out of the portals of the FCO to the real world, Godfrey and Nigel had sent an electronic memo *upstairs* and everywhere East of Suez, to say appropriate action was under way to secure the extradition of Willy Winkle and the recovery of Britain's good name in the Lao People's Democratic Republic.

The appropriate action consisted of sending one Gurka Colonel, retired, and his kukri, to do what the might of the British constabulary had failed to do almost three decades previously. Of course, this was not just any old retired colonel, it was *the* Colonel, a man who, awake or asleep, on or off track – as sure as the sun rises in the West and sets in the East – knows precisely where he is at every instant of his being. A man like the Colonel simply does not *need* tracks. *De facto*, tracks are created by others. Tracks get in the Colonel's way. And the Colonel's ways are all his own.

The Colonel, cunning linguist that he is, knew he would need a direct path to the Lao language. One track the Colonel could have taken would have required him to spend one year studying the language at London's School of Oriental and African Studies. By the end of the year, the Colonel would have spoken pretty reasonable modern Lao and Willie Winkle would be thumbing his nose, or other parts of his anatomy, at the great laws of England and selling his story to a tabloid for more money than Godfrey and Nigel together earned in a decade. Such a course of action would have been unacceptable to FCO budgets, would have ensured failure of the objective, and was *not* the way of the Colonel.

Instead, the Colonel took a linguistic detour that cost fifty pee and a minute of his time. While standing in the economy-class check-in line at Heathrow, the Colonel flicked through a Lonely Peanut Lao phrase book, bought second-hand for fifty pee with a price tag still on it of six and ninepence. This was enough for the Colonel's computer-like brain to recall that, although he had never been to the country in this life, he already spoke the Lao language fluently, knew the culture, give or take a millennium, and knew the lie of the land. This was achieved by one whole minute of perfect *om* stillness; which surely only the Dalai Lama and the Colonel could manage at Heathrow. During this little detour of the mind, our Colonel had run through each of his twenty-three reincarnations. His mind's cog-wheels, like the Buddhist roulette wheel of life and fortune, spun, slowed, and clicked to rest at reincarnation number thirteen, Royal Courtier, Lu-ang Prabang, Kingdom of Laos, seventeenth century. Of course, the Colonel knew that the Kingdom was now the People's Democratic Republic. But mountains don't change. And the Lao People's Democratic Republic, when the Colonel bumped down onto the tarmac in the year 2005, was still mostly mountains. So that was okay then.

At 19.30 hours, just one hour later than scheduled, and seven hours distant from the wine bar at which Godfrey and Nigel sat finishing off their shepherd's pie luncheon with a second round of house red, their shoes, patent, shiny black in the case of Godfrey, Clerk's everlasting in the case of Nigel, sprinkled with the genuine sweep-away sawdust that was enjoying a temporary round of London fashion, the Colonel stepped from a little turbo-prop onto a short metal stairway and almost knocked Kimpen down the steps. Well, she was awfully small, and he had not been expecting to be met. The Colonel liked to enter an arena quietly and anonymously. It was usually quicker and saved any awkward questions.

"Good evening, Colonel," said the sweet little voice of sweet little Kimpen, blowing his cover, had anybody been listening and interested, before the Colonel had even set foot on sweet little landlocked Laos, sleepy little southern neighbour of China, long western neighbour of Viet Nam, cornered northern neighbour of Thailand, bejungled eastern neighbour of Burma and almost forgotten northern neighbour of

Cambodia. That's a lot of neighbours to stay friendly with, and for a country with no coastline, no port, no railway, no industry and no major highway, sleeping, or pretending to sleep, was, to the Colonel's finely-honed sense of political analysis and judgment, the very best way of keeping those five encircling tigers from gobbling up sweet little Laos. Thus, although more used to serve under the Union Jack than the Hammer and Sickle, the Colonel, being British and favouring the underdog, arrived in Laos inclined to like the country. That was, after all, why he had come to save it from the likes of Winkle.

Paused at the top of the roll-out steps, the Colonel looked in vain for the mountains that do not really begin for a hundred bumpy kilometers outside the capital. In fact, all the Colonel could see, held up in front of his eyes, was a very large bunch of flowers. Suddenly, the Colonel had a cold feeling down his backbone, and froze. The passengers piled up behind him.

The pilot opened the door of his over-air conditioned cockpit and wanted to know what all these people were doing bunched at the exit. Perhaps, the Colonel thought to himself, he should, after all, have brought along Kaziman Limbu and D.B. Rai to watch his back and deal with such unknowns as flowers.

"Good evening," the flowers said again sweetly and innocently, as passengers jostled the Colonel's behind and a hostess took his arm to move him forward on his quest.

"Come on mate. I don't wanna sprout roots up 'ere," came to the Colonel's ear from behind. Kaziman would certainly have spoiled that one's holiday with a simple unseen three finger jab to the mate's backbone; Kazi would have stopped short of taking the man out for keeps but he would never allow disrespect to his Colonel to go unpunished. But Kaziman was not there and the Colonel had to swallow the insubordination.

"Good evening," the Colonel said to the flowers to buy time for his mind to find an appropriate detour around the huge bunch of talking foliage. As first man out, or almost out, of the plane, the Colonel feared he might have made a tactical error before even setting foot on the tarmac. Always watch your back. That was the Colonel's motto. Always watch your back. Always. If not now, then later, somebody, somewhere will want to put a kukri through it.

Yet even a man like the Colonel, one of the few hot-bloodied beings in the world above water who could naturally switch to fish-eye vision and get a 360 degree view of the world, even if that world got a bit distorted in the process, could not be permanently tuned-in to his superhuman faculties. Yes, even the Colonel occasionally needed back-up. And the Colonel's back-up usually came in the tightly-muscled form of Kaziman Limbu and D.B.Rai – two men the Colonel could trust to destroy a whole continent before allowing harm to come to a single one of the diminishing number of hairs on the Colonel's sacred head. The Colonel liked men like Kaziman and D.B.; he trusted no others. Well, if he needed them, he had only to call and they would appear – as they had done on Goose Green, where they had saved him from the gnashing jaws of the hounds of death*. He had left them behind because the FCO would not cough up for two extra economy class air tickets.

Ever vigilant, the Colonel was all too aware that there could, right now, be a deadly syringe pushing through the flowers, leveled at his heart. And later there would be a small report to the Embassy in Bangkok saying an aging British tourist had a heart attack when entering Vientiane airport. Moving with the speed of light, the Colonel caught the flowers off guard and hurried down the steps to the tarmac, clutching his single black bag which, apart from his beloved kukri, contained all the retired gurka was likely to need to save Laos, or the Lao People's Democratic Republic as it now called itself, from the dregs of British society. After all, this was a small country with a long name and a small bag and a long knife seemed appropriately sufficient. The flowers crowded him in hot pursuit.

"Piss-pot," said the flowers. To stop their infernal chatter, the Colonel finally took them and cradled them in his free arm. Heavy for flowers, he thought.

"Piss-pot," the young lady of the flowers repeated. "You need visa."

A white Land Rover Discovery with erect but flagless pole on its bonnet stood on the runway, the driver's door open, the driver's left leg dangling out lazily and, the Colonel thought, dangling just about as sarcastically as a leg could dangle. "Better do as the young lady says and give her your piss-pot, before she runs out of flux and butt-welds you." *Butt-welds*. **Contact password**. Welder was in communication rather sooner than expected. The Colonel handed over his passport and Kimpen, looking about fifteen, ran off with it. She threw over her shoulder, "Your cookies in the flowers."

As the few other passengers made their way across the tarmac and formed a queue for visas, a light rain cooled the Vientiane May evening to a pleasant Mediterranean temperature.

"Cookies?" questioned the Colonel.

"The Lao don't pronounce the 'r'," said Welder sleepily. "She means 'your kukri's in the flowers'."

"They pronounced the 'r' in the 17th century," countered the Colonel, his thirteenth reincarnation detouring to the front of the roses and carnations and the forefront of his mind.

"Well, they bleeding well don't now," said Welder, without even a "sir" to soften his insubordination. The Colonel let it pass. No choice. Can't change the whole world all at once. Especially welders. Welder looked like a welder if anybody did. The blue tinge to his otherwise healthy and suntanned features gave him away as much as his choice of words and accent. Late fifties, and with a body that suggested occasional maintenance exercises, the man might have passed for handsome if it were not for the tell-tale bags under his eyes, a flabbiness under the chin and a delay of eye-movement that tended to turn a casual look into the kind of stare a stranger would avoid like the plague in an East-end pub five minutes to closing time. It was clear enough to the Colonel that Welder had spent too much of his life behind the mask. Whether that made him a full-blown welder,

---

**\*See** *Red Fox Goose Green* for an account of the Colonel's adventures in the jungles of an English village.

forever in flux between two poles, and a man who could only be trusted to betray, remained to be seen. In the meantime, the Colonel never provided a man, or a woman for that matter, with benefit of the doubt. The Colonel expected his men to demonstrate they were worthy of his trust; until and unless that point was reached, the Colonel's automatic defences would be fully switched on. Welder had nothing to fear, as long as he did not step one inch out of line.

The Colonel climbed in the back seat and rummaged through the flowers for his kukri. A gurka always feels naked without his kukri, especially a retired gurka on a special mission to save the world. Welder blatantly turned and watched with that fixed stare, grinning, as the ex-gurka warrior wasted no time in pulling down his trousers.

To comply with airline regulations, the Colonel's kukri had traveled alone in the hold, the Colonel's only non-accompanied baggage, until retrieved on landing by Kimpen. Laos was not Nepal and carrying a kukri too obviously might invite questions that the Colonel preferred to avoid, like *Hey, matey why you got a kukri too obviously tied to your leg?* The Colonel carried a kukri because, although he did not seek confrontation, he was always prepared to meet it when required by circumstance. With trousers down, he strapped the leather sheath holding the famous gurka curved knife to the outside of the right leg. With belt and trousers again secured, an easy-pull Velcro tab below the right hand pocket would permit immediate access whenever the Colonel needed to whip out his kukri and nip off a head or two.

So far, things seemed to be going surprisingly as they should, although his London briefing had said nothing about an under-age girl greeting him with flowers or an insubordinate driver. The Colonel would have preferred Kaziman to be stationed behind in an independent vehicle, for security, but his super-keen senses told him danger lay ahead of him, not behind. Anyway, the Trade Office only had one car.

In two minutes, Kimpen was back with the passport stamped with a courtesy diplomatic visa, and she had snuggled in beside Welder, clutching his arm as if claiming ownership. The Colonel noticed her breasts were still but pimples in a tee-shirt and revised her age downwards to an early fourteen. Welder on the other hand must have been the Colonel's age contemporary to the day. Welders were like that. So, the Colonel knew, were some colonels.

The Colonel was not one to judge by name alone. But welding had once been a union closed-shop, and the Colonel knew that anybody named Welder would, if he could be bothered to trace his ancestry at all, have descended from a welding ancestor. To be fair about it, the Colonel knew that welders came in many shades, but the Colonel also knew that welders are always essentially blue and not to be meddled with too far. They suffer from dramatic mood swings caused by a lifetime hiding their faces in blue head shields, to retard the onset of baggy blue arc-eyes and ultra-violet radiation burns, which, like too much masturbation, eventually cause blindness and impotence. As a result they have a pallid blue hue to their skin, which a man with the Colonel's perception could pick out at a thousand paces, and a penchant towards the sexually stimulating, believing fervently in getting it up while they still can.

The Colonel, far from being a snob, placed welders in the upper echelons of the occupational castes. They were, of course, ultimately unpredictable and they were, of course, ultimately unacceptable socially, but, in the past, they had proven useful because of the skills acquired over years and generations, skills essential to a heavy-metal Empire. With their heads locked away from the world inside blue screens, welders tend to have blue thoughts, often depressive, sometimes paranoid, sometimes ecstatically happy. Such thoughts are induced by the intensity of the blue arc and the crackle of the reddish-blue spatter coming from it. A welder under the Colonel's direct command had confided in him that welders see things in these hand-held fireworks that other men might never see in their lives, sometimes pure entertainments, naked young girls and boys fornicating, sometimes frightening predictions, and, occasionally, answers to riddles that might net them tidy sums of money. Welders play with power at their direct control. The Empire's most skilled and alienated welders, the Colonel had heard it said, could make a ship's joints to

23

a standard that would pass any test but be guaranteed to split apart under the sea's pressure and sink the battleship they held together… if the price is right. The Empire needed its welders for its logistical and military machine, but wars, like everything else, were bred by opposites, and the Empire's wars, like those wars that succeeded the Empire, bred in roughly equal amounts, both loyalty and betrayal. The Colonel awarded Welder the accolade of being a part of the same history that had produced a fully loyal and trustworthy colonel personifying all that was right and proper. It was in the nature of things that the same process would produce the Colonel's opposite in the form of Winkle, and also produce an equivocal being, a role which in the context of the current operation, seemed to the Colonel, to be filled by Welder.

Welders, like any other caste or occupation, were subject to change. The mushrooming of the universal plastics industry had atrophied the number of real welders in the world, but done nothing to reduce their blueness. Adapting their skills to other employment was difficult, they had spent too long in isolation within their masks. Those remaining as welders continued to speak their vulgar blue trade language of Weldish and group together in loose associations. Some found work in the torture business. There is nothing like a blue flame to loosen a grey tongue. The Colonel, a Child of the Empire if there ever was one, appreciated the skills that had helped Britannia rule the waves. But he knew well enough that only a fool would trust a welder, and the Colonel was nobody's fool.

"What were you doing before becoming a driver with the British Trade Office?" the Colonel asked in reasonable tones, as if making polite conversation.

"I'm not a driver. I'm Head of Office. And before that I was a welder."

"I see," said the Colonel, not really seeing at all. From welder to Head of a diplomatic trade office in, apparently, one easy jump. Surely there was more to that than met the eye. Or there should be, the Colonel thought, but perhaps there wasn't. With a certain reluctance he remembered how the world had been turned upside down, with the colonies of the Commonwealth now calling the shots and the sudden democratisation of government offices, that were British in an entirely different sense to what he had been brought up to respect as British.

"What's it to be then?" Welder asked the Colonel as they pulled away from the airport towards Vientiane town, his right arm free to hug Kimpen because of the British Government's magnitude in giving him an automatic gearbox. "Dinner first or bomb first?"

# 3

# Winkle and Co.

**"Welder just messaged through. The eagle has landed.**
Welder says the Colonel looks a bit disorientated. He doesn't sound too
impressed with the man we sent to save Laos." Nigel was looking at an
email on his screen.

"Well," replied Godfrey. "Way I see it, the Colonel looked a bit disorientated even here in London. And it's not as if we were looking for
anybody too impressive for this job. After all, all the Colonel's got to do
is deliver a letter and hang around for a few days so we can say he is fol-
lowing-up. I expect he'll enjoy himself in Laos. Sounds a bit like Nepal.
Another land of mountains and hill tribes, and the Colonel has never
been there."

"Yes he has," countered Nigel.

"When?" asked Godfrey.

"I think he said it was the mid-seventeenth century."

The Colonel and Welder shared a Britishness marked by a superficial tolerance of differences rather than homogeneity. To the Colonel, Welder was a mass of contradictions. Of course he would never say that to his face. To Welder, the Colonel belonged to an obsolete past. Two world wars had been fought, with limited success, to destroy the power of the colonels, not British welder against British colonel of course, both sides had used surrogate Germans to fight against. Welder saw himself as a realistic and pragmatic getter done of what needed doing. The Colonel saw himself as a solid child of the Empire, somebody you could rely on when the chips were down, somebody who would, if it came to it, risk his life for what was right. The Colonel was the perfect blend of imperial fact and imperial fiction, fused inseparably into one person. Not just any person, but a colonel of the modern world who maintained meaningful values. A warrior who embodied the wisdom of ages. A man to trust.

Apart from his kukri, the Colonel carried no gun or other bulky armament and preferred to rely on the reflexes of tightly-packed muscles and finely-tuned senses. His personalised survival kit fitted neatly into the inside pocket of a stylishly bulletproof and flameproof parka, designed to withstand plus or minus eighty centigrade and to turn inside out and double as a well-armed dinner jacket, which bore a lapel pin in which was coiled a spool of nylon thread on a pre-shrunk solar-powered grappling hook that expanded to full size at the touch of a tiny button and with the help of which the Colonel had twice climbed Everest's North Face, once going up and once when he thought he was going down. The amazing lapel pin also contained, believe it or not, an extra-strong condom with a capacity for five hundred litres of non-corrosive fluid and an inflatable mini-sub capable of holding twenty gurka frogmen. Next to the lapel pin was, if one ignored the inch-thick lenses, a seemingly innocuous pair of infra-red enhanced night-vision eyeglasses. From the little he had been told in London, the Colonel might well need most of this collection to bring this mission to a successful conclusion.

The Colonel did not, of course, smoke. But clipped to his bush-shirt sleeve pocket was a cigarette lighter which would, when required, snap into two primed three-second fused mini-grenades. One would blow three people apart at ten metres and one would release a cloud of smoke mixed with a gas that would send a whole platoon into deep slumber for hours. The lighter was not quite standard issue. Neither was the packet of twenty cigarettes he carried in the left pocket of his bush shirt. Each one contained a deadly mini-dart invented by the Colonel himself on the basis of his knowledge of the Malaysian blowpipe, the dimensions of which he had effectively reduced from two and a half metres to the length of a king-size filter cigarette, with absolutely no reduction in accuracy and with greatly improved killing power. Each of the ten tiny white darts would blow a precise ten centimeter whole in any target at twenty metres, and each brown dart would release on penetration one of the world's most powerful and rare poisons. This military masterpiece, the miniature blowpipe, had been achieved through the Colonel's application of one of the basic truths of existence: it is not the length that counts but what you do with it.

What the Colonel had done with it was to replace the common-or-garden deadly poison on the blow-dart tips with a highly-secret poison more deadly even than nicotine, a poison found only in virgin forests on the Indonesian Archipelago. Made from mixing the semen of a freshly castrated male chieftain, the venom of a cobra in full strike and the breast milk of an enraged orang utang, this poison could drop an elephant in its tracks. It was fiendishly difficult to obtain.

Since the Colonel was not traveling incognito and this was to be a come-as-you-are party, he did not feel an immediate need to check his makeup set with its hair dye, false eyebrows and moustache, lipstick, eye shadow, rouge, anti-wrinkle cream, vitamin E stay-harder-and-longer cream, clip on eyelashes, inflatable bra and artificial vagina. In fact the trial he was about to face would require many of these items. Noting the insolent stare of Welder looking at him via the rear view mirror, the Colonel resisted the temptation to run loving fingers over his chemical kit, instead he mentally counted off from the left, suicide pills, uppers for prolonged aggression, downers for rest between hostilities, maxi-strength Viagra for breaking down the resistance of prisoners under interrogation, and drops for turning water into wine.

This was the Colonel: gurka retired, ex-husband, the only Westerner with a Certificate in Nirvana, tending towards a little middle fat on an otherwise wiry light frame, balding slightly but only in bright light. The Colonel was old enough not to have a dandruff problem anymore. He was a man impeccably trained to kill quietly or noisily, to climb, to jump, to ski, to snorkel, to ride – to do all of these at once while moving like the wind against the Queen's enemies, and living on a grain of rice a day as he blew everything sky-high above and below the water. A man infinitely adaptable in the service of Queen and Country. The Colonel was, most of all, a man capable of the highest intellectual gymnastics. A man who had absolutely no problem at all to convince himself that early retirement from active service had been entirely his own idea.

As an ex-gurka, it would not have been difficult for the Colonel to settle comfortably into a security company and live out life in the UK. Indeed, he had tried retirement, but every time he turned on the news, it was clear the world was not yet ready to allow a man of the Colonel's capacities to hang up his kukri and put up his feet. So, the Colonel, at age 59, had set out to set the world to rights. Like Robin Hood, he robbed the rich and powerful and bad to feed the poor, disenfranchised and good. And like Robin Hood, he kept a little for expenses.

"Should the girl be with us?" the Colonel asked, ever gallant and mindful of danger.

"You don't like girls?" Welder responded, moving his protective right arm to draw Kimpen even closer into his body. How dare this trumped-up Colonel question Kim's presence. "They can be very useful."

"In what way can you see such a young girl being useful in this mission. She might get hurt."

"Lots of ways. Nobody is going to connect a thirteen-year old girl with setting a bomb."

"Thirteen?" questioned the Colonel. Welders have a reality that other men dream of and publicly condemn.

"Well, she will be in five months. In Laos, we often give the next birthday rather than the last one when stating age."

"So, the girl is twelve! She is *not* setting any bombs." The Colonel spoke as forcefully as he dared. "Who is she anyway? Your daughter? How come she speaks English?"

"Daughter, friend, wife, what's the difference? I've looked after her since her mother sold her. She picked up English very quickly."

"Her mother sold her? Who to?"

"Me," said Welder, wondering what planet the Colonel came from. "Eleven at the time. Now, if Kim is not to be setting any bombs, I presume you'll be doing that yourself?"

"I don't like bombs," said the Colonel, deliberately suspending moral judgment of Welder's morality. "Unsporting and unreliable. Last resort stuff only."

"These people are not sports," said Welder. "They enjoy what they are doing. They enjoy hurting people. A little bomb would only be justice."

"So far as I know, Winkle's associates are thieves. Particularly nasty ones maybe, and perhaps British thieves at that. But we don't just blow them up."

"You'll see," said Welder. "You can hardly arrest them all and take them back to British justice. They know that, that's why they're here. And you want to get rid of Winkle. I tell you, a bomb can be marvelously effective and anonymous. It not only removes the target but blows up any evidence as to the bomber."

"Let's have a look at them before I decide what should be done." The Colonel had to admit to himself, Welder had a point. The boiler-room bunch had chosen Laos for a reason and to prise them out of the country by legal means alone might prove difficult.

"You'll see some of them, including Winkle, if we have a beer at the *Khop Chai*. Winkle will be stopping by there early evening, and he's never alone."

"How do you know where Winkle is going to be at a certain time?"

"If you are going to question every bit of intelligence I put your way, I'm shutting it," said Welder in a factual rather than hostile way. Typical welder, thought the Colonel. All closed up, his very own code of morality, but not stupid. He would have to handle this one carefully; after all he needed Welder and could not afford to alienate him.

"Okay. I appreciate that can be annoying," said the Colonel. "I'll try not to do it again. Promise."

"Actually, it's no great secret. Winkle is there most nights these days, sussing out the place."

The Colonel wanted to ask why Winkle was sussing out the place, but knew that if and when Welder wanted to tell him, he would do so. It was the old game of office intelligence, what you know and what you choose to tell is as important as what you tell and to whom you tell it. So, instead of asking about Winkle's motives and how Welder knew what those motives were, the Colonel asked simply, "What kind of place is this *khop chai*?"

"Open air. Small scene pick-up place. Good beer, good food. Good place for a little bomb."

"No bombs," said the Colonel.

"Just a little one?"

"And let them know we are on to them?"

"Everybody is on to them. Burn them out, that's the only way."

"If you don't mind me asking," the Colonel asked as they pulled up next to the *Khop Chai* and climbed out, the Colonel easing his kukri in its oiled sheath, Kimpen taking Uncle Welder's hand trustingly. "What's in all this for you?"

"And if I do mind…?" Welder left the question hanging.

A half-Lao, half-black woman in a short black dress sat on a stool at the square bar in the middle of the small garden. She stretched her long legs down from the high stool, making them even longer. Her best feature, the Colonel noted *en passant*. Also hair fetchingly kinky, and what, when clad at least, looked like a nice bum. Nice bum was important. And the Colonel liked them a bit dark. He didn't much care for the aging transvestite with whom she was sharing a two litre pitcher of draft beer. The Colonel placed the half-breed at around thirty, certainly the oldest female on the premises, undoubtedly conceived at the end of the period when the Americans were here and were not here. The time of the secret army. He sat at a table nearest the open grilled entrance to get a better look at this remnant of history.

"Wouldn't sit there," said Welder to the Colonel.

"Why not? Tables all look much the same."

"They are. Only this one has a bomb underneath it. See that little bag that Kim just propped against the leg?"

"You're going to blow up an empty table?"

"Would you prefer blowing up the Black Princess at the bar? It's only a warning after all. Lot of noise. Harrass them at play. Viet Cong won the war that way."

"Yes they did, after thirty years. Where's Winkle's bunch?" The Colonel spoke without making any attempt at moving. He presumed Welder was not mad enough to blow himself up in his warning process. For the moment he had forgotten the welder's reputation for unpredictability.

Welder nodded his head across the garden to where a group of six men and four girls sat under a wooden vine-covered trellis, pouring beer from glass pitchers and laughing. All of the men looked alike. All except one. All had shaven heads. All wore tee-shirts proclaiming International Investments Unlimited. All were fit looking, muscular and around the thirty mark. All except one.

"That's Wee Willie Winkle, the one who looks like an unmade bed. Ropey chin-stubble, long, stringy hair on the sides tied by an elastic band in a pony tail at the back, and balding on top. Twice the age of the rest. Weakness: young things like the one pouring his beer. Scruffy bastard but don't let looks fool you. Dangerous as hell. Spends lavishly, buys his loyalties and crushes those who don't fall into his line of thinking and doing."

"This table menu says cheapest draft in town. Can't see him buying much in the way of loyalty here."

"Later we'll go to his club."

The Colonel looked at the disheveled figure. "He belongs to a club?"

"He *owns* a club. The *Blue Member Club*. And word has it he will soon be making an offer for this place, which is probably why he's here."

The Colonel studied the group. "We'll do it my way.

Turning on and tuning in his zoom senses of hearing and sight, the Colonel recognised a predominance of East London accents, and an entirety, Winkle apart, of fashionable shaven heads. The shaven heads, the accents, the youth, the tee-shirts and even the well-kept physiques made Winkle's encourage difficult to distinguish as individuals. They appeared to the Colonel as members of a tribe that deliberately set itself apart from others, adopting a uniform that represented nothing. The Colonel had every sympathy with real tribal homogeneity, and every dislike for those who pretended it.

Winkle himself had an accent which was London but not quite London. The Colonel ran Winkle's vowels through his computer-like mind and came up with Stevenage, but a Stevenage tempered either by education or a middle-class childhood. He also ran the young thing next to Winkle through analysis and in spite of the nicely developed breasts and very acceptable legs, came up with predominantly male, a lady-boy as they are known in Vientiane, a species Welder said was well tolerated in this particular communist state.

Not far from Winkle's group sat a lone fifty-ish figure of a man of enormous size. The Colonel noticed the man had to slouch in order to get his legs under the table at which he sat alone and calculated that when standing, the man must be around the two metre mark or taller. The man's hair was closely cut, military style, but was not shaven like Winkle's tribe. His arms, resting lightly on the table top, appeared strong and muscular. Was he, the Colonel considered, part of Winkle's group? Perhaps a body guard, placed as the Colonel would have placed DB or Kaziman, only a leap away from instant assistance but far enough from the group to appear no part of it, and with his back to the wall and a full view of the garden and bar. The man sipped cosmetically at a tall drink and without moving his head swung his eyes to take in all and everything, pausing occasionally, but not conspicuously lingering, on the figure of the Black Princess.

As far from Winkle as the small garden would permit, and obviously not part of Winkle's group, sat a comparatively smartly-dressed foreign male-Lao female couple, apparently sharing dinner with a middle-aged Lao couple. The Colonel, more used to sub-continental rather than Southeast-Asian norms of social interaction between sexes, and in spite of the ugliness of the Lao man, the fatness of the woman, and the contrasting beauty of the young Lao girl, thought the group father, mother, daughter and foreign husband or suitor. Good, he thought, that at least some people in this country know how to behave.

"Know that group over there?" The Colonel asked Welder.

"Yep," answered Welder, allowing his reticence to hang a full minute before continuing. "Fellow's called Norman. English. Nice guy. Nothing to do with Winkle. Sixty this week and retires from his UN job. Girl's called Souk, dirty little tart, fourteen or sixteen, whatever you want her to be. Now she's getting married to Norman over there, she's suddenly got an ID saying she's eighteen – there are very few laws in Laos, but one of them stipulates a Lao has to be married to a foreigner before she can sleep with him or her and she can only get married after age eighteen. Woman's her mother, in prison for major drug trafficking. Man's the Chief of Police of a big station near here."

"I can't hear that well above the noise of Winkle's group, but it sounds like the man, Norman that is, is being asked for five thousand dollars as marriage price for the girl. That sounds a lot."

"It is. But many foreigners give that and more. It will all go to free her mother from prison."

"But it looks like her mother is free right now. She's eating dinner just over there."

"With Chantavong beside her. He released her just for tonight so she could get the money out of Norman. He'll take the lot and arrange for her release."

"You mean bribery and corruption?"

"Sure. The bitch is down to get fifteen years. Beats me why Norman is getting her out. She's done nothing but sell his beloved Souk since before her first pubes. He's giving up a god sent opportunity to get rid of her...and paying through the nose to do it."

"What is it then?" asked the Colonel. "He cuckoo or simple."

"If only," replied Welder. "Then he would be a happier man. Fact is, Norman's one of the best brains in Vientiane. An intellectual if there ever was one."

The girl had gone down on her knees in front of Norman. "Thank you. Thank you. Thank you. I am yours and yours alone forever. The $5,000 will free my mother from prison. We need only another thousand to complete the smaller bribes, collect the signatures from the various ministries, obtain a letter of non-impediment from the British Embassy in Bangkok, and complete documentation that would normally take a foreigner wishing to marry a Lao a year to put together. One thousand dollars and we can be legally married within the week, and I will be yours, and yours alone, forever. You were the first man in my life No'man. I gave you my virginity. And now you will be the last. No other will ever see or touch me, I promise you. I would die before allowing another man to touch me."

Beautiful girl, but expensive at a tenth of the price, thought the Colonel as he listened in to the discussion of bribery, treachery and marriage. An interesting situation, the Colonel concluded, but one with no apparent bearing on his mission. However, the Colonel's all-embracing vision noted that Winkle was clearly fixing eyes on the girl Souk. And if Winkle was interested in young Souk, so was the Colonel.

Norman would be sixty in a few days, the girl Souk, whatever her papers said, hovered around the age of consent, which, in Laos, was not written down but in people's minds was generally based on neighbouring Thailand – where Welder might have got a life sentence if he entered his girl before her thirteenth birthday but after age fifteen anything went. Norman would be within the law if Souk had an ID card showing she was eighteen and papers promising marriage. Such contrast in ages seemed to be an unexceptional norm in Laos, at least in that tiny part of the foreign gerontocracy that he had observed within his first hour in the People's Republic.

Winkle, eyes fixed on Souk, moved his hand in the Asian way, fingers down, and waved her over to where he sat under the false-grape bower. That she so readily left her $5,000 true-love and immediately answered the older Winkle's beckon came as a surprise to the Colonel. And such surprises always had explanations. The Colonel focused his hearing onto Winkle to hear what it was. Winkle also spoke in Lao, bad Lao, not a scrap on that of the white man now sitting with the presumed parents of his fiancée. Winkle ushered the girl in close to him and placed a hand hard on the cleft of her backside to pull her nearer still. Her dinner companion began to rise from the table as the blood rose to his face.

The Colonel's honed sense of intuition told him: trouble coming. He reached his right hand to the cigarette packet in his shirt's left pocket and, without taking packet from pocket ran fingers along the front row of sticks, counting to number four. This he withdrew and placed, filter end first, between his lips. He patted his other pockets as if searching for matches or a lighter, while pretending at the same time to study the black princess, as Welder had called long-legs, but looking straight past her to the group of Englishmen.

"Let's see your tits," Winkle said in a calm matter-of-fact voice used to being obeyed instantly.

"Here?" the girl asked.

"Of course. Nice tits are what counts." Then switching to English, "Isn't that so, boys? Nice little titties are what counts." The shaven-headed boys agreed that nice little titties are indeed what counts.

Winkle moved quickly, raised the girl's tee-shirt with his free hand, lowered her skimpy bra and addressed his cronies. "There you are boys. I told you. Very nice tits indeed." Winkle kissed a small nipple to emphasise his point. "Work for me. The *Blue Member Club* only employs quality. Two hours dancing a night, serve a bit of food and some drinks at the same time, one thousand dollars a month, plus all the tips your fanny can hold. Okay?"

It was hard for the Colonel to know if the girl, who made no obvious struggle to free herself from Winkle or to put her tits away from his attention, was simply slow in reacting or was considering the offer. Before he found out, her angry boyfriend reached Winkle's table, pulled the girl away and swung a fist wildly at Winkle, who simply flicked his head to one side, leaving a space for Norman's fist to connect with a surprised lady-boy's face. The Colonel heard knuckles crack against the rouged cheekbone.

"What's the matter, Norman?" Winkle asked coldly and calmly. "Gone off lady-boys? I was only offering this young lady of yours a well-paid job. After all, you've been shagging her since she was four-teen. You and everybody else, of course. You've had your money's worth and more, let some other guys have a go." With that, Winkle brought his knee up between Norman's legs and Winkle's compan-ions fell on him with kicks and punches as he went down. The wait-ers all moved their attention to the other side of the garden. The tall man set aside from Winkle's group remained a totally impassive spectator, although the Colonel thought he perceived the faintest of frowns on the man's high forehead.

The Colonel had seen enough. He had been in the country scarcely more than an hour and, to judge from what he had seen so far, what the long-rangers at the FCO had told him was clearly true: an Englishman named Winkle was leader of a rabble of British thugs held together by a common cause of criminality, to which the Colonel thought he could probably add a common activity of lust for under-aged girls and a love of violence. The Colonel wasted no more time. He aimed the cigarette between his lips at the vertical bamboo pole supporting the bower nearest to Winkle and puffed.

As the dart struck the pole, there was only an unremarkable pop, hardly an explosion, but the bamboo broke cleanly in two and the bower came down on the whole brood. The first blow against the forces of evil had been struck.

"Impressive," said Welder impassively. "But Winkle is just going to think the bower fell down as part of the natural course of events. He's not going to put two and two together. He's not the subtle sort. That, by the way, is why I think it's time to move away from this particular table, to the bar." Welder reached down to Kimpen's bag under the table. "Welder and company will be off in a couple of minutes," was all he said, clicking in numbers on a mobile phone. Kimpen moved quickly to the bar. The Colonel thought it wiser to follow than to argue.

Winkle and his company suffered little more than a dusting and had no trouble extracting themselves from under the bower's debris. Making no attempt to pay, Winkle made straight for the exit-entrance, walking past the Colonel at the bar. The man who had sat passively throughout the small affray unwound himself from his table, stood to display fully his giant proportions, and followed Winkle at a distance.

"Hello, Colonel," Winkle said pleasantly as he passed by. "It is the famous Gurka Colonel, isn't it? Heard you were coming. Like to have a chat, but this place seems to be falling down. Never mind, such things are good for business – all reduces property prices you know. Get Welder to bring you along to the *Blue Member* later on. Courtesy membership for you of course. We can talk there without disturbance."

Without stopping for an answer, Winkle and his boys and girls and the bloody-nosed lady-boy walked past the table the Colonel had just vacated and out through the gate at precisely the moment Welder pressed the call button and the explosion split the air. The Colonel, who generally saw bombs as the anonymous and cowardly antipathy of the hand-held kukri and therefore disapproved of them, had to admit to himself that Welder's timing was perfect, injuring nobody, shaking those it intended to shake. As table and chairs went flying, Winkle's men hurried out into the waiting fleet of three Land Cruisers. Winkle turned his head back to look directly at the Colonel, raised a thumb briefly in the air, and said unemotionally and almost conspiratorially, "Bingo!" He made no pause of pace and turned not a hair. Cool customer, the Colonel noted.

The anonymous giant was near enough to witness what might have been, had Welder moved his thumb a second or two sooner, but far enough behind the group to remain untouched. He stepped over the broken metal table and maintained his composure.

"I think another pitcher of draft," said Welder to the barman.

"And I think some ground rules are in order," the Colonel said to Welder.

4

_____

# Norman's Conquest

**"Indeed there is,"** Nigel replied in answer to Godfrey's enquiry as to whether there was any news of the Colonel-sahib. "Seems to have spent his first evening in close contact with a Winkle-inspired brawl, and to have blown up an arbour – whatever that is – over Winkle's head and an empty table in a restaurant. At the time Welder texted this through, the Colonel was invited as guest of honour to a Winkle orgy of under-aged girls and transvestites."

"That's all right then," Godfrey replied and opened his copy of The Guardian.

"Now," said the Colonel. "As leader of this mission, I appreciate your assistance, Welder, but some ground rules seem to be in order," The Colonel, expecting police sirens to interrupt them at any moment, spoke calmly but as forcefully as he dared to a man like Welder. The lady of mixed race, who seemed not to notice the twisted metal table in front of her, turned on the bar stall next to the Colonel, one long dark leg pressing against the hardness of the kukri, she raised her beer and clinked the Colonel's glass. As the Colonel gave a non-committal glance into her eyes, the Black Princess thought to herself, ah, another one falling in love with me, ah, it's such a responsibility. She pressed harder. All right, Colonel or whatever they call you – she said with her eyes – I am not one of these easy girls like you see around here, but maybe you can fuck me, why not?

"No problem," responded Welder, who had been on the edges of the diplomatic world long enough to perfect the art of misunderstanding. "Ground rules are no Bangkok-type bar fines and no pimps. You want her, you take her. Twenty dollars, whatever." And moving his eyes around the Colonel, Welder switched to Lao, "Tik-Tok, meet the Colonel."

"That's not what I meant," said the Colonel as Tik-Tok's fingers ran around his hard, long kukri sheath hidden inside tropical-weight perm-prests. Surely, Tik-Tok thought, it's on the wrong side. She moved her fingers to play the inner thigh of the Colonel's right leg and struck straps. She wondered what kind of perve Welder had befriended this time, someone who has to strap it on or strap it down.

"You like my legs?"

"Yes," said the Colonel honestly. "I like your legs." Then he turned back to Welder and let his voice convey the measured authority of the British Raj dealing with its own lower caste members. "You can't just go blowing up tables like that."

"Why not? I'll blow it back together again tomorrow. No problem. Still keep all my welding gear. Like to keep my hand in."

The Colonel reminded himself he was not here to reform Welder but to catch Winkle by fair means. "Where are the police?" he asked. Tik-Tok moved her fingers up the Colonel's groin and studied his eyes over the rim of her beer glass as she finally found her way passed all the straps and connected with a stirring John Thomas.

"You like my arse?" She asked. "It's black and beautiful. They call me the Black Princess." She turned on the stall to give the Colonel a better view of the short, tight-skirted arse in question.

"They don't respond to calls after ten at night." Welder informed.

"But it's not even nine. Yes I do like your arse. And that was a bomb."

"Bomb? Bang more like it," said Welder. "Bomb, bang, arse, what's the difference? Wouldn't think the police would be too interested in a little bomb like that. Nor a piece of black arse for that matter. Everybody here wants white meat. Nobody else seems to be interested in the bang – nor in the black arse for that matter. Anyway, the police are already here, and they don't seem bothered. Chantavong is not only Chief of Police in Sa Meung, that's the big police station nearest to here, he's in charge of investigating all crimes involving foreigners. Hand-picked for the job because of his complete ignorance of the English language and hatred of foreigners. I'll introduce you if you like. Strange type 'though. Tricky. Can't be trusted."

"Later." The Colonel zoomed his senses into Chantavong's table. Norman had dusted himself off and retaken his seat. He looked less the worse for wear than might have been expected.

"No'man. You know I love only you." The girl said to Norman. "There is only you for me. Please forgive me. I beg you to punish me. Punish me. It will never happen again. Mother and *Thhan* Chantavong are my witnesses."

The bruising and cuts on Norman's face resulted from kicks and punches received from Winkle and company; the bower's structure, now being tied back in position by waiters who moved slowly and deliberately as if practicing a nightly event, was but light spars and flimsy lengths of split bamboo and, while its fall had undoubtedly, the Colonel thought, saved Norman from a worse beating, the collapse itself had done harm to nobody. Chantavong, ten years younger than the foreigner paying for his dinner, had a face much more in need of repair than that of Norman, and Chantavong had the misfortune of knowing that his face, unlike that of Norman, would not look any better in the morning's mirror.

Chantavong smiled rows of rotten teeth, moved his bad breath nearer to Norman's nose and said in Lao, "Mister No'man, Souk is for you and you alone." He made it sound as if Norman had just been sentenced to life in a remote Lao prison. "Better punish her now and start again."

Norman, as the demonstrated enemy of the enemy, held a potential for the Colonel, who watched fascinated as the girl begged for punishment. The mother looked on with obvious contentment and refilled the beer glasses.

"Okay," said Norman, a weary note to his voice, "on your knees."

Souk left her chair and fell to her knees, her palms held together at her forehead, her face looking down, waiting for Norman to erupt into violence or forgive her, or both.

"The important thing, Souk, is that you really feel sorry. Otherwise, you might do it again." Norman was, the Colonel thought, probably using reason with the unreasonable. The Colonel was not an unnecessarily violent man, but if somebody begged for violent punishment, they were either insane or unreasonable and the Colonel would not have tried appealing to reason.

"Never. I've changed," the girl replied. "You can trust me now."

"Okay, I forgive you for when you went to Luang Prabang for three days with that American."

"I never did," said Souk. "That's lies from your *khatoey* friends. You can't trust *khatoeys*. Transvestites always lie. I went because my father called me on my mobile and said he was leaving the country quickly and had some money to give me before he left."

"The Polish Ambassador saw you there. He's no transvestite. Anyway, you told me your father died two years ago, I remember you asked for money to pay for the funeral."

"He's not dead. That was my step-father, my mother's second husband. Do you forgive me? I needed money at that time to help Mummy. So I said my father had died. My real father is in Luang Prabang."

"You lie to me a lot, Souk."

"I lied. Forgive me. The alternative was to sell my body. But I loved you, so I did not. You gave me money, so I did not have to sell myself."

"But in the end, you did sell yourself. You told me you were going to visit your sister in Bangkok. You stayed there five days and I met you at the border on return, and you had $4,000 in your bag. At first, you said your sister had given it to you. But then I heard your sister left Bangkok two years ago for America. Then you admitted selling yourself for four nights for $4,000. I can't believe somebody paid that much for just four nights, and you won't tell me what you had to do to get such money. And on return you even called me from the bridge to pick you up, saying you missed me and wanting to go to dinner. You behaved so normally and lied so naturally. If I hadn't looked in your bag and found the money, I'd have believed everything you said."

"I know that was wrong of me. But I've paid for that. Two months in a police cell you gave me." A peculiarity of the Vientiane policing system is that not only can people be released from Chantavong's cells on paying a bribe, but they could also be thrown into cells on payments made to support *Thhan* Chantavong's football team. On that occasion, Norman reminded those at the table, he had paid for Souk to be detained one month in the police cells and extended it to two because he was still angry with her after one. He had gone along to the police station every day with a package of excellent food and snacks for this errant child he loved, and visited her every Friday. By the end of two months, he had actually felt guilty. He had kept the $4,000, and, after deducting the one thousand he gave Chantavong to put her inside, had given the lot to a charity to buy wheelchairs for the handicapped, telling Souk he would not allow her to profit from prostitution.

"It always comes down to money, Souk. You need money to pay the gambling debts of you and your mother. You need money now to get your mother out of jail, otherwise she will go for trial and the police have recommended fifteen years – and she will get it." Souk's mother, released by Chantavong only for this meeting, began to plead, saying what a good man No'man was, how she would never survive fifteen years in prison and that if released she would make sure Souk was never unfaithful to No'man again.

Norman explained the saga of Souk to the Colonel later, when they were friends, but it fits to set it down here. Norman had decided he would ignore the eagerness with which, even as he discussed with Chantavong the release of the mother, Souk had tripped over to meet Winkle's beckoning command. He decided to ignore it because, in spite of everything, Souk fulfilled him like no other girl could. Souk had lied to him, he suspected throughout the three years since he had intervened, as Welder had done with his Kimpen, to stop Souk, at the age of fourteen, being sold by her mother to an agent from Pattaya. At that time, he had found himself *de facto* owner of a girl who had experienced her first period just a few months before she came to his bed. An illiterate girl, he hired a teacher for her, built a small house for her family with a stocked roadside shop attached and purchased a huge cold drink dispenser to put in the shop. He had given them a chance in life only because he had fallen in love with this child. And all he gave had been thrown back in his face. Souk never learnt, no matter how many times Norman changed the teacher. She seemed quite incapable of learning to read and write her own language or even of making any effort to do so. One day, without a by-your-leave to Norman, the great benefactor, the mother had sold the house and shop to pay her debts and moved the family away without a word to Norman.

Norman, like so many old European men who fall for young and beautiful Lao girls had little choice but to excuse or lose. Not that Souk had appeared in any way promiscuous, at least not for the first two years. And Souk was, everybody agreed, very beautiful indeed, so beautiful that at 16 she won the Miss Vientiane title without sleeping with any of the judges; her easy victory had attracted the attention of every *falang* in town but she, at that point, had apparently not wavered in her devotion to one *falang* in particular, namely Norman. Other residents referred to her at the time as *Norman's Conquest*. Later, they referred to her as *Norman's Folly*. Betrayal tore Norman apart, but, he reasoned later to the Colonel, Lao teenagers were not so different to the average European of the same age. At least, he had been first, he was fairly sure of that, and Souk, whatever she did, at least measured herself against a patchy code of conduct that lingered on in Laos more in the breach than in the reality. That is to say, Souk knew in some way she had done wrong – most Europeans would have laughed at the idea that one-night-stands, clandestine lunch-time meetings in shady guest houses and dirty weekends were in any way contrary to what good people do. And, after all, Souk was right in her last line of defence, they were not actually married. Norman blamed himself for that. True, Souk was now only 17, a year too young to marry a foreigner. But he had known her for three years, and he could easily have paid the money and got an identity card and passport for her adding on a couple of years, then married her, as she wanted. And, last but not least, Norman, much as he loved Souk, had not kept himself exclusively for her. In fact, even on that evening when they discussed marriage and the release of the mother – the two subjects being inextricably linked – Norman had no doubts as to his capacity for infidelity in the future. He liked a fling more than occasionally, and Vientiane offered daily opportunities for uncomplicated liaisons. Now he was ready to initiate the paper work that would lead to marriage and to pay bride price through the nose, knowing that it would go to pay for the release of Souk's mother, an evil drug peddler who deserved the threatened fifteen years in prison if anybody did. Once married, he would have his unique rights. Once married, he would beat the shit out of her if she so much as glanced at another man.

Chantavong pulled a sheaf of papers from a plastic folder. "This will all need to be signed by the village headman where Souk is living now, but he will sign when I tell him to do so, once you and Souk and Mother Kham have signed. I can write in now that you agree to a marriage settlement of $5,000?"

"Why did you have to trip over so eagerly when Winkle beckoned you just now? You know I don't get on with that guy." Norman, struck by a pang of sudden jealousy, could not avoid the subject after all. So he let Chantavong wait, holding the papers, and addressed his question to Souk, still on her knees.

"I was just going to the toilet. I thought it better for you and *Thhan* Chantavong and mother to talk without me. Winkle grabbed me, you saw, I couldn't get away."

"Okay, Souk. For the last time, you are forgiven. And for the last time I'm paying for your mother's release. Come and sit here, if you want to get married." At the same time as cursing himself for being a fool, at the same time as hating Souk and loving Souk, Norman knew he had no choice. Over three years, he had molded Souk into exactly what he wanted in a sex partner and companion. Several times he had tried to live without her and after a few days he would take her back, or even ask her to come back. He had tried plenty of others, none had come near to Souk in giving him satisfaction.

"The marriage settlement," Norman said, pulling five thousand dollars in hundreds from a top pocket as if it were a handkerchief and passing it across to Mother Kham, who put her palms together around the money in thanks and passed the money quickly to Chantavong, who counted every note below table-top level and pocketed it with one of his ugliest smiles. "Bit steep at five thousand, but never mind. Although asking for an extra thousand now for documentation sounds a lot, can we reduce it to 500? After all, I'll have to give a party, and buy a ring."

"Ah, the five thousand. You know that Souk is a good girl and looks after Mother Kham just as she will look after you. Neither Souk nor I get one *kip* of that money. It is not so easy to get drug dealers released these days."

"But *you* arrested her."

"What else could I do, Mister No'man? She was caught with 49,793 amphetamine pills, and customers in the house buying them. She stayed only seven months in my police cells. If I'd had more time, she'd have been free in the natural course of things, in a year or so. But the laws have become tougher, drug dealers can be shot now. And I'm sorry to say this, but one of my own men precipitously rushed the documentation through and Mother Kham would have been tried and sentenced to fifteen years tomorrow, had I not intervened to get the papers back – but at that stage it takes a lot of money to reduce the documented 49,793 pills to 3 and arrest the neighbour for planting even those three on Souk's mother.

"Souk's mother will be released tomorrow, as soon as the village headman signs her release papers; he'll sign your marriage papers at the same time and make sure all the signatories in the ministries sign your application to marry Souk."

"Well, it's done now," said Norman. "And of course we are grateful to you for obtaining the release. But one thousand for a few signatures?"

"For that you should ask Mister Welder, and your own British Embassy. It's that *non-objection certificate* causes the trouble. Some people at your Embassy in Bangkok seem to think that being married already in England is cause for objection. Anyway, it will all be ready in a week. You can go ahead and plan the wedding party."

The Colonel turned to Welder. "Just what kind of nut is that Norman over there?"

Welder shrugged as if in despair. "Naif, romantic," he replied. "Loves that girl. Bought her mother land and built a small general store on it, so the girl and family had no reason to go bad. Mother lost the lot gambling. Whenever Norman's out of town and even when he's in town, the girl disappears for days on end with other foreigners passing through and, if Norman finds out, she invents ridiculous stories – the Lao love to tell on each other, national pass time, sometimes they tell the truth sometimes pure lies, usually a mixture. They have a fight; Norman's quite a reasonable person but I've seen her with a swollen lip and black eye, then she is back with him again. He's completely besotted with her, and in the end she will be the death of him, her and that horrible mother. That's what I can't really understand: Norman finally gets the chance to be shot of the mother and he pays to get her released. He's in love with Souk, that's all too clear, but he must also be in love with his own ruin. Otherwise, quite a nice, and very intelligent, man. In fact, were it not for his stupidity regarding that illiterate girl, I would say he comes closer to meriting the title of intellectual than any other *falang* in Vientiane."

The Colonel could not help but note that neither Welder nor little Kimpen seemed to relate the parable of Norman and Souk to their own particular circumstances. Well, that was a problem of their own making that thankfully in no way concerned the Colonel – or so he thought at the time. At this stage in his mission, the Colonel would follow standard procedures and attempt to build allies against the enemy, and Norman and Chantavong sounded worthy of follow-up as potential allies.

"What does Norman do in Vientiane? Why's he here?"

"Norman's very different to Winkle and that bunch of Winkle followers, who change at Winkle's whim, or Winkle kicks out as soon as they fall foul of anything really illegal. He's very different to most westerners living in Vientiane. A Lao scholar – got several books out on the people and the country and has access to the highest levels. He'll be sixty in a day or two and gets retired from a nicely-paid job at the UN here. Decided to stay on and pursue a hobby that has occupied him for years – locating the Laotian crown jewels. He definitely has an *idée fixe* on the subject, but most people think it's driven him a bit nuts."

"What do you think, Welder?"

"He's not nuts – apart from throwing his money away on that girl that is (Welder gave his own little girl a hand-squeeze and a smile) – and over the years he has had the chance to see all the documentation, including the old Soviet satellite pictures of possible wreck sites, related to the missing treasure, which *must* be somewhere still in Laos, since there is no whisper that it is anywhere else. If the royals in exile in Paris had them, they would certainly make a big thing out of it. Artifacts like that have intrinsic value, that's to say their component parts are worth money in themselves, but worth far more in conferring legitimacy on would-be rulers. And Laos is still a country contested – although not seriously anymore, at least not in much of a military way. Personally, I'd like the UK Government to mount an expedition for the jewels, led by Norman rather than some

Foreign Office twit. The British Government could then hand them back to the current government, communist so be it, which would museum them, making the positions of UK personnel – like me for example – more secure and the UK the beneficiary of special trade privileges."

The Colonel was surprised to hear Welder talk such sense. And the idea of treasure sounded interesting. More interesting in fact than getting Winkle extradited, and far more profitable. After all, the Colonel would receive from the FCO, precisely the same meager expenses whether or not he managed somehow to bring Winkle to justice. No harm in a bit of freelancing to keep the home fires burning. No doubt, the Colonel thought, and the thought surprised him, the Black Princess pressing her knees into his inner thighs would say much the same thing. He reached out a hand and lightly touched the black buttocks in a black dress. Nothing too public. This was Laos, after all, and a degree of subtlety a million times greater than that shown earlier by Winkle's exposure of Souk's breasts was the norm. The Colonel dropped two ten thousand kip notes on the bar and told the waiter to keep the beer coming for the Princess.

"Norman doesn't seem to get on with Winkle?" The Colonel asked Welder.

"Understatement. Winkle wants the treasure too. Offered to use his resources to locate it and go fifty-fifty with Norman. But Norman refused. Lots of people are interested, including Gem Mining, which is an expat company, 50% Winkle. If they find the jewels, they might just break them up and sell them off for their intrinsic value, or they might try to sell to the royals in Paris, if that pays more – although if Winkle sold to the royals, he'd have to worry about keeping on the good side of the current Lao authorities, at least for the next thirty days. But for my money, Norman is the only one likely to find them."

"Why so?" asked the Colonel.

5

---

# The Blue Members

**"Upstairs is asking** whether the Colonel has met Foreign Affairs yet to hand over the extradition letter."

"Phew, Nigel. They might give the guy a chance. After all, he's hardly arrived. With the connection to Vientiane it is a sixteen hour flight. They can't expect him to rush to the Ministry in the middle of the night."

"Right, Godfrey. But *upstairs* said to remind the Colonel of his priority and that he is to inform us as soon as he has handed over the formal request for extradition."

"Sounds as if they know there are other attractions in Vientiane," said Godfrey with a smile.

"No apostrophe," stated the Colonel with disdain, as Welder drove him under the large electric sign that proclaimed *Blue Members Club* at the entrance to what was probably the newest and certainly the most glitzy building in town, although at kilometer three on the road to the bridge, edge of town might be a more appropriate guide to location.

They were stopped at the gate by heavies in jackets and bow-ties, who made a show of the Trade Office's Land Rover parking where they wanted it to park within the almost-empty car park. Welder followed their instructions and parked bonnet facing the wall. It would take a three-point turn to get out again through the gate, a subtle indication that the Colonel would not be going anywhere in a hurry without the blessing of the management. Welder instructed Kimpen to wait in the child-locked car and under no circumstance to open any door. Kimpen opened the glove compartment and started happily on the assortment of children's electronic toys that Welder kept to occupy her. The Colonel wondered how long it would be before the child graduated to more adult toys.

Winkle did not come down to meet them. Instead the Colonel and Welder were kept at the elaborate double interlinked-heart-shaped entrance of the building, while more well-dressed heavies politely but efficiently ran hands over their bodies, removing the kukri from the trouser pocket of the Colonel. The Colonel was handed a courtesy membership card and ushered into what looked like an up-market disco, but was still just a disco. Most of the dancers were young Lao girls, dressed normally enough for Vientiane, that is to say in clothes that had been fashionable in Bangkok a year ago and were now being sold on one of Thailand's neighbouring second markets. A few sat in groups at tables, fewer still had any contact with the male clientele. The usual disco ball spun lights around the large room and waiters served beer in smaller bottles and at higher prices than in most other places. Nothing unusual or illegal here.

An English heavy, muscles bursting out of his formal wear, looking like a very overweight and overgrown schoolboy unhappily forced into a croupier's jacket and bowtie, greeted the Colonel politely and awkwardly. "Good evening, Colonel. I am Mr Biggs. Mr Winkle invites you to eat upstairs." Having said his piece, Biggs turned, slowly, the way a heavyweight wrestler turns. The Colonel's automatic guard system, located within the emergency and security section of the Colonel's brain, tacked a warning light on Mr Biggs, noting that he was very powerful but awkwardly slow and therefore should not be tackled from the front. The Colonel and Welder followed Biggs up a winding staircase set with small ground-level emergency-exit lights like those that are supposed to come on when a plane crashes. They were shown into a large reception-dining room with a central rectangular table. Four very young and very naked girls danced Thailand style, holding onto two poles set in the table top and gyrating their body parts against and around it. At their feet a lumpy white sheet covered much of the table's surface, like a funeral shroud overlaying a body. Apart from the new-comers, and not counting four body guards who hugged the walls and six other nubile and naked young ladies who circulated with silver trays of canapés and champagne, the Colonel counted eleven other guests, all of whom looked very much at home, as if they owned the place, which some of them, as shareholders, did. Winkle stood up, waved his hand to lower the volume of the music and spoke.

"Colonel, so glad you were able to take up my offer. Let me introduce you to some of my partners." The Colonel noticed that the guests included none of the draft-beer guzzling rabble he had seen at the Khop Chai.

A giant of a man, about the same age as the Colonel, every bit as thick-set with muscle as Mr Biggs but seemingly lighter on his feet, dominated the room by his enormous presence. The Colonel remembered seeing him sitting alone at the *Khop Chai*. Winkle introduced him as ex-SAS and manager of both Sucksabit Security and Gem-Mining. The giant went by the unforgettable name of Rupert Sweetheart. Apart from the Colonel and Welder, he was the only white guest. Rupert spoke with a friendly East-Ender accent, a bit over-friendly the Colonel thought, as another warning light came on in his mind.

The Colonel wasn't at all sure what to make of Rupert Sweetheart. The man was undoubtedly as strong in his body as in his dominating presence. His strength and muscle were emphasised by close-cropped hair and a military bearing. But there was something more than size and strength in this man. Something that struck a chord with the Colonel. Rupert Sweetheart, while superficially very friendly, had a strong sense of commitment to something. The Colonel had felt the same vibes in those fellow monks who had meditated with him for three years and three days in a total silence in Tibet. Each separated from the sight of all others, yet knowing they were there, had developed a confidence, a mission; each became something more than normal. Grasping Rupert's hand now in a friendly handshake, the Colonel felt a similar sense of purposeful resolve. A man with a mission, the Colonel thought. But the warning light was still there.

Rupert Sweetheart undoubtedly had a bearing that had been totally lacking in the bunch at Khop Chai; a bearing helped by his towering height; Rupert was well over the two metre, or seven foot, mark. He held the Colonel's hand in his own massive paw and grasped it in a Mason's signal, to which the Colonel responded. No harm in throwing confusion among the enemy. If, indeed, Rupert Sweetheart was to be considered as enemy. Something told the Colonel, he'd better waste no time in finding out what Sweetheart was all about.

"What we need here is a good gurka trainer," said Rupert. "Very well paid. Understand you are freelance. Let me know if you might be interested – after you've concluded your business here of course."

"I thought your Sucksabit was SAS trained?"

"To an extent. But I have to admit Colonel that, having spent most of my life in the SAS, the Gurkas seem to have a moral edge that seems to help them obey without question and fight without fear."

"Having spent most of my life with my gurka companions, I would have to agree. But don't forget there is a culture of loyalty and courage among our gurka recruits that you might not find among the Lao. Our chaps sometimes have generations of loyal service within the family to keep them charging the enemy guns. No matter how good your training, you can't teach that kind of loyalty."

"I'm sure you'd agree, however, that it would be interesting to see just to what extent such loyalty and bravery could be trained."

"Interesting yes, Mr Sweetheart, but it might take years of training for meditation, clearness of mind, spiritual development and all these things which have been bred through generations in Nepali gurkas. And our training is for active warfare in the most dangerous of situations. It seems that you are here talking of security guards. Do they need such a degree of training? It would hardly be cost effective."

"Very true, of course, Colonel. But I certainly need some help from somewhere. At the moment, there is only me to do the training. And there are limits to what I can do. All together we employ over three hundred Sucksabit guards – the largest non-government employer in Laos. Can't train that lot to any extent. So most get a two week course in how to blow whistles and so on and I train only an inner elite, fifty-odd chaps, the blokes who guard and move the money and gems and look after the boss and the rest of us in our slumbers. And the dogs. I personally train the dogs. We have the most marvelously obedient dogs. Whistle and they do a paw-stand."

"Dobermans?"

"Yes, Colonel. You like working with Dobermans?"

"Prefer Alsatians. Like something with a tail."

"Well, there's certainly plenty of tail here tonight." Rupert picked a canapé from a tray held up to him by a tiny girl whose naked goose pimples showed she was unused to air conditioning, and, perhaps more to the point judging from Rupert's stoopingly keen observation of her nethermost region, she had yet to sprout a single pubic hair. "God, that one must be twelve years old," he said, his voice full of undisguised disgust.

"You think too young?" asked the Colonel.

"Legally and morally. Even in this country. You are not even allowed to employ a maid until after age fifteen. And believe you me, Colonel, these children are not employed as maids. Are you familiar with the words of Jesus Christ?" Rupert's personal mission was beginning to show. "Suffer little children…"

"Not overly so familiar with the words, but quite familiar with the spirit behind the words," claimed the Colonel, wondering if he could find an ally against Winkle in the heart of the enemy camp. "I can't imagine Jesus would have approved of all this – or for that matter of kicking a man when he's down."

"Ah, your referring to that incident with Norman West earlier tonight. I understand. Goes against the grain for me too. Great pity really. Of course the real problem is that girl of Norman's. One day he'll wake up and see her for what she is. I don't like to see a good man go down because of a little slut like that. Don't like to see Norman making enemies of Winkle for that matter. Not good for him. Not good for anybody. Know what I mean, Colonel?"

"I think so," said the Colonel. So Rupert Sweetheart was not only a high standing man, he was also a man of high moral standing. How did he fit in with Winkle & Co? Loyalty would be high on his code, but there must be exploitable differences there. Another possible ally, and one best placed within the Winkle camp. But something about Rupert Sweetheart spelled caution, like a sword with two edges, the Colonel felt sure he could cut both ways. "And regarding an ex-gurka trainer for Sucksabit, I'm sure I can suggest several good gurkas to choose from. Let's talk again, when my business here is over – one way or the other."

As the Colonel shook hands all round and names were exchanged with the Lao and Thai guests, Winkle, the only one who hadn't bothered to dress for the occasion, spoke pleasantly, and with a smile on his stubble-encrusted face that could almost be called charming, in a slightly raised voice that reached to everyone in the room. His words, or rather the fact that he spoke so openly, surprised the Colonel. Winkle spoke first in English, then interpreted for himself in Lao. He clearly wanted everybody to understand. Even the girls stood stock-still and stark-naked as he spoke.

"The Colonel is here to try to catch me out. He hopes to do in a few days what the UK Government has not been able or not been bothering to do in twenty-nine years and eleven months – drag me back for a trial long-forgotten in the UK. You see, I'm a bit of an embarrassment for dear old England. They even issued me a new passport from the Embassy in Bangkok five years ago – isn't that right Welder? Lucky for me the left hand doesn't know what the right hand is doing. The Colonel has three options. Option one is to persuade the Lao to extradite me back to the UK, a bit difficult since Thailand would never allow passage, although I suppose things could be arranged through Viet Nam. Fortunately, Laos doesn't rush into things. Option two is to kidnap me and somehow get me on a plane to the UK, perhaps passing over the bridge to Udon, taking a domestic Thai flight to Bangkok, wheeling me in unconscious to the international terminal – there are plenty of possibilities and I'm sure the Colonel is thinking of them. Option three would be to make things so difficult for me here that I would have to leave Laos and sanctuary before the thirty-day deadline. That would mean my committing some major misdeed, like trying to take over the Government – and why on earth should I attempt that?

"The Colonel is only doing his job. But he no doubt thinks he is doing it in secret. This is to put him right. We now know his plans. Let him visit all my enterprises tomorrow – we sell shares worldwide quite legally, we deal in gems, helping the Lao PDR, one of the poorest countries in the world, obtain scarce foreign currency, and we provide Sucksabit, a security service to protect the airport and foreign embassies. We also have a few entertainment places, so the Colonel should have no trouble enjoying himself in Vientiane. No reason for us to be enemies. And as he will soon be aware, I am very generous to my friends. So, my friends, let us welcome the Colonel."
A ripple of applause went around the table and some present even shook the Colonel's hand a second time. The Colonel reminded himself he had come to bury Caesar, not to praise him, and made no reply.

At this very moment, given time differences that make a late dinner in Vientiane coincide with a late lunch in the UK, Godfrey and Nigel were sitting in the FCO restaurant – the word canteen could never do it justice – the highlight of their day. The white table cloth was decorated by a solitary English rose in a short-stemmed glass vase that sat comfortably among the condiments. Each table had one, cut fresh each morning and nicely arranged by the Welsh lady. It was definitely an English Rose. Not a Foreign and Commonwealth Rose.

The two men were going through precisely the same three alternative courses of action that Winkle was outlining in Vientiane. "Of course, there is a fourth," said Godfrey very matter-of-factly.

"Is there?" said Nigel.

"Yes. Just top him. Kill him."

Nigel drew his face back in disapproval. "Nigel! You know the Colonel could never do that!"

"Why not?"

"He is not licensed to kill."

"So, license him."

"Don't have time," Nigel said sadly. "A military matter."

"Wonder what he's doing now?" said Godfrey. Eating dinner? Playing with the girls?"


At that moment, the girls stopped dancing on the table and lifted up the sheet at their feet, revealing a feast of king prawns and tasty sauces set out decoratively on the naked body of Norman's girl, Souk. Six large and peeled prawns stood up like an open fan, their head-ends cleverly tucked into the cleft of Souk's hairless virginal cavity. The Colonel's eyes almost popped out of his head. This was indeed exciting stuff. Very, very exciting stuff. He just wasn't used to seeing prawns of such size and succulence.

The guests were indulged in every way. Sucking mouths were served tasty morsels and champagne by long fingers, and soon began to find their way to the more sensuous parts of each girl's personal menu. Later, Welder would disclose to the Colonel that these guests were police and army from neighbouring sides of the river. A mixture of high-ranking officers. No ministers or government people were present. The prawns between Souk's legs disappeared fast. Winkle was complimented on the new girl. Souk, the new girl, was wiggling as mouths and tongues sucked and licked remaining sauces from her nipples and hands fondled any free parts of her, reaching round to get a good feel of what had many times been described as the nearest thing to a perfect bum in Vientiane. A forest of hand turned Souk's thighs and buttocks this way and that, squeezing, prying, poking, as if trying a chicken at the market prior to purchase. The Colonel was of course extremely embarrassed, particularly when Winkle took hold of Souk's ankles, pulled her towards him and placed his mouth and tongue into her vagina, making piggy slurping noises and drawing some laughs. The Colonel would have happily taken out Winkle right there – which would certainly have brought a smile to Godfrey's face should he hear of it in London – but in the name of what cause? If Souk were being violated, she made no move to save herself. And the Colonel was not only bereft of kukri but hopelessly outnumbered, and outnumbered mostly by representatives of the law.

Some guests were openly beginning their orgy on the chairs or dining table, or took their choices off to behind the closed doors of the rooms adjoining the dining room. Welder passed the Colonel, willing to leave his little darling in the car building bricks on the electronic game while he took somebody scarcely any older into a vacant room.

"Winkle will invite you to take a girl," Welder whispered in the Colonel's ear as he passed. "Take any you like, but don't take Pon, that's her over there, the only one wearing clothes. She's Winkle's personal property – nobody else allowed. Understand?" The Colonel understood.

The Colonel and Winkle looked across the table at each other. Winkle's face remained buried between Souk's thighs. The Blue Member Club had revealed a side of Winkle's power, even before the Colonel visited his many other less exotic but probably more profitable enterprises.

"You know," the Colonel said to Winkle because he felt that at some point it had to be said, "you can always come back voluntarily. I'm sure an undertaking could be negotiated so that you retain your freedom in the UK, pending trial. And the trial could be arranged as quickly as you wish. It would after all count in your favour to return voluntarily rather than be thrown out by the Lao – who would then probably take away everything you have built up over the years."

"And what would I get," Winkle asked without withdrawing his head from Souk, "if I win the case?"

"Well, nothing," said the Colonel. "But you would be free."

"And if I lose?" said Winkle.

"Probably thirty years," replied the Colonel.

Winkle smiled, prawns and drool oozing from his lips. "Don't think much of the odds," he said as he finally took his face from the stubble-chaffed thighs of Souk, rolled his tongue around his teeth, and asked the Colonel casually if he would care to pick a lady or two and use a private room – a very private room. "After all," he said laughing and wiping his lips of Souk-prawn mixture. "I suppose the government service has to maintain a certain discretion."

The Colonel immediately requested Souk. Winkle frowned just a little, having got a taste for her, he had rather been looking forward to a full tryst with Souk himself that night. Plus, he had already set aside somebody to treat the Colonel to her specialities. But it took only a moment's thought for Winkle to realize that having Souk with the Colonel was even better than his original plan. So Winkle smiled his assent. "And I insist you try the Vientiane sandwich. You will find that Souk and her friend make a very nice team." He led the Colonel, Souk and the only girl wearing clothes, the one that Welder had warned him *not* to choose, into a luxurious room with one huge double bed and mirrors on the walls and ceiling. Rupert Sweetheart looked down his nose at the Colonel from on high, making no attempt to hide his great disappointment.

The Colonel locked the door behind the three of them, left the key in the latch and tested it was indeed closed firmly. As he turned, Winkle's girl friend, the forbidden flesh, eased her long gown from her shoulders and allowed it to drop slowly to the ground, revealing a naked and very beautiful body, above the eighteen mark but the flush of youth maintained by an expert shaving of the pubic region, a light blush of rouge on the facial cheeks, a light glistening red lipstick, and very long black hair that she untied from her neck and, shaking her head provocatively, caused to cascade down almost to her knees, framing the unblemished whiteness of the nether region.

"I'm Pon." Red lips moved into the Colonel's ear while Souk was cleaning herself of food and human spittle in the marbled bathroom. "Be warned," Pon whispered, "the mirrors are one-way. Winkle is filming all this." She spoke so softly and gently into the ear of the Colonel that he found himself going hard with a speed that surprised him and was actually not in his plan at all. Pon gently lay the Colonel down on his back and worked his trousers down over his erection, undoing the straps of the empty kukri sheath with a look of confusion as she moved downwards and the Colonel's member moved up to greet her. His resolve – his plan – was fast disappearing as the Colonel's eyes fastened on the buttocks reflected in the mirrors above his head – the Colonel never could ignore a good, firm bum, and this one, like that of Souk, which had returned to lie cheeks up on the bed on the other side of the Colonel to Pon, came close to what he had been searching for all his life, the perfect rump – and here were two of them. He found himself growing harder between Pon's fingers and switched his mind into slow gear. He might as well enjoy this, he did not want it over too soon, and there was the plan to think about. Souk, meanwhile, was rubbing her young breasts and pubic mound along the Colonel's back.

"You can eat the cream," said Souk, the other half of the Vientiane sandwich, as she lifted a slim leg to reveal strawberry ice cream, before curling it expertly around the Colonel's neck. She was not to know that the Colonel always favoured chocolate or lemon sorbet. One of her slim legs curled around the Colonel.

"What are you up to?" said the Colonel stupidly.

"You can lick me out," said Souk. "Strawberry ice cream."

No way, thought the Colonel, extricating his head. Chocolate or lemon sorbet only. Never could stand strawberry.

"We must go through the normal sexual actions," Pon whispered so quietly into the Colonel's ear that he had to switch his mind to amplified soundtrack. "I will explain later. If there is trouble now, you may never leave here alive. Winkle wants film to blackmail you, and to curtail any cooperation between you and Souk's boyfriend." With that her mouth moved down to take, play and embrace the Colonel's member, bringing it to full attention and salute.

Souk, strawberry ice cream dripping onto the sheets, was relegated to a supporting role; the Colonel would rather she not be there – he had selected her so that nobody else had her and in the hope of learning more about Norman. He did not know Norman at that point, but still he felt a measure of guilt as Souk rubbed her body against him, although much stronger than guilt was the confusion as to what Souk was doing there at all. He was also confused as to why Pon, the only girl wearing clothes, the one girl Welder had warned him off, had been presented to him by Winkle, and had confided in him about the filming.

The Colonel, foiled in his plan by the need to whisper in ears and the presence of a witness, was perfectly able to put his confusions aside and enjoy his sandwich. He had in fact, much earlier in the evening, thought of inviting the Black Princess to his bed, but that particular morsel was probably over the admission age for one of Winkle's soirees, anyway the Colonel had to admit that it would be hard to beat his tryst with Pon, with Souk quite literally acting as back-up. It had been some time since the Colonel had enjoyed the attentions of two young ladies – or, for that matter, *one* young lady – and when he finally freed his mind of all restrictions and allowed Pon's lips to free him of accumulated tensions, the Colonel felt well and truly drained. The girls showered their guest and dressed him before seeing to themselves. Winkle was waiting as the Colonel unlocked the door.

"Take them with you, if you like. My little treat. Nice for breakfast. Staying with Welder I suppose?" Winkle grinned. "Now, *his* little girl really is something. Waiting in the car downstairs, I bet. I understand why he doesn't let her in *my* door, but he must know that one day I'll be in *her's*. He'll get tired of her eventually, or her of him, or she will need to build her mother a house; they all do, you know. Then Uncle Winkle will be there to lend a hand. Well, not a hand exactly, har,har."

"I'll do just that, take them back to Welder's place," the Colonel smiled back, pretending bonhomie. "And thanks for the hospitality. I look forward to seeing your other business activities tomorrow. By the way, where is Welder?"

"Oh Welder. Well, he's like us all. Madly in love with his little mermaid, but likes some variety in the menu. He'll be out very soon. Never takes very long does Welder. I think he's scared somebody might steal his baby. Ah yes, Colonel, don't forget your kukri on the way out. Although you seem to have coped well enough tonight without it – so far, har, har."

"I wanted to say goodbye to your Mr Sweetheart. But I suppose he is busy like everybody else."

"Not Rupert!" Winkle exclaimed. "He hasn't had it, at least he says he hasn't, for the past ten years. Some religious thing. That's his business. He looks after mine, and that's all that matters to me. Does a good job, does Rupert. Out checking on our security right now. Don't worry, you'll be seeing plenty of Sweetheart. Ah, here comes Welder now."

The Colonel, Welder and the two girls rejoined Kimpen in the locked and child-locked vehicle. She was still playing with the electric toys as the two girls hugged and kissed her. Welder handed over a parcel of seafood, Kimpen unwrapped it, smiled sweetly and seemed a happy little child. Too young to be jealous, or even to question what was going on. For that matter, too young even to get pregnant. The voice of the Colonel's education told him Welder was an evil man; the voice of the jungle told him Welder certainly had it made. The Colonel was not going to judge the whole country by what he had seen of it so far, but clearly a moral measuring stick built up over years in Nepal had best be packed away in a recess of the mind. Vientiane, so far, seemed to the Colonel to be a symbiotic relationship between a male Western gerontocracy and a female Lao kindergarten.

"Okay if I take Pon back to your place for the night?" The Colonel spoke to Welder as they drove away from the blue neon sign that spelled out in English *Blue Member Club*.

Welder raised his eyebrows, glad to realise the Colonel was human after all. It would make things a lot easier.

"*And* Souk?"

"Souk had better go back to Norman." The Colonel turned to Souk and was jolted again when she looked into his eyes at how very beautiful she was. The Colonel was still rather fazed by her apparently total lack of any sign of morality or conscience. "What are you going to tell Norman, Souk?"

"Earlier," Souk said. "I told him I was going on my motor-bike to get some *som-tum*. My bike's still at the stall. I'll just tell him the truth, that I went to see Winkle about his job offer.'

"Norman is," the Colonel searched for the word in Lao, "certainly naïf, but he will surely not believe you went to see Winkle to get *som-tum*. And Norman must know what goes on in the Blue Member."

"Don't worry about me. The som-tum will be waiting and so will Norman. After all, Winkle offered me one thousand dollars for serving food, and that's what I did, in a way, although I shall say I just looked at the place and turned the job down, on condition Norman and I get married within one week." Clever little bitch, thought the Colonel, wondering how many dollars she had managed to tuck away during the course of the evening, and where, but one day Norman will kill her, he was fairly sure of that.

They dropped Souk at her motor-bike and continued to Welder's large British-government provided house by the Mekong River. As they made themselves at home in the guest room and exchanged pleasantries, the Colonel told Pon he really liked her, which was true enough. Pon complimented him on his Lao and said it was very correct and high class, the kind of Lao people don't speak since the

Revolution, and even before the revolution as far as she knew. She asked where he had learnt it.

"In the seventeenth century. I was Lao," replied the Colonel. "Royalty, of course. I suppose I learnt it in the royal court."

Pon laughed out loud. "You're marvelous. Not a trace of a smile on your face. You really are nice, you know, and fun too. Not like Winkle and the rest of his bunch."

"Thanks," said the Colonel. "And you, my dear, have the loveliest little bum."

"So, you really like me?" asked Pon. "Or you just want to get information out of me? I've been with Winkle for six months now and have good reasons not to like him. You match his money, you get the information."

"Fair enough," said the Colonel. "What I really want to know is what Winkle is going for? With all these enterprises he seems to have, all bringing in money, lots of it, what is his big target? Not, surely, just to wait out the next thirty days and return to the UK as an untried and untouchable criminal-suspect."

"You mean it isn't obvious? You mean, you yourself think you *really* have come to Laos only to take him back to face British justice? That's so funny." And Pon broke into unstoppable laughter.

# 6

## Clean as a Winkle

"Has our Colonel delivered the extradition request? I have to follow-up with the Lao mission in Paris." Godfrey spoke as he reached for his jacket and folded it over one arm. It was warm that May afternoon in London, and no directive had been needed for the entire FCO to enter spontaneously into loose tie and shirtsleeves mode and an almost mischievous air, where long lunches and early after-work drinkies were tolerated to the point of obligation.

"I think he's been a bit too busy enjoying Winkle's hospitality. According to Welder – and I suppose we have to believe him – the Colonel spent his evening starring in a porno movie with one sixteen-year old and one possibly legal. Then took one of them back to Welder's and is still at it."

"Girls?" Godfrey questioned, affecting surprise.

"Of course girls. Nothing queer about our Colonel."

"Lucky old sod. Now that's one set of holiday movies I'm not going to complain about having to watch. Come on Nige, drinks by the river tonight."

The British Government had certainly done Welder proud in terms of accommodation. Built in the more prosperous and expanding days of the early 1960s, the first inhabitant had been the Ambassador to Laos, at a time when the UK, for reasons lost in the sidelines of misty history and a very hot cold war, had a full Embassy in what was then the Kingdom of Laos.

Pon's backside snuggled up against the Colonel in invitation. It had not taken Pon long to work out where her main attractions lay for this fascinating visitor, who went to bed with a long knife under the pillow. For the Colonel, Pon's backside presented the best and most enjoyable way of getting information out of this canny and cuddly young lady. The Colonel reached for his shirt pocket and took a blue pill. It would not be the first time he had rogered information out of a reluctant informant, even one he assumed was well used to being rogered in the normal course of daily life.

The Colonel used the pill's effective waiting time to investigate Welder's guest room for listening and viewing devices, and to remind himself that the only reason Pon was in his bed, and the only reason his John Thomas was becoming as rigid as the flag pole beside the British Trade Office, was because he needed to gather intelligence about this *Blue Member Club* and Winkle's activities.

The naked Colonel looked back to the seductively reclining Pon and looked down to note happily that he appeared ready for the interrogation. Well, he sighed to himself, it's all in the line of duty, and somebody has to do it. Curling up to a sleepy Pon, the Colonel employed his intrinsic knowledge of the Kama Sutra to put the young girl through a hundred positions and it seemed like almost as many orgasms in what was, for the Colonel, a warming-up exercise. It was at the point where the Colonel was still ramrod-hard and beginning to ease himself into the cleft of that delightful little bum, that the master of interrogation popped the big question. "You don't feel like telling me now what Winkle is really up to?"

Pon squirmed, tired, a bit saw, but *so* satisfied. "I feel like telling you everything. Nobody ever made me cum like that. I'm yours now, can't go back to Winkle."

The Colonel didn't collect human possessions or attachments, but saw no reason why Pon could not hang around until he wrapped up Winkle. She would need no cover. She would be what every other old man in Vientiane seemed to have, a temporary sex companion. "You don't have to go back with Winkle if you don't want to," the Colonel told her. "This house is British property, you can stay until you feel it safe to leave. But I would like to know everything about Winkle, his friends and his activities, including the layout of the *Blue Member Club*, and most importantly, his plans. So stay friendly with him if you can and with the other girls, but sleep here."

"You mean, be your spy and help you catch Winkle?" Pon was certainly not stupid. She also showed none of the indecision that the Colonel associated with a female of her age. "Okay then," she said, with no pause for reflection. Pon ceremoniously shook the Colonel's hand to seal their understanding and complicity, then poured herself a glass of water and sat up in bed. The Colonel had to admit she had the most delicious little tits and nipples, perfect complements to the perfect bum. He remained stretched out naked and fully erect, and Pon, who appeared surprisingly ignorant of the effect of little blue enhancement pills, particularly ignorant of the personal formula of the Colonel's customized stay-harder-longer variety, examined his erection and played with it. "Talk in the upstairs of the *Blue Member*," Pon said matter of factly, "is that Winkle is planning to take over."

"Take over the club? Kick his partners out?"

"No. Take over the country. Along with those men you saw tonight – his partners. Declare himself President and turn the whole of Vientiane into one big pleasure centre. Patpong and Pattaya will be nothing compared to the bar scene in Vientiane. But that's just icing on the businessman's cake. He will control the State Bank and Laos will become the centre of the money-laundering world."

"Do you understand what money-laundering is?" The Colonel was already surprised at the knowledge and vocabulary of this girl, maybe eighteen at most, who sold her body in one year for as much as a farmer could hope to gain in ten.

"Sure. Those of us Winkle trusts make regular runs across the bridge with dollars in our knickers. We put it into one of several Thai dollar accounts, or Thai Baht accounts, then take it out bit by bit and either bring it back or pass it to a man who takes it to Bangkok, from where I believe it is sent to Switzerland. We sometimes carry gems too, but only the best quality ones. These go straight to Europe. Winkle pays most of his people here through transfers between banks in Thailand and their banks in countries the UK cannot access. Of course, once he controls the State Bank, things will become less complicated and money will flow in and out at will. At the moment, Winkle is a careful man. He has as many legal activities as illegal. Employs a team of accountants to make sure he pays the legal requirements in both countries, taxes and so on, but whatever he pays legally, he gains a lot more from the illegal activities."

"Such as?"

"Human trafficking for one thing. Mostly underage virgin girls, sometimes boys, sold to Pattaya. You can ask Souk, her mother sold her – wasn't forced to sell her or anything like that, just wanted the money. Sold her once as a virgin to Pattaya through Winkle, then sold her again as a virgin to Norman West. On second thoughts better not ask Souk, Norman might not know about the first time. If it hadn't been for Norman, Souk's mother would have kept selling her as a virgin – Souk hates sex, or used to hate it, not so sure since Norman came into her life. For Souk, sex is just a way of raising money for her mother. A woman has nothing to sell as valuable as her body, and nothing to sell as valuable as first-use of her body. And when the whole village does it, there's no shame involved, and as everybody says, once a girl's period arrives, or even before, a poor girl will lose her virginity anyway. Might as well sell it for a thousand dollars as give it away for an ice cream to the boy on the corner."

"Any involvement in drugs?" The Colonel asked. Pon eased his member from where he had placed it at the entrance to her backside and suctioned it snugly into her virgina.

"He stays squeaky clean on the surface. Anyone at the *Blue Member*, even just a customer on *ma ba*, or anybody working in his enterprises caught with any drugs, is immediately handed over to the police. He even has a dog trained to sniff out drugs and has that same dog tour every activity every day. Even sends Sweetheart and his dogs for surprise inspections of his hotels and restaurants and stuff in Luang Prabang. He's very careful."

"You say he's very careful. Does that mean he is really clean?"

"Winkle is probably not clean of anything," Pon answered. "But when it comes to drugs, he has another man handle everything, one hundred per cent. All the way from the poppy fields and the refineries to accounting the profits in several distant bank accounts."

"And who is this other man?"

"Please don't ask me that. Anyway, you want to catch Winkle. I'll help if I can. But not to the point of suicide. Don't ask me such a question."

The Colonel took his moist and decidedly red member from its comfortable virginal sheath and replaced it firmly between the rear cheeks, turning Pon onto her lovely face. He pushed gently at first. Pon wrapped her fingers around it, to stop it going in too far.

"All right, *thi hak*, my darling. I know that's what you want. But only a little way, okay? And stop when I say so. I'm really a virgin as far as the back door goes. Nobody has entered, not even Winkle."

"Who runs the drug business for Winkle?" the Colonel repeated, pushing through her fingers and making Pon yelp.

The Colonel went slowly, having no wish to turn love-making into torture, but confident that in a few minutes he would have the name he sought. He reckoned without Pon. She groaned and cried and screamed, but her fingers seemed to be urging the Colonel on as much as they tried to keep him out. And the Colonel got so excited he forgot all about the interrogation he was conducting and found himself hugging Pon's waist, pulling her down as he drove home and exploded inside her.

They lay, sweating. It would have been hard to say who had enjoyed it most. Pon turned her head and kissed the Colonel's bruised lips with genuine passion. "Fantastic," she said.

"Yes," said the Colonel. "It was fantastic. Indeed you are fantastic."

"Nobody has been up my bum like that before," Pon repeated. And the Colonel, having no reason not to do so, believed her. But he still didn't know who was the drug-lord, and he had the feeling that trying to find out the next day might be just as much fun, but would produce no more of a result.

Pon snuggled herself up and into the Colonel, who had yet to leave her backside completely, and they lay like two kittens comforting each other after energetic play.

"I can tell you who runs the drug side of things." Pon whispered, a tremor in her voice. "Not because of your magnificent thing, and certainly not to get you to stop! But because I have never met anyone like you, and I want to stay with you. If I tell you, can I stay with you, at least while you are here in Laos? And if I tell you, will you promise to take the utmost care? He would kill us both."

The Colonel gave Pon a squeeze and for a fleeting moment felt something approaching affection for this young whore. "You can stay," he whispered. "And I always take the utmost care. You can give me his name."

Pon buried her lips in the Colonel's ear. "Welder," she said.

_____

# 7

# Calling Day

**Nigel** was just saying how nice it was these days in London where, after a hard day at the office, one could sit and drink in the atmosphere by the waterside and really enjoy a cold lager, when his mobile rang. "My shout," said Godfrey, getting up to go to the bar. "Fourth pint Nigel, better make this the last one or you'll be pissing down your leg again on the train home."

"Message from Welder," Nigel said as Godfrey returned with pints and crisps.

"Colonel still at it?"

"Seems so. But Welder says they have a meeting with the Deputy Minister of Foreign Affairs first thing in the morning. Well, Acting Deputy actually. So you can bring Paris in tomorrow after lunch."

"_If_ the Colonel's up to it," said Godfrey, with a snigger. "What's with the Acting? I thought Laos had four Deputy Ministers. Surely one of _them_ could have spared half-hour for the Colonel."

"You never cease to amaze me, Godfrey." The slight sneer had crept back into Nigel's voice. "Last week you didn't know where Laos was, now you're an expert on the governmental structure. Where did *you* get that snippet of information?"

"Just following my competency-enhancement work plan," replied Godfey with a hint of sarcasm. "Couldn't find anything on the FCO websites, so went straight to the source of all knowledge."

"Which is?"

"Lonely Planet. Four Deputy Ministers of Foreign Affairs. Or was it Four Deputy Prime Ministers?"

"Never mind," said Nigel.

"That's the national motto," said Godfrey.

"What is?"

"Never mind," replied Godfrey. "*Bo pen nyang,*" as the Colonel might say.

Nigel groaned. "What other cunning gems of information have you encumbered yourself with?"

"Well, there's the national currency. Sounds like it's good for a laugh."

"And what, Godfrey is the national currency of the Lao People's Democratic Republic? Can't be funnier than the Vietnamese Dong, divided into a hundred zoos."

"May not be funnier than the Vietnamese money, but it's in the same bed. The Kip. Divided into forty winks."


Next morning, after a full English breakfast on the weathered wooden boards of Welder's wide and high terrace, perched discretely within a tropical garden and reaching out and over a spectacular bend in the Mekong River, Pon gave him a goodbye-kiss that the Colonel felt had more passion and affection in it than he had received from his wife during their entire fifteen years of progeny-less liaison. Welder fondled Kim and asked if she wanted to come and sit in the car while they made some calls. She declined and said she would rather stay with Pon and help her make dinner for everybody.

Welder has it made, thought the Colonel…again…pity he's an international criminal.

The Colonel brushed aside the cloud of Welder the Suspect Drug Baron. He felt unusually lighthearted and recognised the feeling from long ago – happiness. He had not started a day feeling this good for years. His step had a bounce and his face had a smile. For the first time in over fifteen years, ever since he separated from his English wife, and long before it, the Colonel was actually looking forward to coming home for dinner, and very much looking forward to coming home to the woman, well, girl, who would cook it. He wasn't going to let a little drug-dealing darken his mood – or a lot of drug-dealing for that matter. He would decide what to do about Welder later.

"What's that you said?" Welder asked.

"Nothing. Didn't say anything," said the Colonel. "Just singing."

"Singing?! Crikey, I think maybe I had you pegged right upside down. Singing, eh? Good screw, was she then?"

The Colonel laughed. Yes, he thought, she was a very good screw.


It was to be a day of tea-stops, unhurried and polite. Welder drove and introduced. The Colonel made diplomatic chat and delivered the letter requesting Winkle's extradition.

The first stops were the essential ones, required by diplomatic courtesy as much as by the objective of his mission. The Acting Deputy Minister of Foreign Affairs stood up from his desk, walked across a worn track in his carpet, grasped the visitor's hand warmly, and twisted his free arm around the Colonel, to turn on an air-conditioner that hung, at the height of a sitting ear, from a hole in the wall and vibrated with the noise and frequency of a pneumatic drill. "Gift of the Soviet Union," the Acting Deputy said, speaking within the noise not over it, or that's what the Colonel thought he said. "My name is Gop, the name means Frog."

The Colonel had added some Gurka insignia and all of his medal bars to his reversed parka dinner jacket. He had borrowed a tie from

Welder – a bit too bright and flashy for the Colonel's tastes, but Pon had said he looked absolutely gorgeous, so maybe he would change his tastes. From the waist up, which was the only part that would figure in the photograph the Acting Deputy's assistant took for the *Vientiane Times*, the Colonel was reasonably presentable. However, the permacrease trousers and rubber-soled canvas combat boots did rather subtract from the swath and serious diplomatic image, and the Colonel felt somewhat *mal en soie* on seeing the Acting Deputy Minister dressed in a shark-grey suit, unblemished and uncreased silk tie of pastel hue, white shirt with just the appropriate amount of cuff extending beyond the jacket sleeves to show his mother-of-pearl cufflinks, and black dress-shoes that, had they been a little closer to his closely-shaven face would have reflected the handsome features of this fifty-eight year old man who looked forty. There was nothing very Che Geuvara-ish about the Acting Deputy Minister of the People's Republic.

In spite of a youth spent struggling for the revolutionary cause, Acting Deputy Gop had retained all his shining white teeth and a full head of well-groomed back-combed hair. The Colonel had been briefed by Welder that Gop was one of the youngest in the hundred and fifty or so men and women in the Central Committee, but within the top twenty in terms of power and closeness to the President. The Colonel thought him as nice as pie. The Acting Deputy took in both hands the formal letter requesting extradition of Winkle, saying politely that he would ensure that within the day the Minister and the Prime Minister saw it and that of course the matter would need to be discussed with the President at the earliest opportunity. At least that's what the Colonel, straining to hear through the noise of the Soviet Union's gift, thought he said.

The churning airconditioner was making so much noise and the Deputy Minister was speaking in such quietly respectful tones, that the Colonel had to turn his super-hearing powers on full just to make out that the Deputy was speaking English, and then he was not too sure.

Fluent in Russian, Vietnamese and Czech, the Acting Deputy

Foreign Minister had chosen English as the language of this meeting. Rather a pity, the Colonel thought, since clearly it was a struggle for both of them.

"Laos is foreign investment necessary, and the biggest Winkle in the country. We like big Winkle."

The Colonel waited until he could be sure he was supposed to say something. Whatever he said had to be simple and short and, with all respect for protocol and Lao sensitivities, delivered in a voice soft enough to indicate respect but loud enough to be heard by both the Deputy Minister and the girl who sat as faraway as she could get from the airconditioner, in the far corner of a long room, taking note of every word in a well-used exercise book in pencil. He looked across to Welder, who, having shook the Acting Deputy's hand and introduced the Colonel, had propped himself in one of the heavy and uncushioned wood chairs and had no intention of saying a word.

Welder had already briefed the Colonel that Winkle was probably the biggest of the few individual or corporate investors in the country, and, coming at a time when the Lao Government was pulling out all the stops to encourage foreign investment, extradition of Winkle could not only damage the economy but be reported in the region, and especially on Capital Hill in the US of A, as a crack-down on foreigners. The Colonel's reply kept to the brief he had been given in the FCO and resolved the acoustics problem by saying everything twice, once softly to show respect and once loudly enough to be heard.

"Winkle maybe big thief. We try in court. Guilty, Winkle go prison. Not guilty, Winkle come back Laos with extra money from England." Spoken softly and spoken as near as the Colonel could get to the Acting Deputy without kissing him. The Colonel then turned his head to the note-taker and threw his voice to her at a decibel-level slightly above that of the stay-behind Soviet aircon, a much louder voice, but one which would appear to the Acting Deputy as quiet and respectful. It arrived slowly and the note-catcher missed not a word.

"We appreciate that Mr Winkle appears important to the Lao

economy at this stage but you need fear no adverse reaction on investment if you grant the extradition request. Quite the reverse in fact. The UK would be happy to upgrade the Trade Office here, open and staff a business-school here, have the Department for International Development and the British Council discuss the opening of offices and programmes in Laos, and encourage Jardines, already here in a sense since Sucksabit had been part of its world-wide interests until it went independent, to expand into other areas of service compatible with the objectives of the Government of the Lao People's Democratic Republic, such as the creation of a duty-free zone. In anticipation of the advances we expect Laos to make in the coming years, I am also delighted to inform you that the UK will be fully supporting the Lao request for WTO entry and has already made its decision known to the United States, which is unlikely to go against the wishes of its staunchest ally in the war against international terrorism."

"Laos open Embassy in England?" the Acting Deputy said with a smile. The Colonel had to stop himself from replying in pre-kindergarten English.

Godfrey and Nigel had briefed the Colonel that the Lao had once had a very fine embassy in London – until the new communist government had sold it at a huge profit. No way they are going to get another one, at least not as a free gift from the UK, and no way the UK is ready to reciprocate by opening a full British Embassy to Laos. The briefing was not a lot of use to the Colonel in forming a diplomatic reply now. So the Colonel did what all diplomats do when cornered by an embarrassing question, he changed the subject.

"I love your new book," the Colonel said, taking a copy from his jacket pocket. "It teaches me a lot about the evolution of Laos. Will you sign a copy for me. And the English is very good."

The Acting Deputy Minister beamed as he signed the book. The Colonel thanked him and rose to go.

"You want girl?" asked the Deputy Minister of Foreign Affairs. There followed a long pause in which the Colonel was genuinely at a loss as to how to answer. He looked down the room. The girl taking notes was certainly pretty enough. She smiled to the Colonel.

The girl rose. Very trim indeed, thought the Colonel, beginning to be fascinated by the possibility that Foreign *Affaires* sanctioned non-marital sexual interaction between foreigners and Lao – proscribed somewhere within one of just thirteen laws then in the Lao penal code. The girl wore the long traditional Lao *sin*, this one of plain blue silk hugged tightly into a tiny waist by a thousand-dollar gold belt and embroidered elaborately at the hem. She turned in front of the Colonel. Nice tight little bum he thought, and very nice feet.

"Yes," said the Colonel, glancing over at Welder, who was keeping a straight face with difficulty. "Yes. Very kind of you."

The girl sat on the settee next to the Colonel, took his hand and shook it. "My name is Latda. I am the Head of the interpreter unit. The UK funded my training. This is what I have noted today." The girl spoke in fluent English and showed the Colonel her note book. Indeed, every word he had uttered was there, along with a revised-English version of statements made by his interlocutor. "Is there anything else you would like to ask the Acting Deputy Minister? Or anything more you would like to state, particularly regarding the exchange of embassies and the extradition of Mr Winkle."

"I shall inform the FCO of our discussion on this subject. As far as I know, the FCO has no objection to a Lao Embassy in London, *eventually.*"

Acting Deputy Foreign Minister Gop remained smooth and polite as he squeezed the Colonel's hand and promised to follow-up on the matter of Winkle, regretting only that time was so limited, just twenty-eight days. But they might find a way. He then lapsed into Lao and asked again if the Colonel would be so kind as to carry back to the UK with him the advance information that the Lao PDR would greatly value opening an embassy in London and granting the UK every assistance, to the extent of free land or an existing building of their choice to build or open a British Embassy in Vientiane.

The Deputy and his assistant escorted the Colonel and Welder down the stairs to the ever-open front doors of the building, lazily folded half-way back on themselves as if the folder was not sure if the building were open or closed. The Colonel noticed that closing them would anyway have made little difference, as at least two door frames were completely lacking in glass and could easily be stepped through. Nobody sat behind the reception desk to note their departure (or, for that matter, their arrival), there were no guards at all, and the echoing concrete corridors, badly in need of a good attack of detergent and a paint job, were empty of personnel. The Colonel had been briefed in London that the Lao civil service was 30% overstaffed. Where were they all?

As he closed the door to the Range Rover and waved farewell to the Acting Deputy, the girl and his official extradition request, which remained in the hands of Acting Deputy Foreign Minister Frog, the Colonel thought out loud. "This is not at all what I was expecting from a communist state. What is to stop a couple of men with guns walking into that building, going up to the offices of the Minister and Deputy Minister, opening the doors, shooting both between the eyes, and walking out?"

"Nothing at all," replied Welder. "Indeed, a dozen fairly determined men could do the same in the half a dozen ministries of any substance, all of which are within a few hundred metres of here, then take out the Prime Minister in his compound over there – like to drive through by the way? – and simply toss a decent-sized bomb through the President's living room window without stopping the car. And all before lunch. Winkle's been trying to get them to accept Sucksabit protection at give-away rates, but the Lao don't seem interested."

The Colonel was tempted to ask Welder why security of top people appeared to be non-existent. Then he remembered that Sucksabit, ultimately under the control of Willie Winkle rather than Rupert Sweetheart, *was* guarding the airport and most embassies, and he remembered the words of Pon, given under no duress, regarding Winkle's ambitions. *Take over the Country*, she had said. And he remembered Pon's whispered accusation that Welder himself ran what must be the biggest money-earner in the country, the drug trade, and the Colonel changed the subject.

"Sounds like they are quite keen on an exchange of embassies?"

"Well, don't fancy yourself as Ambassador in Paradise just yet. For at least two years now, the Lao have raised the same request for an embassy with every important visitor. At least it means the Foreign Ministry thinks you are important, even if you did only get to see the Acting Deputy. But don't expect anything much to happen following the extradition request. Real power in this country lies with the President and five or six people close to him, but any discussions or decisions are made with the whole eleven-man – ten really, one's dead – Central Committee of the Politbureau present, and they meet at Party Headquarters, out at Kilometre 6. Mind you, they would have Winkle out of the country tomorrow and all be singing *God Save the Queen* if the FCO suddenly agreed to an exchange of embassies."

"It's all nothing like I expected to find in a communist country."

"Right," said Winkle. "Laos doesn't meet expectations."

"In the nicest possible way, of course. It just seems surprisingly open and, what's the word?…free."

"In many ways it is. That certainly makes it easier for Winkle to operate. Did you keep that kukri strapped to your leg when you were in the Ministry?"

"Yes. I never thought about it. Stupid of me. Might have provoked a diplomatic incident."

Welder shrugged.

They drove around the Victory Monument, a copy of the Arc de Triomph, begun by the French, continued under the period of American influence, and finally completed – if the rough cement finish, and hole where the lift should be, could realistically be described as completed – after the communist victory of December 1975, with cement left behind by the Americans to construct a longer airstrip, a fact that gave rise to its local nickname of 'the vertical runway'. Welder described it with the mixed affection residents feel for this anomaly of a memorial to an unknown victory. *Victory Gate* was unambiguously Lao in its ambiguity. "One thing's for sure. Put some guys with bazookas on top of that – and anybody can just walk up it – and you wouldn't need to bother shooting ministers. You could take out every ministry and the Prime Minister's Office in five minutes. Make a lot of noise though and Vientiane is a quiet place, people might notice."

"You seem to have given the matter some thought," the Colonel said.

"What matter's that?"

"Blowing up the existing government," said the Colonel as Welder swung the car around in a large loop to take in the real National Monument, the Buddhist stupor known as *Thhat Luang* – the Golden Stupor – and next to it the Lao Parliament, the *National Assembly*, He approached the Victory Monument again from the other side, where no single vehicle occupied the recently constructed wide and tree-lined parking area, and drove straight into the Ministry of Justice, where the Colonel had a repeat performance with a real Deputy who, if anything, was even nicer than his Acting counterpart in Foreign Affairs, and who complained openly about the corruption of his own police officers, joking that perhaps they should all be sacked, or locked up, and replaced with Sucksabit or a few British bobbies.

Welder then took the Colonel on a little tour of Vientiane, driving down the pot-holed road connecting the Victory Arch with the official President's Palace on the River. They passed the *Morning Market*, which closes after 5.00 p.m. Welder pointed out *Wat Pra Keo*, "The Thais stole *Pra Keo*, the Emerald Buddha, from that temple, still have it in Bangkok," and Wat Sisaket. "The only temple left untouched when the Thais torched the city." He drove past the main Catholic church and the Seventh-Day Adventist church. "See the light bulbs on the doors? They light up at night and it looks like a burning cross, the Ku Klux Klan would surely be happy here."

"And what about all that talk of religious persecution?" the Colonel asked.

"Talk. That's it. Just talk. I can take you to two mosques, one Baha'i Centre, a hundred Buddhist temples, and even evangelical churches. You can't stop talk."

Not far from the British Trade Office, they arrived at Winkle's Headquarters. At six stories, one of the tallest and most modern buildings in town. Certainly the only one crowned by a sea of high antennae, which Winkle later explained allowed his staff to tele-phone anywhere in the world at any time, which was the essence of the operation.

They were directed to a specific parking area and accompanied by security guards through automatic glass doors that carried the message "Welcome to Investment Unlimited" and responded only to the correct punch-in number code. As the Colonel walked through into a pleasant air-conditioned atmosphere, the doors buzzed loudly, causing more guards to appear, these ones big boys holding big guns in front of them. Lao, but with a greater sense of discipline and re-solve than the Colonel had noted generally among those Lao he had met during his short stay so far; he guessed them to be part of Rupert Sweetheart's hand-trained elite. The doors locked behind them. The Colonel surrendered his kukri and was provided with a numbered ticket to reclaim it. The guards escorted him and Welder through the immaculate marble entrance hall and up Vientiane's only escalators, from which the Colonel could note the moving surveillance cameras and laser alarm-beams, switched off to allow their passage, before reaching a smiling Winkle at the third floor.

Winkle was dressed in much the same disheveled way as he had been the night before, and looked to the Colonel as if he had not bothered to shave. His careless profile seemed to thumb its nose at the world – like a born-again teenager making a statement, 'I have arrived, I can dress any way I want.' He took the Colonel's hand and, at least two guards constantly by his side, introduced him to some of his technical staff.

Winkle's staff was overridingly British; almost all seemed to have East London accents. They sat in lines at banks of computers talk-ing to people they did not know, selling or trying to sell shares that according to the FCO existed in virtual space or in reality, or were in passage between locations. The Colonel wondered how *he* would respond if a cockney voice telephoned out of the blue and tried to sell him shares he had never heard of at a knock-down price. He found it difficult to believe anybody could be so gullible. But then he remembered Norman, obviously an intelligent man, and his gullibility regarding Souk. Greed, love and the need for human company were emotions, and as such were much stronger than reason. The Colonel spun his super hearing around the room and realized that many of the conversations sounded like old friends talking. Most, Winkle confirmed, were repeat calls.

Winkle invited the Colonel to pick up any of the spare earphone sets attached to all computers and listen in. The first sounded like an old lady, "It's so nice of you to call, Harry, and I do look forward to your calls. Nobody calls me these days and you say the calls cost nothing, that's marvelous in this day and age. My son, who hardly ever calls, told me it was all a con trick, but he has a computer and so I gave him the website thingy you gave me last time, and you know what? He came back and said he'd looked at the site and checked the trading price of the shares and what you are offering is below the trading price. He said if I bought them and sold them immediately, I could not lose. Not that I'd do that, Harry, since, as you say, the price has already come down and the only way is up. So I think I will go along, not that I can do very much you know, but I can afford a hundred pounds, if I can pay by cheque, I don't hold with credit cards." The Colonel heard Winkle's operator give details of a bank in the UK that would accept the cheque and assure the caller that without waiting for confirmation of clearance, a share certificate would be sent out today.

Winkle took them up further escalators showing the third and fourth floors, which were repeats of the second, the fifth floor, where his website team explained how they stayed up to the minute on constant revision of company websites, to the sixth and top floor, where he proudly showed off his private offices and personal quarters, and finally to the rooftop garden, where Winkle used the vantage point to indicate the location of some of his other interests and part interests, including a five-star hotel that appeared to be going up in the very middle of the swirling waters of the Mekong River. The Colonel noted at least one huge electronic screen in every room, constantly monitoring changes in share prices. Everything looked very clean in all senses of the term.

"Up here, among the antennae, this is a private beer garden where the men can unwind any time they want to, they are all on commission, so working hours are left up to them. There's a canteen on the first floor and the second and third provide accommodation. My men are well looked after and rarely need to go out of the building. Girls are issued passes and can come and go. So you won't find many of my boys disturbing the local population balance." The Colonel remembered Nigel and Godfrey at the FCO telling him of a messy incident when Winkle's boys had badly beaten some Lao after a disagreement emerged during the directly-televised World Cup, and a separate incident when some of Winkle's drunken rabble had badly beaten police called to the Fountain on New Year's eve, when a group of naked computer operators had decided that the fountain's waters looked better with some red paint and detergent thrown in. Winkle himself had taken that group to the local police station the next day at gun point, where Chantavong had, at Winkle's insistence, locked them up in an air-less small room for one month. Winkle had provided Chantavong with five hundred dollars for his expenses and provided another five hundred as compensation for the injured police officers. When the men were released, they were deported with Winkle's blessing and without back-payments owing. Winkle ran a tight ship.

"Your operation is very impressive," the Colonel said.

"I like to think so," said Winkle. "You have just seen what some people call my *boiler room*. No idea how that term originated by the way, my premises must be the coolest and most pleasant in Vientiane. We are only doing what is done on any stock exchange – just providing better deals for our customers and staff and all-hours' trading."

"And the Lao don't mind all those antennas and foreign phone calls?"

"Some of our best customers are Lao. Why should they mind?"

Before leaving, the Colonel asked Winkle if he could borrow Pon for awhile.

"Of course. She called through to me earlier from Welder's to ask the same thing. Seems she likes you a lot. Said you were very nice to her. Of course if you do want a change, just pop along any time."

Winkle offered to show the Colonel Sucksabit and his other enterprises, but the Colonel said he could see Mr Winkle was very busy and he was sure Welder would do a good job as guide. He thanked Winkle pleasantly and shook hands with a practiced sincerity.

As they left the front door, the Colonel gave his opinion to Welder. "Very nice place. Certainly beats any office you will find in the East-End of London. I should think any union in the UK would cry if it saw the beautiful conditions Winkle's men work in. Good security too. Very well organized."

"Has Winkle converted you so easily then?" Welder asked.

"He appears to be as clean as a whistle," answered the Colonel.

"That's a con-man's stock in trade," said Welder.

Perhaps, the Colonel thought, studying the suspect drug lord's face as he drove, perhaps we are all con-men in some way.

8

---

# The Colonel Strikes

**Godfrey was just beginning** the news when the telephone rang. He hated having the news interrupted. "You, Nige. Can't it wait until after the news?"

"It could, Godfrey, but I thought you'd like to know the Colonel has delivered the letter of request for the extradition of Winkle. So you can get on to the Lao Embassy in Paris first thing in the morning."

"Right. Would be a lot more convenient though if the Lao had an Embassy in England."

"That, Godfrey, is exactly what the Lao said to the Colonel."

"You mean they *want* to be here?"

"Crying out to have their man in London."

"And we won't let them?"

"Come, come, Godfrey. We'd never say no to such a request. Just might take a long time saying yes. It's all politics, even if we pretend it's all economics. Not our concern of course, unless a memo comes down from *upstairs*."

"Say no more, Nige. I'll be on to it first thing. Apart from delivering letters, the Colonel been up to anything else?"

"The grand tour of Vientiane, which took an hour, and of Winkle's enterprises, which the Colonel describes as very modern, clean and impressive. Apart from that our Colonel seems to have had a quiet day, dinner at Welder's and early to bed."

"Who with this time?"

"Same one," said Nigel.

"That's nice."

"Maybe, Godfrey. But Welder says she's a recent girlfriend of Winkle and has probably been planted on the Colonel."

"What does the Colonel say?"

"Same thing, Godfrey. But also that the girl has given him vital information upon which he is about to begin action."

"Begin action? I thought his action was confined to the bedroom."

"Ah, Godfrey. Nice boy but such a lot to learn. Now, *your* Tony Blair has just appeared on the screen so I'll leave you."

"Not *my* Tony…" but Nigel had already rung off.


At three in the morning, a time when night owls were for the most part already tucked up in somebody's bed and a time when almost three hours of dark night remained, the Colonel drew a black ninja-like hood over his face, and put on an all-black action suit, into which he placed his special instruments of combat. He left Pon, Welder and Kim asleep and ignorant of his departure and jogged the three kilometers through empty streets. His kukri was now strapped to the outside of his trouser leg. His mind was 100% keyed for action as he climbed carefully over the wall surrounding what Godfrey and Nigel in London had referred to as Winkle's "boiler-room", the spankingly modern Investment Unlimited he had visited the day before and about which Pon had provided useful ground plan detail.

The Colonel had decided to strike early in his mission, at the stage of *entant cordiale*, when the enemy was friendly, and therefore most likely to be off-guard. Always attack when unexpected – it was his off-track philosophy. He would search Winkle's personal offices, on the top floor of the building and gather whatever evidence he could to support the request for extradition and hurry it through Lao procedures without unnecessary violence. The most obvious evidence, the Colonel thought, could be the films and photographs that Winkle made and kept in readiness to compromise or blackmail his clients or guests, including the Colonel and members of the Government. While these were made at the *Blue Member Club*, the Colonel had noted during his tour the day before, a sophisticated editing and VCD production unit in Winkle's top offices, and Pon had confirmed that the videos were edited and stored at the Investment Unlimited office, where entry was more tightly controlled and restricted than at the raucous *Blue Member Club*.

As his soft-soled combat boots touched the manicured lawn inside the compound, the Colonel's developed sixth sense told him he was not alone. He reached for his night-sight glasses, and had put them on just in time to see three Doberman dogs jumping silently for his throat. The dogs, Pon had warned him, had been de-barked by Sweetheart on the orders of Wilder; their purpose was not to warn off intruders but to attack and kill. The Colonel's right hand responded automatically. Even as the dogs sprang, the kukri was drawn from its oiled sheath and swung in a wide arc. As the dogs' bodies hit the Colonel, sending him staggering and spattering blood over his nicely-pressed combat fatigues, all three dogs were already dead. Only one managed a whine as the breath left his body for the last time.

With the aid of his night glasses, the Colonel noted guards at fifty metre intervals surrounding the building. All were Lao and all wore the uniform of Sucksabit. The difference with other Sucksabit guards, at the airport and foreign embassies, was that these men were armed, and heavily armed, the Colonel noted, with AK-47s in their hands and side arms on their belts. Any honest company would not need nor could afford such a wide use of security personnel.

Even the Colonel could not take out all the guards, had he wanted to do so. But the Colonel avoided bloodshed whenever possible. These men were only doing a job they were paid to do, there was no substantive reason to kill them and to do so would certainly alert those inside the building who were still working at their computers, selling shares across the world. No shades were drawn and the Colonel would need to pass these floors on his way to the top.

After careful surveillance, the Colonel selected a back corner of the building as offering the best chance for an ascent: the inside lighting was dimmer and there appeared to be less activity. Two guards were stationed at the corner, smoking and chatting. The Colonel moved silently into position behind them, sheathed his kukri and placed his hands on the neck and shoulders of both men, a comradely action. As the men turned, the Colonel pinched neck nerves and both men dropped quietly to the ground. They would be paralysed for three hours, plenty of time for the Colonel to complete his mission and be far away.

The Colonel unfolded the arms of the tiny grappling hook with which he had three times climbed Everest, pointed it to the top of the building and pressed the release button. A muffled pop sent the hook flying like an arrow beyond the six floors of Investment Unlimited to hook its barbs among the branches of a tree in the roof garden. It trailed behind it a nylon cord invisible to any naked eye except that of the Colonel, who had, during his many incarnations, trained his vision to exercise supernatural powers. The cord connected with the buckle of the Colonel's belt. A touch on the buckle and a tiny winch whirred, taking in the slack, then lifting the Colonel, kukri in hand and feet walking on the glass, up past the second floor, where a naked heap of white flesh was bouncing on a little brown girl, past the third, fourth and fifth floors, where eyes were too directed at computer screens and minds too directed to the commission they were earning to notice a dark figure passing on a dark corner, past Winkle's dimly lit personal offices and quarters on the sixth floor, to the roof garden.

The Colonel peered over the parapet wall and noted with some surprise that activity in the roof garden was in full swing. Winkle's policy of paying by results, in terms of commission earned, and the provision of accommodation and recreation, appeared to keep most people in the building. A couple of dozen young girls moved between tables, serving beer and being fondled. The Colonel allowed himself to wonder what percentage of Vientiane's youth were camp followers of Winkle enterprises. Perhaps, he thought, it would be easier to calculate what percentage was not. He scanned the tables and was jolted to see Winkle himself sitting at a table, talking seriously to a small group of men and, as usual, surrounded by fawning girls. The Colonel had assumed Winkle spent his nights at the *Blue Member*. He would have to make haste.

Descending on the cord to the sixth floor, the Colonel placed a suction pad on the glass, ran a finger-mounted diamond ring in a large circle around the pad, and gently pushed the glass inwards, laying it on a convenient desk. He listened carefully for any alarm bells before entering through the hole he had made and unhooking his belt to allow him full freedom of movement.

He was in Winkle's personal office. But before beginning his search, he checked the whole floor. Opening one door, he found Winkle's bedroom, complete with two naked girls on his bed. The girls were twins. Wide awake, they were waiting for Winkle's return. On seeing a hooded black-clad figure in the doorway, both started to scream. The Colonel launched himself upon them and used both hands on both throats to stifle the screams. The twins, children really, struggled, lashing out with thin arms and legs. Fighting children was a new experience for the Colonel. He could not kill them, but could not allow them to raise the alarm. Reluctantly, for he knew it did not send to sleep but merely paralysed temporarily, leaving the paralysed fully conscious and afraid, the Colonel used the same technique he had used on neck nerves of the guards. As their little bodies sank into immobility, the Colonel whispered that they should not be afraid, and they would recover complete normality within three hours. He arranged their bodies so they were hugging each other, a pillow under each head, and covered their nakedness with a sheet.

The rest of the floor revealed a full kitchen, a large sitting, a larger meeting room, and the film editing facilities, but no videos or disks. There were no obvious threats or alarms, but the important unknown factor was when Winkle would return. The Colonel went through Winkle's desk and found nothing of interest. He turned to the safe and noted that in addition to a combination dial, it required two keys to open. Nothing for it. The Colonel took plastic explosive from a pouch around his waist and placed it on the safe door, inserted a detonator into the pliable materials and ran back into the bedroom, where the girls were curled up in apparent peace. The Colonel closed the door as the blast shook the apartment. It would surely bring guards running. He had very little time. He prepared his defences by taking the cigarette lighter from his sleeve pocket.

The jagged edges of the safe door looked like a sardine can opened with a kukri. The Colonel reached inside and removed stacks of VCDs. Quickly he looked at the labels. The very top one was labeled "Colonel", the others had names that the Colonel did not recognize but that Pon certainly would. He put all into a stretchable nylon bag. A singed file labeled "Crown Jewels" caught his eye. That too went into the bag, along with a stack of loose papers. Then the Colonel's eyes lit up as he pulled out a bundle of one-hundred dollar bills and a large brick of Lao kip. As the Colonel stood up, he could see guards outside the sixth floor door, with Winkle's outline behind them.

The extra-strong glass resisted assault with a fire extinguisher just long enough for the Colonel to snap open his cigarette lighter, automatically priming a three-second fuse for both explosive and asphyxiating smoke screen. The Colonel threw both halves at the entrance door as the glass gave way and guards spilled through. The explosive charge blasted apart the three Sucksabit guards who had climbed through the broken door and sent shards of glass into Winkle, who was thrown backwards by the blast and found himself dazed in front of what was left of his own apartment door and asphyxiated by the smoke which filled the sixth floor with a gagging cloud. The anarchy provided precious seconds for the Colonel to make his escape.

The Colonel leapt to put on his belt and jumped through the window. Rounds of AK47 fire whistled around his head. He descended at maximum speed, noting with satisfaction as he went that all guards were rushing into the building and up to the sixth floor. His escape over the outer wall thus went unchallenged.

The guard at the gate of Welder's compound was fast asleep as the Colonel easily scaled the diplomatic defences and slipped unseen through the gardened grounds. At the entrance to Welder's house, the small piece of folded paper the Colonel had inserted between outer door and its frame was still in place, nobody had left to follow him. Dawn had yet to break. All was as it should be as the Colonel let himself quietly into the house and into the guest's bedroom.

Pon pretended to be asleep as she peeped through long lashes. The Colonel took off a black hood and black clothing, pushed it all into a black bag, hid the bag in the wardrobe and slipped into bed and into Pon. She backed herself snugly into the Colonel's embrace and began to play her role, then became genuinely aroused as the Colonel energetically released the tensions built up by action.


Winkle cuffed the Lao Sucksabit guard at the tracking screen. "There's a tracer in every article of the Colonel's clothing, why did you not inform me he was on the move?"

"Look at the screen," the shaking guard mumbled. "The red dot has been static all night. The Colonel has not left his bed."

"Then who came here?" growled Winkle. The *Investments Unlimited* doctor had patched up with iodine and sticking plasters several cuts on Winkle's face caused by glass shards and given him a whiff of oxygen to clear the effects of the smoke. Winkle looked as ugly as his mood. Attacked in his own office and home, and all his security had proven worthless. "Send Biggs and Stamford and two guards to Welder's and find out if the Colonel ever left the house during the night. And have Pon brought back here. And tell Biggs to remove this Colonel permanently." Wilder stormed back to his bedroom and a whole new sexual experience.

"What's the best hotel in town," the Colonel asked as Pon washed him down in the shower. The outside world was rapidly becoming lighter outside the open shower window.

"Setta Palace is the most expensive, but very small. Lao Plaza is large and international."

"Good. Get dressed and we'll go have breakfast there."

The Colonel took the black bag with them and they left through the main gate, saying good morning to the guard who opened it and, at the Colonel's request, stopped an early morning tuk-tuk. The Colonel climbed into the rear of the vehicle and sat on the narrow benches full with chattering women going to market. As the tuk-tuk pulled away from the house, a Land Cruiser pulled up at the gates and Winkle's bully boys jumped out. Pon saw them and shrank back, pulling the Colonel further into the vehicle and down among the baskets of the passengers.

"Colonel on the move," the guard said into the phone to Winkle, watching the red dot move along Thadeua Road.

"Phone Biggs and have them followed and stopped. Deal with the Colonel and bring Pon in alive." Winkle barked into the mobile phone, cut the connection and went back to contemplating a new delight: necrophilia. Double necrophilia at that. The bodies were still as warm as life, but totally unresponsive, their young, open eyes registering only confusion and fear. He could find no trace of how they had died. Interesting, Winkle thought, as he pushed his way into what he rated the tightest little cunt he had ever entered. Interesting, and exciting, he thought, they must have been overcome by the gas while asleep – although why are their eyes open? Well, it's done, so better not waste an opportunity. He managed to achieve entry from the rear of one totally unresponsive virgina – better, he thought, than any virgin – while looking directly into the fear-ridden eyes of the second twin. Winkle had never been so turned on in his life.

The tuk-tuk stopped at the market. Pon removed a tracer-bug from the cuff of the Colonel's trousers and another from inside the collar of his shirt. "I'm sorry," she said to the Colonel. "Winkle made me put them on when we were together at the Blue Member. They can trace your movements on a computer screen."

"Any more?" the Colonel asked.

"Your underpants," Pon replied giggling.

Immediately, the Colonel unzipped and Pon's fingers groped inside his loin. The women stopped gathering their baskets together and stared. Pon threw all three bugs into a woman's basket as the passengers left the back of the tuk-tuk.

As the Colonel and Pon continued to a sumptuous breakfast at Lao Plaza, the Sucksabit operator, trembling, again phoned up to Winkle. "They've gone into the Morning Food Market".

"Tell Biggs, not me. And get the doctor up here quickly. And some soapy water. I'm stuck."

"Stuck?" questioned the Sucksabit guard. "Stuck where?"

"Cunt," replied Winkle.

And cunt to you, you bastard, thought the guard as he phoned for the doctor and watched the red dot moving slowly among the vegetables.

"I've been Winkle's favourite for the past six months, but not any more. He wouldn't have given me to you if he still fancied me. He told me to stick those bugs on your clothes. I had no choice."

The Colonel reached across his huge helping of everything he had piled on his plate from the buffet and touched her hand caringly. "That's all right. I understand." That means, the Colonel thought, they will not have traced me to the intrusion at *Investment International* during the night. Luckily, he had dumped his knickers, along with other clothes, on the bedroom floor – the Colonel always went knickerless into battle. But how far could he trust Pon? Quite far, his inner dialogue concluded. After all, there was no reason for her to have taken off the bugs. And hell hath no fury like a woman scorned, he reminded himself. And Pon had been discarded by Winkle. But Pon was certainly no fool, she knew Winkle only too well and she was not likely to risk his wrath willingly.

"Just imagine Winkle's heavies rummaging through the women in the market looking for us or the bugs," the Colonel said lightly, laughing at his mind's image.

"When he doesn't find us," Pon replied, "he will punish me. Normally when he kicks a girl out, he gives her a present. But when he finds me, I'm finished. As good as dead."

"Don't worry," replied the Colonel gallantly. His speciality was saving damsels in distress, a speciality built up over centuries of honourable reincarnation, and honed to its finest point through years of service in the gurkas, where death before dishonour was the norm of the men he led, and nothing was more merit worthy than rescuing damsels. True, the rescued damsels were usually a tad more virginal than Pon, but he was happy to make an exception. He looked around at the empty restaurant; nobody knew where they were. "I will protect you. Do you believe me?"

Pon gave a "Yes" so hesitantly, it sounded like "No".

"They will find me easily at Welder's," she said.

"We're not going back to Welder's."

"Then where?"

"First, I want to see the manager here and rent a private business room. Then we send one of the hotel staff to buy tickets in our names for the next flight to Luang Prabang."

"Winkle has Sucksabit at the airport there."

"I said we buy tickets. I didn't say we go there. I have another destination in mind. But I need some time to go through some things with a computer, a gallon of coffee, and a locked door."

"Those 'things', are they in that black bag? Did you steal them from Winkle? Is that why he sent Biggs and Stamford after you?"

"Yes," said the Colonel calmly. "I took them from Winkle's safe.

You can help me identify them. As for Biggs and Stamford, no idea who they are."

"They lean on people. And they kill people. Winkle thinks nothing of knocking out anybody who gets in his way, and you are a major threat to him. Biggs is Winkle's personal assassin." The Colonel now remembered the heavily-built bouncer at the *Blue Member*. Powerful but slow.

The soapy water had no effect. Winkle was stuck tight. "Get your scalpel and cut her open," he said. "I've got things to do."

The terrified girls heard every word, but could not move a muscle. Not even blink a fearful eye to show they were alive.

"Strange they should both die at once," Winkle's doctor said. "It looks like a suicide pact or a double murder, but there are no signs of struggle, quite the opposite. I suppose you're right, they died in their sleep from the effects of the smoke or gas or whatever it was. But I've never seen anybody die in their sleep with their eyes open – and both girls at that."

"Maybe that's a peculiarity of the gas. You can analyse it all you want once the Colonel is dead and you have his possessions. But for now, just cut me out of here."

The doctor laid fingers on the neck of one of the girls and spoke with surprise. "She's still warm," he said. "And she seems to have a faint pulse. I think she's still alive."

At that moment, as if to confirm the doctor's diagnosis, both girls gave little groans as the effect of the paralysis-pinch began to wear off. The groans were accompanied by a pulsating of loosening virginal muscles which excited Wilder and prompted him to complete the sexual experience which he had enjoyed at first but would not wish to repeat. He came with a huge groan and popped out.

"Okay. Bring them round to their normal dim intelligence and find out what happened. I've got to catch or kill a Colonel."

9

_____

# Wanted Dead or Alive

**"Do you know what time it is?"** Godfrey complained into the phone.

"My feelings precisely. That damn new urgent signal on my mobile sent me downstairs to check the email – after all it could have been from _upstairs._"

"Well get on with it, Nigel. I'd only just got to sleep. Is it _upstairs_ stuff? And what's so urgent it can't keep 'til morning?"

"It is morning for the Colonel in Laos, early morning. The e-mail's from him, not Welder this time. Top Confidential, Top Urgent."

"You woke me up for that? A nutter of a colonel sends an email about a twenty-nine year old case – and it can't wait until tomorrow?"

"I think we'd better not ignore it, Godfrey. The Colonel asks for a reply within two hours. He has scanned through to us a list of all foreign personnel working for Winkle, together with the numbers of their bank accounts, their passport numbers and date of expiration. All the bank accounts are in non-EU countries, so we probably can't access them. The passports are all British, and some are coming up for renewal soon, and some have been renewed recently – sent to the Bangkok Embassy by Welder."

"That might sound exciting to you, Nigel. But my response is 'so what'. Get to the point matey, or I'm turning over and going back to doh-doh."

"Point is, Godfrey, there are 250 names on this list. That's suspicious in itself – one hell of a lot of Brits to be working under one boss in a little place like Laos. The Colonel wants us to get the police to run a check on the lot, to find out if any have criminal records in the UK or are wanted here. I'm forwarding this across to you now. You can have the pleasure of getting Scotland Yard on the job. Colonel says its super urgent and that he will be going into hiding for a few days. Seems to think the information might strengthen the expedition request with the Lao – at least give him an excuse for seeing Foreign Affairs again, before he disappears from sight."

"Okay, Nige. I'm sure Scotland Yard will be delighted. I'll get my old mate there on the job. Sounds like a simple criminal records check on their computer. Can't imagine it will take long. What's the Colonel going into hiding for? Stepped on somebody's toes has he?"

"He doesn't say. But I think it's a bit more than stepping on toes. There's also a mail in from Welder. Not marked urgent. I'll read it to you:

'Colonel has overstepped boundaries of his mission and eye – that's spelt out e-y-e Godfrey, and you think *I'm* old fashioned, Welder thinks he's sending a telegramme for Christ's sake – request his immediate recall. Just visited by two British security personnel employed by Winkle. They tell me the Colonel broke into Winkle's office during the night, leaving three guards and three guard dogs dead and paralyzing two other guards and two female domestics. He forced entry, blew the safe, and made off with administrative documents and a large sum of money. Colonel has not returned to my house or made any contact. This unauthorized and unilateral action by the Colonel will place Winkle on full alert and jeopardise extradition maneuvers. Eye understand that Lao police now searching for Colonel on suspicion of murder. Colonel should be withdrawn at once for own safety and for continued harmonious UK-Laos relations.'

"That's it, Godfrey. Putting two and two together, I would guess this personnel list the Colonel sent comes from Winkle's safe. Before we consider withdrawing the Colonel, I think we should find out what sort of Brits are in Winkle's employment. By the way, the Colonel asks us not to communicate with Welder on the police check."

"Okay, Nige. Forward everything and I'll get onto my mate at the Yard, sure he'll be delighted. Sounds like it might be nothing or might be everything."


Norman withdrew from Souk and lay back satisfied. He had not bothered with a condom this time. Souk had what she wanted, they were on the way to legal recognition of their marriage, and Norman saw no reason not to give her a child. She was still only seventeen, or sixteen, Norman still was not sure, but Souk's friends all had children by this time, even if the children had no known fathers, or fathers who could not possibly support them. A child would cement their relationship. Norman, naively, could not imagine Souk betraying him once she was pregnant and had his child.

Apart from the daily moments of ecstasy with Souk, which nobody other than Souk could give him — Norman had tried alternatives several times — Norman led an introspective life of constant internal dialogue. Souk was Norman's opposite. She was social, spontaneous, unthinking, often impetuous, a chatter box who enjoyed life by the minute. Norman knew, not so deep inside, that their relationship stood very little chance of long-term survival, even with a child or two. It wasn't so much an age thing — Norman was more than three times Souk's age — although that would become increasingly important as he got older and she remained young. Norman couldn't really say what it was. He thought that Souk really did love him, as he loved her, but he knew that if he did not have money, he would not have Souk.

Norman's mind constantly replayed a rose-tinted video of the Norman-Souk love affair. Norman had cared for Souk since she was fourteen, a short but gangly teenager, thin with just tiny dimples of breasts, but already with those wide eyes and that gorgeous smile, and that tightly pouting backside that had turned him on since the first day he saw her. He remembered that first day, although he suspected that Souk had already forgotten it, after all, it was a quarter of her life ago.

On that day, he had been sitting in a small noodle shop not far from the office, drinking Lao beer and watching a very small part of the world go by. A group of *thamnuat baan* had arrived – what are often called "militia" in English translation – local men who work under the direction of the village headmen and receive small payments from the villagers they "defend". (Vientiane is a municipality and as urban as most other third world capitals, but remains divided into "villages".) The militia was fully uniformed and armed – which meant fearsome looking camouflage suits, including long-peak caps, and an assortment of automatic rifles. They ignored Norman but busied themselves with a group of squatters on the opposite side of the road. Norman could hear the yelled commands to pack up their things and get out now. The squatters got their things together as a bulldozer approached and stopped at the end of the line. Norman had carried on drinking his beer. After years in the UN, he was well able to witness injustice, death and destruction and, unless ordered (and well paid) to intervene, say to himself, "nothing to do with me". Souk had crossed the road with her younger half-sister, leaving her mother and step-father to put their things on an old hand-cart. Souk, as if this happened every day, appeared totally unmoved by the police action, even as the bulldozer began slowly to move along the line, crushing flimsy shacks in its path. She sat at Norman's table and Norman asked what was going on. "Oh, we have to move," Souk had replied matter-of-factly. Norman looked at her and thought she looked delicious.

"Where are you moving to?" Norman had asked.

"Nowhere," answered Souk.

"Everybody's got to be somewhere. You mean you don't know where your parents are going?"

"I mean that," said Souk with a note of childishness and maturity. "I also mean, we have nowhere to go. My step-father is Chinese and has no relatives here; my mother has annoyed all her relatives by falling into a heavy gambling debt. They won't take us."

When the mother and step-father came across, with a mattress and few possessions on the hand-cart, they confirmed what Souk had said. They sat and watched philosophically or apathetically (Norman found it hard to distinguish the two things when it came to the Lao) as their home was flattened in seconds. Norman looked at Souk. Lovely little girl, homeless, mother in debt. It would be so easy. And, he knew, it would lead to trouble in the end. So he put a bundle of kip notes on the table and left to return to his very comfortable home by the River, which could, at a small pinch, have held all of those he had just witnessed dispossessed. Heavy machinery and an army of workers moved in and they had begun construction on the land the very next day after the squatters had left. Within four months or so the tallest and most modern building in Vientiane was complete and the sign went up: *Investment Unlimited*. But by that time he and Souk were bound together like a pee in a pod. Replaying their beginnings in his mind, Norman reached his arms around Souk and drew her tightly towards him.

Fate had taken a hand in their meeting. In Laos, fate takes a hand in everything. The evening of the very same day as the dispossession, Norman had been invited to a funeral at a nearby temple. The funeral was for a girl of twenty five, who had returned from Pattaya a couple of years previously to die of AIDS in her home village. Her picture from happier years, a picture taken in Vientiane when the girl was barely older than Souk and almost as lovely, was on the coffin. A group of children played cards for money in front of the coffin, unaware that they were literally representing the fate that controls all of life's actions and leads eventually to the manner, time and place of death. Men sat watching TV and drinking rice wine. Women sat in a group. Souk was one of those playing cards, unaware that just metres away, her mother was deciding her fate.

It had always seemed to Norman repulsively ironic that, at a funeral for an AIDS victim returned from Pattaya, Mother Kham was selling her daughter, through a Thai go-between, into prostitution in Pattaya. Fate had definitely sent Norman to the funeral to intervene. And he did. He had paid what he had in his wallet as deposit and paid the remaining twenty-five thousand Baht, about $500 at the time, the next day and Souk was his. He took her home as his maid.

Norman, in spite of his desires ever the gentleman, had put Souk in his guest room. On the first night she had come into his room because she was afraid to sleep alone and he had allowed her to slip into his bed, put a comforting arm around her and gone without sleep himself, unsure what to do with his erection. For weeks Souk had shared Norman's bed and remained a virgin. Norman would have been happy to keep her that way, were it possible, for ever, every day playing with the child in her and adoring her young innocence, coming everywhere on her beautiful body as she lay still and not really comprehending, marveling at the *honey*, as she called it, that spurted out and at first not believing she could be turning on this funny foreigner. It was Souk who eventually had asked him, and had to ask him several times, to enter her, and then on the rather unsound reasoning that all her girlfriends had boyfriends who did it. And when Norman finally did it, he was so gentle, so considerate, Souk showed no signs of pain. So gentle had Norman been, there was no blood on the bedsheet, and Souk was a virgin no more. But she was uninterested in sex, which suited Norman perfectly. She would just lie there and let Norman do whatever he wanted, and smile that wonderful smile. Norman never knew that Souk's virginity had been sold to a Chinese shortly before he met her.

Souk adored Norman as father, brother, friend and lover and for the first two years at least of their union, knew no other man. During that time, Norman bought her a small piece of land, paid off her mother's debts, paid to get the mother out of prison the first time, where Chantavong had put her for having drugs in her house, and gave the mother enough to build a small house. He had done more than enough, but he went further. He wanted nobody in the family to ever again need get involved in prostitution or drugs. So he had a simple shop constructed on their land fronting onto the road. He put in a large and expensive cold drink machine and stocked the shop fully. Two days later Mother Kham had sold the lot to pay off new gambling debts. Norman gave up on the family, but could not give up Souk, although he tried. He threw her out and got a real maid and tried other girls. Within days he had rented a house for the whole family, including Souk, paying a year's rent in advance. It was about this time that Souk began to talk of marriage. Slowly, also, her attitude to sex changed and she began to enjoy it. During the third year, they remained deeply in love, but both lied about their adventures with others. Norman slowly began to hate Souk. He hated her because he was so infatuated with her. He could leave her in the morning, vowing that they would never be together again and search for her in the evening because he felt so painfully alone in the world without her. He hated Souk because she betrayed him. Souk's excuse for everything was that Norman did not marry her. Now he wanted to do things right, to get married, and to give Souk children. Today Mother Kham would be released after seven months in Chantavong's cells, and this afternoon they would invite all neighbours to a *ba si* ceremony and feast, to announce their marriage. Things would be okay from now on. He hugged Souk tighter. Today they would, in the eyes of the Vientiane world, be married. Tomorrow, he would begin to resolve the question of the Laotian Crown Jewels – hopefully the newly arrived British Colonel could help there.

Behind the locked door of the business centre's office to rent, the Colonel emptied his black bag on a desk. Dozens of VCDs, bundles of documents, and bundles of money. Both he and Pon first counted the money. The Colonel counted $15,000 in one-hundred notes and Pon counted the equivalent of another five thousand dollars in kip. They both looked at the money and at each other. Pon was no stranger to good payment for services rendered, but the most she had ever held at any one time was one thousand dollars, that Winkle had given her one time on her birthday, soon after they had come together. "Pon," the Colonel told her, "I'm taking out four thousand dollars and kip to the value of another thousand. This I'm putting in my shirt pocket for expenses. The rest, fifteen thousand dollars is yours if we manage to extradite Winkle." Pon brought her palms together and held them at her forehead as she expressed her thanks. The Colonel put Pon's money back in the bag. This was the Colonel's guarantee that Pon would not betray him to Winkle. "We have to corner Winkle first. And I need your help."

First thing in the line of action was to identify the men in the compromising VCDs. Pon knew them all and as the Colonel played each disk in turn, Pon noted down the names and positions of each government employee, businessman, policeman and, in a few cases, high ranking army officers. She wrote neatly, in Lao script. The compact disks starred a large proportion of top Government personnel as well as people outside the Government that Winkle might need to exercise a hold over – the Colonel himself was there, so was Welder and Norman West. The films featured many young girls the Colonel did not recognize, but prominent in frequency was Souk, Norman West's fiancée. Pon was absent, which no doubt was explained by the attachment to Winkle at the time. While he wanted something or somebody, Winkle was all possessive; when he no longer wanted, he discarded or gave away.

After an hour watching the sexual antics of some of the bastions of Lao society, the Colonel found his hands caressing Pon in a way that he would never do had she really been his secretary. He found her particularly attractive in the long Lao *sin* she had worn for respectability in the best known hotel in Vientiane. They kissed and fondled as the last disk played and soon the Colonel was indulging another fantasy as he slowly lifted the silk material of the *sin* up over that beautiful rounded bum, stroking Pon's perfect legs on the way and entering her from behind, in the manner police chief Chantavong was entering Souk on the TV screen before their eyes.

The office, rented for the day, came with attached bathroom, convenient after their lusty "tea break". The Colonel put the pile of disks back in his black bag. He was disappointed to find nobody at all from Foreign Affairs – direct blackmail, which the Colonel felt was justified in the circumstances, was therefore out of the question. On the other hand, he thought, this might strengthen our hand, as he could ask the Deputy Minister to take action without requiring him in any way to betray a close colleague. Pon surprised the Colonel by offering to type out the list in Lao, which she did on the computer while the Colonel turned his attention to a VCD that he had kept until last – like a small boy deliberately keeping his favourite chocolate until the end of the assortment.

This particular VCD stood out from the pile because of its title – instead of the name of a prominent person, the label bore one simple and beautiful word: *Treasure*. It distinguished itself further, when the Colonel played it, because of its total lack of sexual content. The Colonel put aside the fast-forward remote control that he had used for viewing most of the other VCDs, and concentrated. Pon's eyes also were glued to the TV set, after all it was the history of her country they were looking at.

The first part of the video was a transcription from some other media that showed a French-language documentary shot before the change in regime in December 1975, which overthrew the monarchy. This went through the King's Palace in Luang Prabang, showing the King's remarkably modest living accommodation and the contrasting, almost gaudy, large reception room that was all usual visitors saw. The Crown jewels were in locked glass cases in the reception room and the documentary went through them item by item. There was no crown in the Western sense. The place of crown was taken by a tall broad-rimmed hat. The kind of hat a witch would wear, or perhaps a man in one of the small religious groups in the United States of America that rejected modernization. Interesting, but apparently of no intrinsic value, thought the Colonel. Similarly, the gold thread weavings of royal *sin*, which anyway would probably have long ago perished if the conclusion of the documentary were correct. Interest perked as the many silver and gold artifacts were shown, along with the collection of gifts received from foreign visitors and early ambassadors, and the monarch's personal collection of antique Buddhas. As the crown jewels of nations go, the Colonel thought, those of Laos were intrinsically valuable, yes, but not much on a world scale, and certainly not worth spending millions of dollars to locate – which, he thought, was probably the reason nobody had really bothered to find them. The real value of the national treasure, the Colonel thought, lay in national symbolism, it belonged in a museum, preferably a museum within Laos; to break it up and sell the bits on the market would not bring in a fortune, and would be an act of vandalism against the Lao nation. The documentary ended with the statement, which the Colonel translated for Pon's benefit:

*The Crown Jewels of Laos were last seen by man in the 1930s, shortly before the world war relegated their redemption to the lowest priority. The national treasure had been loaded aboard a French gunship and was on its way down the Mekong at the height of the rainy season, when a small vessel could navigate the river's flood waters as far as Saigon and the oceans beyond. It was bound for exhibition in France. Its departure coincided with fierce storms – some Lao said the heavens were angry at the treasure leaving Laos. In places the Mekong River is still dangerous to navigate, with rapids and deep pools distant from any human settlement, bordered by thick jungle and swamp. The assumption is made that the gunboat was capsized and sank with the loss of all hands in a remote deep pool at the height of a fierce storm. The Crown jewels of Laos have never been seen again.*

The VCD continued without commentary, showing the Mekong River from a helicopter that traced the route of the French gunboat from Luang Prabang, through the forests of Sayaboury Province. Certainly the river looked wild and at places was indeed remote from any habitation. The helicopter film was shot in the dry season, when the waters were at their lowest and jagged rocks and shallows made navigation impossible. Even so some deep pools remained. And it was in one of these pools that the camera picked out a dark shadow under the water that might just have been the lost gunboat – or a large rock, or the viewer's imagination. The camera panned for kilometers round both banks but showed only swamp and forest. The nearest place for a helicopter to land must have been a clear ten kilometres of very difficult terrain, no roads, not even a path. Whoever went looking for the national treasure would have a tough time, and from the banks at ground level it was doubtful even the ambiguous shadow would be seen. And if the location of the gunship were to be found, recovery of the treasure would require a diving or salvage operation.

The Colonel turned to the singed file he had taken from Winkle's safe. He opened it and was surprised to find on the inside cover, written in English and Lao: *Property of Norman West.* Turning the loose-leaf pages, the Colonel saw more helicopter photographs of the supposed submerged wreck. More interestingly, there were satellite pictures of Sayaboury and blow-ups which suggested the shadow indeed had the shape of a gunboat. Lastly, there were a series of maps, one marked with an X on the spot where the treasure had supposedly lain, undisturbed for over six decades.

"Pon, can you find out the telephone number of Norman West?"

"No problem Colonel," Pon replied with the air of an efficient secretary, reached into her bag, and pressed a short-cut number. Souk came on the line and Pon told her the Colonel would like to speak to Norman. She passed the phone to the Colonel.

"Is that Norman West? I have something that I believe belongs to you and would like to return. I would also like to talk to you about a project of interest to you and perhaps to the UK Government."

"Is that the Colonel speaking?"

"Can we meet face to face and discuss things? If you can come immediately, my secretary will meet you at the front door of the Lao Plaza and bring you to me."

"Excellent. I've been trying to get hold of you. I'll be there in ten minutes."

Ten minutes later, Norman was face to face with the Colonel

within the business center room. He had brought Souk with him, which the Colonel was not too happy about, but had to ignore. Anyway, she did not understand English and she was a companion for Pon, leaving the two men to discuss and conspire. They established an immediate empathy, which delighted the Colonel as it was the best indicator of a useful alliance.

Norman's face lit up when he discovered his file. "Did you get this from Winkle's office? He had somebody steel it from my house a couple of days ago. Took a VCD on the subject as well."

"Which is right here," said the Colonel. "Winkle had put them in his safe, so he must attach a value to them. I got a lot of other video recordings too from the same place. One is of interest to you personally, but this is not the time to hand it over." The Colonel glanced over at Souk by way of explanation.

"Well, I'd certainly be happy to destroy that. After all, I'm getting married this afternoon – well, officially its engagement, but as far as anybody is concerned it's the same thing. You must come. Bring Pon along too. She certainly looks different dressed up like a secretary."

"She could be a secretary too, if she wanted. Look at this list. Pon typed it out in Lao with no problem. Don't know where she acquired such skills."

Norman looked wistful. In spite of the money he had thrown away on private tutors, Souk, who had never been to school in her life, had failed or refused to learn to read her own language. He ran his eyes down the list. "Phew. You've got some pretty important people here. Mind if I ask what the list is for?"

"It's Winkle's fail-safe list. People he can blackmail or pressure to get his way, if he ever needs to resort to it. He made video of all of them, same as the one featuring you. His insurance nobody would interfere in his plans. An insurance policy that has just run out – all the VCDs are now in my bag over there."

"I heard Winkle's place was attacked last night. Don't know what else he lost, but he certainly lost a lot of face. He spends a fortune on security precautions, which are said to be far and away the best in the country, and one man gets through them all. You're the prime suspect, I've heard. I've also heard there is not one shred of evidence against you. All anybody saw was a black-hooded shadow jumping through a window. Apart, that is from the two young girls in Winkle's bed. They say a fierce black spirit grabbed them by the throat, paralysed them, then told them in antiquated Lao not to worry. But nobody saw your face. That doesn't change the fact that Winkle is sure it was you. So, the police are looking for you right now. Probably checking all hotel lists and going through the bedrooms of the little guest houses. Three of Winkle's guards were killed and three of his dogs. He's offering a ten thousand dollar reward for you – dead or alive."

The Colonel looked across at Pon, glad now that he had promised her fifteen thousand if they caught Winkle, but a bit worried about Souk, who as far as he could see, seemed to be motivated only by money. "I'm afraid that rather scotches my attendance at your wedding party. Somebody would certainly be tempted – perhaps Souk's mother."

"Your right of course. It would be foolish to take a chance. But where are you going to go? You can't stay in this room forever, and if you did, Winkle or Chantavong would find you eventually."

"Early on I sent a hotel boy across to the travel agent to buy tickets in our name on this afternoon's flight to Luang Prabang. Thought it might turn the scent. Could I ask you to do me a favour and get tickets for Sayaboury in the names of you and Souk? We would then use them. There's a flight this afternoon at fourteen hundred."

"Would do you no good, Colonel. First, because in Laos foreigners have to show their passports even on domestic flights. Second, Winkle's Sucksabit men would pick you out like a sore thumb – the Sayaboury flight is entirely Lao passengers, not like the Luang Prabang, which has a large *falang* element. No tourism in Sayaboury. And third, Chantavong has road blocks everywhere and the militia searching all houses. You would never get to the airport. Colonel, you're the most exciting thing that's happened in Vientiane for years."

"Sounds like it's time to practice the art of disguise," said the Colonel, who always carried his make-up kit with him, along with his array of mini-armaments and his trusty kukri.

"Might be a good idea, just to get out the hotel door without being spotted. Winkle must have taken a picture of you when you visited the *Blue Member*. Anyway, your face is probably known to everybody by now. Just now, when Pon met us at the door, we were handed your portrait." Norman reached into a shirt pocket and produced a folded handout carrying a nice picture of the Colonel, who in dim lighting could still look quite handsome, and the legend in Lao and English *Wanted Alive or Dead. $10,000 Reward*.

"Hmm. Quite a flattering picture," said the Colonel. "Don't worry. I shall leave here a bent and wizened old man, with grey hair, a moustache, a limping game leg, wearing a dinner jacket and traveling on a US passport under the name Henry Jones."

"And where will you go?"

"I wanted to go to Sayaboury as the first leg in verifying the sinking of the French gunboat and estimate how difficult it might be to dive for the treasure."

"And if you found it?" Norman asked, rather possessive on the subject of national treasure.

"Offer it as a gift from the UK Government. Stick and carrot. Treasure is the carrot. The stick is the stock of videos showing members of the Government and armed forces enjoying themselves. I'd offer to hand them all over to Foreign Affairs in exchange for a rapid extradition of Winkle. Lao Government should be happy. UK should be happy; they will have nailed Winkle and greatly improved relations with Laos – and of course it's one in the eye for the French, who lost the treasure in the first place."

"Brilliant, I hoped you would say something like that. Handed over by the UK's temporary representative in Laos – that's you, Colonel, unless you can get the Ambassador up from Bangkok. Welder's all right in his way, but he doesn't have the clout or class. UK assistance in recovering the crown jewels would ensure they go into the National Museum and not into somebody's pocket. That's been one of my biggest problems so far. Plus of course, Winkle, who shows a surprising interest in having them. Since he stole my map showing exactly where they are, I've been afraid he would move ahead of me. Why he's so interested, I don't know. They are really much more valuable as a symbol of national power than for the price they might fetch if sold outside Laos."

"I think that just might be why Winkle is so interested. But for the moment all this is academic, since the national treasure is lying on the bottom of a distant and remote stretch of the Mekong in the Province of Sayaboury."

"Did your military training include aqualung-diving?"

"It did. And I've put it into practice on a number of occasions. I can see you have something going through your head."

"Yes, I have," said Norman. "Another reason I was trying to get to you is that I have the diving equipment, but can't dive myself. No point in trying to learn either because I can't swim either. Never learned – lived all my life in a landlocked country. Well, that's my excuse. Truth is, I'm terrified of water, even a swimming pool. I've tried to learn to swim many times. Just can't. So I was looking for someone I could trust and who had the experience necessary to make the dive. Found nobody so far."

"You have now!" said the Colonel. "But that still leaves the problem of actually getting to the shipwreck site and back again. I think my disguise and another passport I carry would get us past any police, but perhaps going to the airport and taking a domestic flight would be tempting fate a little too far."

"I can take you to the airport. But not the passenger airport. We go in a side entrance and direct to a helicopter."

"Private charter?"

"Not really. I'm a director of *Lao-West Helicopters*. I'll telephone now and get flight clearance to take a sick old man to Udon hospital across the river. What did you say your *nom de guerre* is? Henry Jones? When we take off, we go across the river, then turn and follow the river on the Thai side, recrossing the land border into Laos where the river turns inland. I can fly a helicopter, but we will take a pilot with us – we'll need him to carry the diving gear, and Souban's a useful chap. It will be almost dark when we land, in a very deserted area. We camp the night and walk the next day. About ten kilometers I'm afraid. Very swampy and muddy. If Pon is coming, she will need to dress more appropriately – I'll bring along some of Souk's bluejeans for her; they're about the same size. I should tell you I have already been to the site of the wreck and know it's there, and the way to get to it. Of course, there is no guarantee that the treasure is still on board, for all we know perhaps one of the crew survived and made off with it back in the 1930s, perhaps it was never really loaded on board in the first place, perhaps it has been carried off bit by bit by the river waters, perhaps villagers or Japanese soldiers found it long ago, broke it up and sold it. Lots of perhaps; after all, it's almost seventy years."

"Well, you might be a romantic, but you're a realistic one. And if it does all come to naught, at least it will get me out of Vientiane. A tactical retreat seems to me to be the most productive of actions at this time. But what about you, aren't you supposed to be getting married or something today?"

"Oh, that. Yes. But it doesn't take all day. I've already handed over the money to buy lots of food and beer and that's the main thing. We'll sit down soon after noon, there will be a *ba si* ceremony, everybody will tie threads on our wrists, then it will just be drinking until blotto. I'll be glad enough to get away by four o'clock. Not sure Souk will, but she will have no choice. And she'll be wearing a nice new gold necklace and bracelet, so she shouldn't complain. I'll tell everybody I'm taking her to Thailand for a few days holiday. I'll time my arrival here for five o'clock precisely. Can you hobble down to the main door at exactly that time, with Pon assisting you and looking like you're about to kick the bucket?"

Norman then called the airport to request emergency evacuation for a very sick old man called Henry Jones, US passport, to cross the river border by helicopter, as his heart condition was too dangerous to risk the twenty kilometers of pot-holed road to the bridge and the sixty kilometers on the Thai side to Udon hospital. Norman would bring Professor Jones's passport into immigration immediately for an exit stamp.

"I must say your Lao is absolutely first class," complimented the Colonel on hearing the telephone conversation. "On the phone, I would never know a foreigner was speaking."

"Oh, I just speak village Lao, the everyday language that Souk speaks. And only Vientiane dialect. But you, Colonel, where on earth did you learn your Lao? It sounds like *lajasop*, court language, but a very old form of it, with Luang Prabang inflections. Of course, Souk thinks you just can't speak Lao properly, but I can tell you are speaking a high form of the language that certainly hasn't been heard since the revolution – probably not for centuries before then. It's like somebody speaking Shakespearean English in today's East End of London. Intriguing. Where did you learn it?"

"I learnt it in the Court, in Luang Prabang, over three hundred years ago. I was, I think, minor royalty or a hanger-on. Of course, at that time Luang Prabang was more important than it is today. That's about all I can recall. If I went into intense meditation for a few months, I could probably call up much of the incarnation. But for the moment, I just have shadows of my past."

"Amazing," said Norman, looking, indeed, quite amazed. "Spontaneous recall of language, particularly period language, must be one of the strongest arguments to support a belief in reincarnation. I know there are some senior monks who would be very interested in meeting you. You must promise me that when this is over, you will allow me to record your Lao and see if you can read some scraps of manuscripts I have from the 17th and 18th centuries."

"Delighted," said the Colonel. "but by the time this is over I might be speaking market Lao!"

Norman took Souk with him and left. The Colonel told Pon of the plan and she insisted absolutely on going along. Their fates had met. For the moment at least two fates were intertwined. Strangely, the Colonel, who feared nothing except emotional attachment, seemed quite content with this situation. Pon also seemed happy enough to have her destiny temporarily tied to that of this amazing Colonel.

The two destinies hugged each other tightly. Then Pon took some of Winkle's kip and, not daring to venture into the hotel restaurant or use room service, went down to the bakery and brought back some ham and cheese sandwiches.

At precisely five o'clock in the afternoon an ambulance pulled up at the main door of the Lao Plaza Hotel and two hospital orderlies jumped out and took charge of the waiting bent old man who limped slowly and painfully through the open glass doors, assisted by a respectable girl wearing her Lao *sin* and with her long hair tied neatly at the neck and flowing correctly down in a line as straight as her young backbone.

Norman handed Henry Jones his US passport, with the visa page ready stamped out of the country, as the Professor settled onto the stretcher bed. "Don't worry," he said, "we'll get you on a helicopter in ten minutes and to a good doctor in another twenty."

They drove down the hotel ramp onto Sam Sen Thai, the road that led from the commercial center of town to the airport. Almost immediately they met a barrier of police across the road. The ambulance driver turned on the siren and slowed down, expecting the police to step aside. They did not. Norman turned his head and looked out through the windscreen. "It's Chantavong," he said in English. "And he's brandishing a pistol in the air." Then in Lao to the driver, "Better stop."

# 10

## Treasure Trove

**"'Morning Nige," said Godfrey,** hanging up his fur-collared leather jacket as he complained about the weather, boiling hot one day and freezing cold the next, and the traffic, as if these were fully to blame for his daily late arrival and as if Nigel, who lived much further out in a satellite town did not face exactly the same elements. "Any news on the gripping saga?"

"Quite a bit, Godfrey. Message from Welder says there's a manhunt on for the Colonel, whose wanted dead or alive."

"Go on," said Godfrey in tones of incredulity. And to think I rated the Colonel a boring old fart when he came for tea."

"Just shows you, Godfrey. Even a red-brick educated, working class origin, soul-brother can be wrong."

"Couldn't resist that one, could you Nige? All right, I admit I was wrong about the Colonel. Although that doesn't necessarily mean you were right. It all rather depends on *why* he is wanted dead or alive."

"Probably for service to the crown over and above the call of duty," Nigel wasn't one to avoid rubbing it in, not when Godfrey gave him so many opportunities.

"As opposed to service under and below the call of duty rendered by us red-brick and black chappies?" Godfrey played his two habitual colour cards but did not drag out the daily routine. He was too interested in knowing how come the Colonel, okay *not* a boring old fart, had come to be wanted dead or alive. "Go on, then, Nigel. Sock it to me. What's with this manhunt for the Colonel?"

Nigel noted the use of his full name, rather than the diminutive 'Nige' *and* a direct request for information. Coming from Godfrey that almost amounted to saying please.

"Your mate at the Yard phoned in a very interesting reply to the enquiry about all Willy Winkle's men. He asked for you, but I said you weren't in yet, so he spoke to me." Nigel paused; hanging onto information was contrary to the professed ethic of teamwork and transparency emphasized in every FCO training course and assessment of personnel. It was also basic trade craft in the civil service, a survival craft learned through daily practice.

"And you're not going to tell me what the reply says, are you Nige?"

"I might. Wouldn't mind having lunch outside for a change today. What do you think Godfrey? Duke of Wellington, lunch of the day and a pint."

"All right, all right. My shout. God, Nigel, I'm not sure which of us two originates from a poor and corrupt third world country."

Nigel smiled smugly, point won. It wasn't every day he had info of interest to his junior partner.

"You remember that list of 250 names, Godfrey?"

"Yes, Nige, I do remember the list of 250 names. Please Nige. Pretty please."

"Well, Godfrey, you might not believe it, but of the 250, you know how many have criminal records?"

"No, I don't Nige. That's why we made the enquiry."

"Oh be a sport. Guess how many."

"Probably all or none of them," said Godfrey.

"That's right," said Nigel.

"Well...which?"

"All of them. Every single one of them. All kinds of offences, but mostly with some element of violence. Some are decidedly danger-ous – your mate asks us to tell the Colonel to approach any of them with the utmost care. A dozen have jumped bail. There are six mur-der suspects. And there are four escapees that the police have been hunting for a long time. The Yard asks us to express our thanks to the Colonel for this very useful information and to request a reliable address in Laos to which may be sent official requests for extradi-tion for the most wanted, these requests are currently being pushed through as fast as possible in a democratic country."

"Christ, Nigel. What a can of worms. We'd better advise the Colonel. And reply to the Yard: have to give the Trade Office's ad-dress, I suppose."

"Haven't been just sitting on my arse since 8.30, Godfrey. At 15.45 Vientiane time I forwarded everything to the Colonel, includ-ing a full list of offences of the 250 bad apples. Suggested he inform Foreign Affairs – if he can do so without jeopardizing own safety – that we will eventually be sending extradition requests for the fourteen worst cases. Also to inform Foreign Affairs that the UK will in no way object should Laos decide unilaterally to push these particular British subjects over the bridge into Thailand. As for giving the Trade Office as mailing address, that would involve Welder, and I think we should avoid that until the situation clarifies itself. So I've advised the Yard to send everything to the Ambassador in Bangkok – this thing is surely big enough now to merit his lifting cheeks and getting up to Vientiane. After all, to believe Welder – and I do in this instance – Winkle has put a ten thousand dollar reward on the head of our emissary and Vientiane is teeming with armed police, the people's militia and, for some reason of which I am ignorant, armed Sucksabit, that's Lao Securicor, all looking for a British subject – our Colonel."

"Good on you, Nige. But with the Colonel on the run or in hiding, will he receive any e-mail you send?

"He acknowledged receipt immediately. He also said he was just about to leave by helicopter to a distant and remote destination within Laos, where he hopes to recover the Laotian National Treasure or Crown Jewels, missing since before WW 2. If he finds it, the Colonel wants to know if he, or the Ambassador, can present it to the Lao President as assistance from the UK – on the understanding Winkle will be extradited immediately. Wants to do a deal, through Foreign Affairs. I have replied that I agree in principle, but must get the green light from *upstairs*."

The ambulance came to a stop directly in front of Chantavong. Next to the Police Major, and dwarfing him, stood Rupert Sweetheart, the ex-SAS director of Winkle's Sucksabit. The ambulance was the only vehicle on the streets. Immediately, armed police surrounded the vehicle as Chantavong opened the side door, pistol in hand.

"Mister West! This is a surprise. And who else do we have here?"

The two orderlies and the driver were quick to show their ID cards from Mahasot Hospital. Norman handed Chantavong Henry Jones' passport. The Colonel lay grey and clutching his chest on the stretcher. "This is Henry Jones, an American University Professor. He has a heart problem and under the terms of his insurance Lao-West is to fly him across the River to Udon Hospital. Here's the flight plan and permission. It is important we get to the helicopter and take off very quickly. It is a question of life or death for Professor Jones."

Chantavong kept his pistol waving generally inside the ambulance as he searched under the bed, looked under the sheet covering the Professor and opened a couple of medical supply boxes.

"Okay," he said. "One American with a heart problem. One girl I've seen somewhere before. You and your wife. What are the girls for? Or are they responsible for the heart problem?" Chantavong laughed.

"This is the Professor's assistant – he was doing research here," Norman replied.

No sooner were the words out of Norman's mouth then Rupert Sweetheart strolled up to the ambulance door and, knowing her from her six months with Winkle, said to Pon, "Professor's assistant, eh? What was the Professor's research topic?"

Pon looked squarely at Rupert, knowing he had recognized her. "Khmer archeology in the Wat Pu Period," she said unfalteringly.

Chantavong appeared not to notice Rupert's intervention. Norman rushed to maintain his attention. "Souk and I were at the wedding when I got the urgent call, so she came with me."

Rupert Sweetheart bent his giant form and climbed inside the ambulance. He looked the Colonel directly in the eyes for a full minute, then said in English, "Okay, we won't detain you further. Good luck…Professor."

"Sorry I couldn't make the wedding myself," said Chantavong. "There's a desperate English terrorist on the loose, so that takes priority. Clearly he is not in here. Warn your staff at Lao-West, just in case he gets through and tries to steal a helicopter – you never know. There are other blocks on the road and the airport is temporarily closed and heavily guarded. I'll give you an escort to Lao-West."

Norman expressed his thanks. Chantavong barked orders to two police motorcyclists, who set off, sirens wailing, towards the airport, the ambulance following. The streets were empty of anybody other than armed police, fearsome-looking militia in full camouflage uniforms waving AK 47s, and Sucksabit guards, who had all been issued arms. As they approached the airport, Norman saw a truck full of armed soldiers heading into town. They passed them all, sirens blaring, and entered the gates of Lao-West helicopters. A helicopter's engines whirred into life and rotors turned as the pilot saw them coming. An immigration officer was at the helicopter together with a heavily armed policeman; he studied the Professor's passport and looked closely at the face of the old American as the orderlies lifted the stretcher bed and carried it to the helicopter. He tried to get on board alongside Souk and Pon.

"Sorry," said Norman. "You are not on the passenger manifest. Can't risk trouble with the Thais, and anyway we are full. This is an emergency flight, no time for discussion. Be back soon." Norman slid the helicopter door closed as the pilot increased the revolutions and the rotors quickly gained speed and the noise drowned out the words of the ousted immigration officer. The helicopter vibrated, straining to be gone. Immigration and police reluctantly backed off, their heads lowered, hands on hats, as the helicopter slowly rose into the air.

Within minutes they were crossing the Mekong into Thai airspace. Norman followed the air path towards Udon for a few minutes more, until the helicopter was out of sight of those on the Lao side of the river.

"Okay," he breathed with audible relief and addressed the pilot. "Soubanh, turn west and fly parallel to the river until it turns inland. We are going to Sayabouli." Soubanh, as if this kind of thing happened every day, did not turn a hair as he turned the helicopter on its new course. "Colonel, I think you can say goodbye to Professor Jones now. And Pon can change into something more comfortable. I must say my heart gave a flutter when Sweetheart came into the ambulance and recognized Pon. Luckily he didn't recognize you, Colonel."

The Colonel sat up, took off the moustache and wiped his face. He knew that Rupert had indeed seen through his disguise, but decided not to worry Norman with such information. "That was marvelous, Norman. Do you do this sort of thing all the time?"

"Never have," Norman replied. "But must say it's all good fun. I feel quite excited. Like a schoolboy's adventure story in the weeklies I grew up with."

"And the wedding feast went ahead as planned?" The Colonel noted that both forearms of Norman and both of Souk were covered with the tied on strings of well-wishers.

Norman put an arm around Souk, who looked now much as

she had done when Norman had first met her at age fourteen, full of childish devotion, sweet and innocent. Souk fingered the thick gold necklace and bracelet and smiled as Norman replied in Lao, for Souk's benefit. "Couldn't have gone better. And thanks to you, Colonel, we were spared Chantavong's presence at the wedding, and that of the local militia. No regrets, eh Souk? This is a very happy day – and now an exciting one."

The Colonel looked at Souk, who continued fingering her new thick gold necklace and bracelet, and for the first time understood Norman. He had himself lay naked between Souk and Pon, and yet now he found it almost impossible to imagine that this lovely little child was the same person who had served herself up starkers, peeled giant prawns sprouting from her fanny, on Winkle's dinner table just two nights before. And the same person who featured so prominently in the filmed sexual antics on the recordings that were tucked away in the Colonel's black bag. Norman, the Colonel knew, was living in a world of wishful thinking, refusing to acknowledge the reality of what Souk always really was or had now become. For Norman's sake, the Colonel hoped that Souk would now change back to the adoring child he had fallen in love with; but he knew that if people changed at all, they very rarely changed for the better.

The helicopter left the Mekong River behind and turned again into Laos, flying over an unmarked border of forests and small villages. For both Souk and Pon helicopter flight was a new experience, fascinating and frightening at the same time. When Souk was not hugging Norman, she held on tightly to Pon.

Following Norman's directions, the pilot turned in a large circle over stretches of what appeared to be endless forest and redressed the river, following its left bank upstream in the gathering dusk. Norman pointed down and indicated to the Colonel that this was the site of the wreck. They turned again back over forested land and circled until Norman saw a small rocky outcrop and a clearing where only an expert pilot could settle a helicopter. They came in to land very slowly, hovering, circling, there was no sign of life below them. Soubanh expertly lowered the machine down a tunnel between tall trees and came to rest gently on rocky ground. Hidden in the forest that surrounded them, several pairs of eyes witnessed the descent and several pairs of hands fingered their weapons.

Welder and Kimpen were pushed roughly into Winkle's personal bedroom at the top of the *Blue Member Club*. The sun was setting behind Winkle's dark profile as he stood looking through the picture window, the town of Vientiane and the curving Mekong stretched out below him. And to judge from the cuts and bruises on Welder's face and the flexing of muscles on Biggs and Stamford, who stood huge and brutish behind them, the sun was about to set on the Head of the British Trade Office and his little lover.

"Do take a seat," said Willy Winkle as he turned, a look of fury on his face. Welder looked around. The only seats were a luxury velvet armchair and a dainty antique stall tucked under a scroll-top writing desk. "I said, take a seat," Winkle repeated, as he moved himself towards the armchair and sat down deeply into its luxury.

With his hands manacled behind his back and blood drying on his shirt, Welder looked helpless and confused. "Where?" he asked hesitantly.

"Well, I think that here is appropriate. Don't you?" Winkle pointed at his own feet. Biggs pushed Welder down on the floor at Winkle's feet. Kimpen sat down beside her man.

"Some overdue questions," said Winkle flatly. But first, I want to remind you that for several years we have had a cooperative and mutually beneficial understanding. Your Swiss bank account is bulging, and why? Because I allowed it to bulge. Now I understand that you have got greedy and are heavily into the drug trade. You know the penalty for large-scale drug-dealing, don't you Welder?"

Welder remained silent.

"Come on Welder, say it. I want to hear it from you."

Welder swallowed blood, and spoke between swollen lips. "Death," he said.

"That's right. Death. And we have enough evidence to hand over to the Lao to ensure your rapid trial and quite legal execution. The Lao would like that. So would the Americans. Good for the reputation of Laos. The kind of action the aid-giving countries want to see – the top man topped."

Welder spoke with difficulty. "I don't understand. I've never been involved in drugs."

Winkle right foot came up and rubbed the sole of the shoe against Welder's bloodied face, then slowly descended to the floor, to rest between Welder's legs. Biggs grabbed hold of Welder's hair with one hand and held both his arms behind his back in with the other. Winkle reached out both hands and let them rest on the cheeks of Kimpen for a few seconds before moving slowly down her neck and throat, circling around where breasts had yet to take form and clasping her slim waist. Then in a swift movement, he whipped her Snoopy tee-shirt up over her head to leave her pre-pubescent nipples exposed. Welder struggled; Winkle raised his foot and kicked him in the groin. Welder yelped like a dog and folded over.

"Such nice little nipples." Saliva dribbled from Winkle's mouth as he spoke and stroked the skin where Kim pen's breasts had yet to bud, rolling a nipple between his fingers and kissing it. "Right you are, little girl, off with those blue jeans and let us see your little delicacy – that must be a nicely tight and tasty one, eh Welder?"

Kimpen remained on the floor, her hands by her sides, her breasts bare. "Stand up girl," Winkle ordered. Kimpen stood up.

"That's better. Little girls must learn to do as they are told. Isn't that right, Welder? Now, little girl, I want you to undo your belt and slowly, very slowly open the zip on those blue jeans and let them fall."

Kimpen made no move and Winkle's foot lashed out hard into Welder's stomach. Kimpen undid her belt. Biggs pulled Welder's head up and turned it towards Kimpen, his knee in Welder's back. Winkle raised his foot and held it poised to slam into Welder's face. "Now the zip. Slowly girl." Kimpen pulled the zip slowly down. "Now ease those jeans off. Come on now, all the way." Winkle flexed his foot.

The blue jeans were pushed down to a crumpled heap around Kimpen's ankles.

"Oh such lovely little knickers. Yellow. I do like yellow. And is that Snoopy again? Lucky old Snoopy, eh? Now pull down lucky old Snoopy. Slowly now. Stamford, are you getting all this?"

"Yes, Boss," said Stamford, moving around Kimpen with a video camera.

Kimpen stood still, unmoving. Winkle's foot slammed into Welder's nose, causing Welder to cry out in pain. Kimpen pulled her knickers down to her ankles and stood, a helpless little child. Stamford panned down and up her naked body, coming to rest on her pubic area and zooming in. Welder had tears streaming down his face from the effect of Winkle's foot in his face. He saw his darling Kimpen through a blur. In the steel-hard grip of Biggs, there was nothing he could do. Winkle was showing his complete power. Kimpen too was sobbing as tears streamed down her face.

"Beautiful. A darling little cunt. Not a trace of any fuzz in sight. Just the way I like them. You like them like that too, isn't that so Welder? Now, no need to cry my little love, I'm not going to hurt you. Come closer and let me see that delightful little fanny."

Kimpen moved closer. Winkle's hands moved her legs apart, inspecting closely, working his fingers into Kimpen's virgina, then turning her round. "Oh, yes, a perfect little bum. All my life I've been searching for the perfect bum. And now I've found it. What do you say, Welder, isn't it perfect? Been up there yet, have you Welder? Like it up the bum, do you young lady?"

"What do you want of me?" Welder cried out.

"In a moment. You haven't been very cooperative so far. Now little girl, down on your knees please."

As Kimpen sank to her knees, Winkle opened his zip and tried to take out his hard member. It would not come through the gap. "Ah, my dear. See what you've done? Made your Uncle Willie's willy so hard it won't come out. Use your hands, little girl, ease it out for me. That's a good little darling."

Tears streaming, Kimpen reached in and withdrew Winkle's hard penis. "Now my dear, just suck on it. Come on now, don't be shy. You can always imagine it's Welder's dick. Better get started, We've a long way to go before we get to the prick up the bum bit. Then, of course, there's Biggs and Stamford. They have been such good boys. They deserve a bit too." Winkle reached a hand behind Kimpen's neck and forced her face forward, pushed her lips apart with his penis and entered her mouth. "Hmm, very nice, very comfortable. You're a lucky man, Welder. No teeth girl, just wrap your tongue around it. By gum, I think I might just come now and save the bum for later."

Winkle took Kim's head in both hands and pushed deeper. She gagged. Winkle turned his attention to Welder. "There's a long way to go yet, you know. Just like on the porno movies. But I don't suppose you let your little girl see any of those. You are very protective of her, aren't you Welder? After this we have the licking out of the virgina, the penetration bit, followed by the backsider – with original screaming soundtrack, and finally, for the benefit of invited viewers in a *Blue Member Exclusive,* we have the facial – coming all over that sweet little face you love so much. But I think before we get to the finale, we'll treat you to a preview of the three into one, featuring Biggs in the mouth, Stamford playing on the fanny and myself making that first entrance into the perfect bum. Haven't been there yet, have you Welder? Saving it for your birthday, were you? Well, be a good boy and we'll let you operate the video camera, since the three of us are going to be occupied at the same time. Would you do that for us? Probably not. I suppose we'll have to call somebody in to handle the camera and let Biggsie break both your legs to keep you still while we give your little Kimpie the first dose of what she'll be getting regularly from now on, as a star performer in the *Blue Member.* Of course, you can stop it any time you want. After all, we've been friends a long time, Welder, and I've no wish to inflict unnecessary pain."

Welder choked, blood was filling his mouth.

"What are you trying to say there, Welder? Was it, 'Go ahead boys, I'm enjoying it'. Or maybe it was a full confession."

"I confess," yelled Welder.

"That's better. Of course, a video'd confession of a beaten and bloody man, with somebody rogering the mouth of his girl friend might not stand up in court. Not even in Laos. So, let Biggs release his hold on you and take you into the bathroom for a clean up and powdering for the cameras. And put on one of my nice, clean shirts. Then sit at the desk there and you can tell the camera how you've been king-pin of the drug trade for years, and how the Colonel is your partner in Europe, and how he uses diplomatic connections to smuggle heroin to Europe and America. You can write it all out too, and sign it. Think you can do that Welder? My dick will stay just where it is until you have come clean. And, oh yes, almost forgot, I'm sure that if anybody can, you can find the Colonel. You kill him. So that's a video confession, a written confession, and a personal promise, on your word from one gentleman to another, that you will deliver the Colonel's head on a plate. Only words, Welder. You only have to say and write the right words. And top the Colonel, of course. Then you can both walk out of here. Of course, if you don't keep your promise, *Thhan* Chantavong will be viewing your confession. What do you say, Welder?"

"I'll do it," said Welder.

"I'm impressed," said the Colonel. "I was prepared to set up a jungle camp, using my kukri and cutting a few branches to make a shelter, and cooking in the fire whatever we can find within a few metres of here – edible leaves and shoots and maybe a frog or two and some juicy bugs."

Norman smiled. We hire out helicopters to the embassies and UN agencies, and the occasional rich tourist. Those people always want a comfortable lunch, and on a long trip, they expect to get some sleep, after a cold beer of course. Soubanh, the pilot, worked almost single-handed. First out of the helicopter was a crate holding twelve large bottles of Beer Lao and another crate of mixed soft drinks. A huge ice chest and a light folding table with four collapsible canvas and wood stools followed and within minutes the Colonel and ladies were being invited to sit and take refreshments.

The Colonel watched and drank as Soubanh and Norman sprayed the ground of the camp area, set up two gas and battery operated lamps, which gave a mellow hue to the camp scene and relegated the natural world of the forest to the engulfing darkness of a quarter-moon night. A wide camouflaged parachute was stretched from the roof of the helicopter and pegged into the ground. Beneath it Soubanh tied up two mosquito nets over sleeping mats, sheets and inflatable pillows. Another large mat was rolled out and a portable gas cooker lit. A saucepan was placed on its flames, a bottle of water was poured into the pan, and sealed aluminium envelopes were dropped into the water. Five minutes later and all five were tucking into chicken and vegetables served on top of Thai fragrant rice. Roughing it, Lao-West style, meant sitting cross-legged on a mat to eat dinner, something the Lao did every day anyway. "Save some space for desert," said Norman, speaking in Lao for the sake of the two girls. "Canned mixed fruits and ice cream from Lao Plaza, with Cointreau of course."

"Of course," the Colonel repeated with a smile. "I have to admit this places my lifetime of jungle living into perspective. No grilled monkey parts and snake stew for the clients of Lao-West Helicopters, I see."

"You will have your chance tomorrow, Colonel. We will need to spend the night on the river bank in a makeshift camp. It's a long walk, some ten kilometers of swampy land and undergrowth, takes about six hours, and we will need to carry the diving equipment. We return the same way, and if we find the treasure we have two options: either abandon the diving equipment at the river and carry the national treasure back here to the helicopter, or, and I don't know how possible this is – can't land on swamp – clear a space near the river so that only Soubanh need walk back, fetch the helicopter and come and collect us and the treasure trove."

"I much prefer the second of the two options," Pon chipped in, laughing. "But seriously, like in the movies, would it not be possible for Soubanh simply to wait here, guard the helicopter and wait until we call him on a mobile. Then he could hover over river bank and winch up each of us in turn and the treasure, if any."

"It would indeed be possible," Norman replied, "– in the movies. In our situation, practicalities are not so convenient. For example, if you look at your mobile phone, you will find we are outside of the scope of any cell, so communication is out – except by the radio in the helicopter, but since we have no portable set, that is not in the game. Secondly, winching people and goods up into a passenger helicopter is much more dangerous than in a large military machine – we don't have a Blackhawk, and with our stability and power, we might just, in an emergency, try winching up little Souk. Even that would be chancy as things are, with trees and undergrowth right down to the water's edge. Get snagged on a tree and instead of Souk arriving in the helicopter, the helicopter could find itself toppling over onto Souk. So, we take chances only if absolutely necessary."

"Glad to hear it," said the Colonel. "From what I've seen from up above on the way in, this jungle looks as thick as any in Sumatra or Malaysia, and the ground is flat, which probably means swampy. And no people means no tracks or footpaths. This will be compass-stuff and I imagine the kukri will come into its own – although if we have to remove a few trees to make a landing area, explosives will be more appropriate. Fortunately, I have a limited supply."

Pon led the general entreaties for the Colonel to tell of some of his exploits in the jungles of the world, and, with a show of reluctance, he provided the camp fire (gas-version) entertainment, as more beer and tea was served.

"I was talking of Sumatra and the thick jungles in large parts of it. During the Malayan Emergency, which you are all too young and distant to remember, and which I won't go into, the gurkas played an important role, being trained for jungle fighting behind enemy lines – and in the Emergency, there were no lines. It was important for all my men to be able to live off the land for days, or weeks, at a time. We could not safely train live-off-the-land techniques in Malaya – Malaysia as it now is – since enemy and friends were indistinguishable, so I would take my men across to Indonesian Sumatra, where we knew they had only the natural elements to contend with. But even in Sumatran jungles, some of these natural elements were not quite natural as you might think of the term 'natural'. In fact some of them were distinctly unnatural." The Colonel paused for effect. Pon filled his plastic beer mug to the brim and everybody urged him to continue.

"What," Pon asked, looking at the Colonel with a look women usually keep for those they love, "was the most unnatural natural situation you've ever been in."

"Hard to say," replied the Colonel, aware that it was better for them to engage in campfire chit-chat than to talk about the treasure, which he felt would only raise expectations and hopes. "That Sumatran mission must come close. If you don't mind me telling it in my antiquated Lao. It was while my men were living off the land that we made the acquaintance of a vanishing culture that's very existence was based on the unnatural, and a culture that was suicidal in essence. It was a culture unique to the last remnants of a deep-forest tribe reduced to only five aboriginal men and ten female orang utangs. This tribe was on the verge of extinction until we came along and saved the day. My infiltration live-off-the-land unit surrounded and overpowered the group by the simple means of appropriate cover – disguise if you like. The men dressed themselves up in open-crotch male orang utang suits and rogered the swooning females from the front – using one of the natural techniques of sexual action developed in the human world, but unknown to the apes. The essential of the tribe's problem was that the males of the group were indulging in frequent sexual intercourse, but only during the ape mating season, when each male did it twenty or thirty times a day, but did it the ape way, from behind. Careful analysis of the problem showed that their acts of intercourse lasted on average 20 seconds – orang utangs are like that – or less than the time taken to eat a banana, which was the group's way of measuring time. More importantly, given those delightfully tempting large red buttocks of a female on heat, and given the cultural measurement of time, which meant anything that took longer than the time required to eat a banana just wasn't worth doing, the males never got around to finding the correct hole before premature ejaculation, and onto the next set of on-heat rosy buttocks. They were therefore exterminating themselves unwittingly through a culture of buggery.

"We saved what was left of the group from extinction by providing a training course based on the only educational video on the subject, starring heterosexual homo sapiens and orang utangs and entitled *The Joys of Cross Species Intercourse*. With a little help from my men and some of the younger orang utangs, who had yet to come onto heat and were therefore able to stay still longer without wriggling their buttocks in the air, the remaining tribal men were drilled in frontal intercourse and correct use of the virgina, which until that point the men had been using as a convenient cleft to park their cigarettes.

"Very soon, the sound of young homo-orangs was heard everywhere, and developed into a super race that could walk upright into any pub and order beer and bananas in perfect English, then swing from the chandeliers and rafters and do back-flips while waiting to be served.

"This was the same vanishing culture by the way that had, before we came along and gave them something a little more productive to do, developed the most powerful poison on earth, a poison more deadly even than nicotine, and a poison not found outside the virgin forests of the Indonesian Archipelago. It was made from mixing the semen of a freshly castrated male chieftain, the venom of a cobra in full strike and the breast milk of an enraged orang utang. This poison was used on the tips of their blow-pipe darts and could drop an elephant in its tracks. It was fiendishly difficult to obtain.

"I was by the way honoured with the offer to stay with the tribe forever as their last castrated chieftain. Tempting as the offer was, I declined, arguing that I had yet many millions of people to save and/or kill."

By the time the Colonel had finished, the whole group had collapsed in laughter. "What?" said the Colonel, feigning offence. "You don't believe me? Well, I happen to have some mini blow-pipe darts in my pocket here – I just hope we don't have to use them on this trip."

Pon hugged her Colonel and asked for more such stories. "Only after each of you has told a story. Only then will I tell you about the incredible culture of fox-hunting in the wilds of England, where I also went on a treasure hunt and ended up in a situation where the hounds were hunted by the foxes."

The beer was almost finished. Norman suggested keeping the last three bottles in the helicopter for their return, to be drunk either in celebration or in consolation. And off they went to bed, each couple sharing the privacy of a mosquito net. The same two girls who had not hesitated to "sandwich" him two nights before, were now shy about taking off their clothing. Soubanh slept outside to act as guard. The Colonel cuddled up with Pon. It had been some time since he had slept surrounded by the noise of the jungle at night and it served as an aphrodisiac – not that he needed one in Pon's embrace. Norman and Souk celebrated their first night of marriage in a similar fashion. Outside, Soubanh looked up at the stars, and the sounds from the tent brought a smile to his eyes. In the trees, other eyes were keeping watch over the camp; it would be the work of an instant to kill everybody as they slept, but they were under orders to wait.

11

# Back to Nature

**"So the Colonel has disappeared,"** said Godfrey.

"As far as Welder, Winkle and the combined Lao forces of order are concerned, that is certainly true," answered Nigel. And given that everybody is after the Colonel's head, I can't say I blame him for doing a disappearing act at this moment."

"Nothing else in from our man Welder?" asked Godfrey.

"Just a sitrep saying that Vientiane is practically under siege pending the arrest of the Colonel. All places of entertainment are closed and people told to remain in their houses, which are being systematically checked by the militia. Road blocks everywhere and only essential travel on the streets. One of those essential travels that Welder thinks worth mentioning is that of the English director of Lao-West Helicopters, Norman West. He filed an emergency flight path from Vientiane, across the river-border and on to the Thai hospital in Udon for an American Professor Henry Jones. Welder says he checked with Lao Plaza

Hotel, where the American was supposed to be staying, but he was not registered there. Jones is also not known at the US mission. Welder says that he is about to check with Lao-West. There's no more talk about recalling the Colonel, instead Welder seems to be directing his concerns to Winkle – which is perhaps something of an improvement from our point of view. He says Winkle is using the attack on his office – which everybody presumes was done by the Colonel but for which nobody has any proof or witnesses – as an excuse to use the combined armed forces of the authorities to track down the Colonel. Welder says that Winkle is reasserting his power over the police forces in a way which he calls 'overcompensation'. It seems that Winkle needs to regain face, and capture of the Colonel will achieve that end. Welder breaks off rather abruptly, writing that there are some of Winkle's men down stairs asking for him and that he will revert. He hasn't reverted so far."

Welder signed off on the confession that he controlled the drug trade and the accusation that the Colonel was his commercial partner, buying and moving the drugs grown in Laos. Biggs took the hand-written document across to Winkle.

"Good, good. You write well, Welder. Very believable. Of course, I shall not use this document unless I have too. I would much prefer that you bring me the Colonel's head." As Winkle spoke, he continued to grip Kimpen's head in his hands.

"Now my dear, you see that your lover has saved you from our further pleasures. And saved his own life at the same time. All temporarily, of course. If he does not keep the bargain he made, he will be tried and shot as a drug dealer and you, my dear, will be back here with me and Biggs and Stamford. Now, put your hands up and say goodbye to Uncle Willie's willy, at least for the time being. Take hold of it and slide it out of your juicy little mouth."

Kimpen did as she was told and took hold of Winkle's penis with both hands and tried to pull it from her mouth. Winkle meanwhile pulled her head harder in towards him. Welder had no choice but to remain where he sat, at the writing desk, and hope he and Kim would soon be free.

Kim did not understand. She did as she had been told and again tried to pull Winkle's penis from her mouth, but every time it seemed to be about to leave her, Winkle pulled her head down and thrust further in. She grabbed it more tightly, but this seemed to make Winkle even harder and more excited. Winkle seemed to be daring Welder to rise from his seat and intervene. At last, feeling the unstoppable surge, he allowed Kimpen's hands to pull it from her lips, at the very moment he came. Winkle took Kim's little hands in one of his own to keep them where they were. With the other hand he held her tightly by the neck hair and rubbed her face around his dick, forcing his cum into her eyes and nose, and neck and hair.

"Whoops," said Winkle. "An accident. Well, accidents do happen, don't they Welder? And it might have been a lot worse – and it will be a whole lot worse if you welsh on your agreement. Now, you can take your little girl with you and when I see you again, I hope for both of your sakes that the Colonel is no longer in this world. Biggs will give you a loaded gun, and I advise you strongly to use it only on the target. Now, I could keep your little Kim here as a hostage until you have completed your mission. But I must say it would be difficult to keep Biggs and Stamford away from her – and I might find her rather tempting myself. So go now before I change my mind. Biggs will give you a pass signed by Chantavong to show when you are stopped by the police and, of course, the pistol with which to shoot the Colonel. And I will give you a tip: Norman West flew a helicopter across to Thailand an hour ago. I would be foolish for me to leave the sanctuary of Laos at this time. But as a diplomat, you can come and go. Biggsie, tag them both so we can keep a track on them – and don't try to be too clever, Welder, remove the tags and Biggs will find you and shoot you. Everything should be clear enough for you by now. Is it? If not, you can lick my cum from your baby's face."

"It's clear," said Welder grimly. "I find the Colonel and kill him, and in return you leave us in peace."

"Bingo! You've finally got it. And Welder, I wouldn't have had to drag you in like this if you hadn't advised your office in London that the time limit for my extradition was coming up. That was not very nice of you. Some people might think you wanted to take over all my operations. Remove the Colonel and we'll say no more about it. I think I'm being more than fair, don't you, Welder? Don't you think I'm being more than fair?"

"Yes," said Winkle simply.

"You can call me Willie, again. After all, we are still friends, I trust? How about, 'Yes, Willie, you are being more than fair. Thank you.'"

"Yes, Willie, you are being more than fair. Thank you." Welder repeated. He would have said anything to get away from Winkle.

"Good. Very good. Now, take your little girl and get her cleaned up. Get yourself cleaned up while you're at it – and you are welcome to see the doctor on your way out."

Welder took Kim by the hand, gave her his handkerchief to wipe her face, pushed the gun into his waistband and went as quickly as he could away from the *Blue Member*. He drove in the dark in silence towards the airport and Lao-West Helicopters. Kim rubbed her face with Welder's handkerchief, trying to remove all traces of Winkle. But Welder knew that was impossible. Kim had been deliberately spoiled for him. He fingered the gun. He would either kill the Colonel or kill Winkle, Biggs and Stamford. Winkle, of course, knew that. The Colonel did not.


While the Colonel and Norman were pleasantly engaged, Soubanh answered the helicopter radio call.

"This is Welder, British Trade Office. I need to speak to the Colonel."

"Sorry, he's occupied. Norman too. Any message I can take?"

"I don't seem to be able to raise Norman on his mobile, Pon neither. Since the whole town seems to be looking for the Colonel, I thought I'd better see he's all right. The police checked and there is no Henry Jones registered either at the Lao Plaza or the hospital, so now the police search has expanded to Norman and the helicopter."

"Where are you calling from?"

"From Lao-West Helicopter office. Your man here was asked by the police where Norman had taken the Colonel. He told them Udon hospital – where he has not checked in – and received a beating. He didn't seem to know where Norman was, but said they had fuel enough only for Udon and return."

Welder was, as far as Soubanh knew, a friend of Norman, but this was not the time to give away their location. "It's not difficult to buy extra fuel if needed," said Soubanh. "I'll let Mr West and the Colonel know you called."

"Where are you? I should be able to get Norman on the mobile if he's in Udon."

"Probably switched it off. As I said, he's otherwise engaged. Married, actually," Soubanh laughed at his own little joke. "As I said, I'll let them know you called. I'm closing down the radio now. I expect Mr West will get back to you on the phone, later."

Welder spread one of Norman West's maps across the table. Chantavong stopped beating Norman's assistant and called Sweetheart across to look.

"With enough fuel to get to Udon and back, they can't have gone far. Ninety minutes max. Draw a circle around Vientiane with a radius equal to the distance between here and Udon. Take into account they are in an area not served by a mobile telephone cell and they can't be in many places. Certainly, they are not in Thailand. Certainly, when I spoke to them, they were on the ground with engines shut down. They could be somewhere in Xiang Khouang, near the Vietnamese border, they could be in the special zone in Vientiane or they could be in Sayaboury. Since Xiang Khouang is full of army, as is the Special Zone, where Hmong insurgents might shoot them down if they tried to land, my guess is Sayaboury."

"If we requisition a helicopter large enough for fifty or so well-armed men, it will become an army matter and we lose control," Rupert Sweetheart said bluntly to Chantavong and Welder.

All three men understood the latent competition between army and police and while Winkle had some influence over some of the high officers in the army, Welder did not intend to ask Winkle's help in obtaining army assistance. Besides, that influence was limited and the army as a whole remained firmly behind the President of the Republic. If the army captured the Colonel, it might rebound on Winkle's plans to seize power in Laos. This in itself was of no concern to Welder. Simply, he was afraid that any period of disturbance, or any activity that might raise Winkle's suspicions, would lead Winkle to carry out his threat against himself and Kim.

"Is there an alternative?" Welder questioned.

"We are here at Lao-West helicopters," Sweetheart replied. "We hire two helicopters and fill them with our best men – 50% Thhan Chantavong's armed police and 50% Sucksabit specials, that makes sixteen in all, plus us, that's max capacity for the biggest Lao-West helicopter – should be enough. Then we fly over Sayaboury until we find West's helicopter. If he can land, so can we."

"But Rupert," Welder objected. "We have no flight permission and hiring helicopters is expensive."

"The Colonel and West also have no permission," said Chantavong. "And we will pay for the helicopters later, from the reward money offered by Winkle – or the treasure that we will reclaim from West's attempts to steal from the nation. But why should we pay at all? After all, West is aiding a fugitive murder suspect."

Welder offered no objection. After all, it was Chantavong's head that would roll, not his. Thus plans were readily agreed with Norman's badly beaten assistant to take off at first light and track down the Colonel using two helicopters and pilots of Lao-West Helicopters. Chantavong and his men would stay overnight at Lao-West, to ensure there was no communication with West or the Colonel. Welder took Kim home. She was still shaking from her experience in the *Blue member* and the next morning he would have to leave her at the house, with the maid, behind locked doors and a promise to stay inside and to open to no one but him. He could not take her with him on one of the helicopters, too dangerous and she would be in the way all the time. And how could he kill the Colonel if she were there watching, and afterwards how to explain that he had killed a man who would never harm her to protect her from a man who would?

Welder did not like to leave Kim alone in Vientiane. But she was tagged and to move her out of town or to remove the tag would only provoke Winkle. Vientiane would be a dangerous place as long as either the Colonel or Winkle lived. Welder did not care which of the two died, but the Colonel, it seemed, would be easier to kill, with a little help from Chantavong.


Morning came comfortably with hot mugs of tea and a full breakfast. "That's more than I can promise you for tomorrow," said the Colonel.

The Colonel felt uncommonly happy that morning and looking across the steam of his hot tea, he realized why. In spite of his avoidance of attachment, he knew that the happiness came from sleeping curled up with a girl who seemed to care for him. It had been many years. And yet this girl was too young for him, too beautiful for him – because the Colonel knew that a beautiful wife does not lead to happiness – and, in the end, although only eighteen and talented in many ways, she was a whore, and, the Colonel knew that you can take a whore to culture, but you can't make her think.

The Colonel had spent his life in the safety of the philosophy that whores are whores, virgins are virgins, and there are no degrees of in-between. He knew that a virgin can become a whore, and that the reverse movement is impossible. Yet, this morning, he felt happy because of Pon, no other reason was possible. And Pon, at a tender age, had decided to become a whore. His mind was now threatening that happiness with such thoughts. He gazed into Pon's eyes and, as if she knew what he was thinking, she said quietly and wisely, like a Buddhist monk, eye to eye, "Just be happy. Just be happy now."

"Let's hope," said Norman. "That by tomorrow morning, we'll have a lot more than breakfast to put a smile on our faces."

"There is already a lot more," the Colonel said, maintaining his eye-contact with Pon.

"By the way," said Soubanh. "Mr Welder, the trade office man, called on the radio from our office last night. Wanted to know where you were. I didn't tell him."

"Good man, Soubanh," said Norman. "Leave the radio shut down until we get back."

Soubanh made light work of repacking everything in the helicopter. He had done it a million times. He carried the diving gear and gave Norman and the Colonel large water bottles and a length of nylon rope to carry and a pack of nylon bags, which everybody hoped would be needed to bring back the treasure. The Colonel expressed concern at leaving the helicopter unguarded, but was assured that the camouflage parachute that Soubanh had stretched completely over its form, would make it invisible from the air – in the unlikely event that an aircraft was passing. And from the land, no paths led into or out of the small rocky clearing. Even so, the Colonel encircled the helicopter with some almost invisible nylon thread trip wires connected to small but powerful explosive charges. "Just don't forget to let me disarm them before you rush aboard on return," he said with a smile.

As the Colonel had sat happily drinking tea and the first rays of the sun filtered through the tree tops, Welder, feeling vulnerable without the child he loved at his side, Chantavong, whose mind was on the $10,000 reward money, Sweetheart , with his eight Sucksabit specials, and eight police armed to the teeth and loyal to Chantavong, took off from Vientiane airport and followed the river to Sayaboury. They were fueled up to the brim and after two hours it became obvious they would need every drop of fuel. Having no idea of the location of the sunken treasure ship, the two helicopters separated to double their chances of finding it. One, with Rupert Sweetheart and his men on board, flew directly to Luang Prabang and would follow the river downstream, the other, with Welder, Chantavong and the police on board, would fly upstream. Both would look for remote pools of water big enough to hide a gunboat and aerial search the area around such pools. When one located the grounded helicopter or saw signs of West and the Colonel, it would radio to the other.

It was a simple plan that seemed certain to succeed, but failed to take adequate account of the number of deep water pools in the stretch of Mekong and the time needed to circle around such pools in search of one small helicopter within a tall and largely uninhabited forest.

In the operations room of Winkle's offices in the *Blue Member*, keen eyes followed the progress of red dots that marked the positions of the tags on Kim and Welder. One dot stayed motionless in Welder's house, the other moved in confusing circles along the Mekong River in Sayaboury Province. Biggs reported the positions to Winkle regularly, but there was no change in the basic pattern. "A bit strange," said Winkle. "Luckily, Sweetheart is there to keep an eye on Welder. Even so, let's bring back in Welder's girl as security. Don't touch her, Biggsie. I mean it. Just sit her down in front of the TV and give her some ice cream and whatever kids eat."

The journey through the swampy forest proved every bit as difficult as Norman had warned it would be. The Colonel led the way, guided by Norman's compass. Very soon the ground became swampy and at times both men were piggy-backing Pon and Souk, to whom at first the difficulties of travel were all part of the game. But when the first snake wriggled through the water, they changed their mind and mood. Souk, like a small child on the back seat of a car on a long journey, asked repeatedly, "Are we almost there?" Pon, on the other hand, stayed close to the Colonel, and her trust in his protection and her closeness lightened the journey for both of them.

The Colonel had been on many a difficult and long journey through such inhospitable terrain; in fact he thrived on it, but the thriving was usually experienced after the journey was over and the beer was flowing. On this day, as long as Pon was within his reach, the Colonel was having the time of his life. With each leach he expertly plucked from Pon's fair skin, he felt the excitement of childish emotion; with each touch, he tingled. The Colonel allowed his mind, and hands, to play with Pon. As a man of developed consciousness, the Colonel was aware of what he was doing, and knew it was both stupid and dangerous. A lifetime's training and experience told him men died because their minds and bodies were not 100% directed to staying alive. He, of all men, should be able to control his mind. But the Colonel's mind was in a devilishly playful mood. It had had enough of discipline and was enjoying itself, like a mischievous puppy.

Apart from stooping now and again to pick the leeches from Pon's neck and ankles and run his fingers playfully over her buttocks and give her a sweaty hug every ten minutes at least, the Colonel maintained as fast a pace as the others could stand. He knew from studying the map they had at least ten kilometers of unfriendly forest to cross before arriving at the river and he kept rest periods to a minimum, and then allowed a lie down only when they came across a reasonably firm and clear piece of land, and only he had inspected it for snakes and poisonous insects. On one such rest stop, Souk refused to leave, saying her legs ached. The Colonel spotted the beginnings of female rebellion and knew that Norman would do nothing to force his beloved to move on. So he suggested that Norman massage her tired little thin legs and, reluctantly, patted the air to indicate stay put as Pon moved to join him. He circled the small area of raised dry land, moving quietly. Ahead of him a particularly tasty snake slipped into the water as he approached. The Colonel drew his kukri but remained hidden in the trees.

Unfortunately, the Colonel was not the only one to be tempted by the snake. He froze as a figure moved away from the forest cover and caught the snake in his hands, lifting it up from the water playfully and looking it straight in the eyes. The figure was naked except for a loin cloth. The Colonel recognized him as one of a group whose name came back to him through the infinite time of reincarnation, the *phi tong luang*, the Spirits of the Yellow Leaves, so called because any attempt to find them ended only in location of their abandoned and yellowing leaf shelters. The *Spirits* were a jungle people who avoided the modern world, a group that declined in numbers as their habitat shank around them, until now they seemed to be reduced to hunting and gathering in the least accessible surviving woodlands of Sayaboury Province. Even here, in an underdeveloped corner of Laos that had changed hands repeatedly between Thailand and

Laos, the Colonel was surprised to see that at least one member of the tribe had survived into the modern age. And their technique of survival, the Colonel noted, had not changed over the centuries – run and hide from the modern world and its attachments and conflicts. The aboriginal saw the stranger, dropped the snake and ran off. The Colonel, while he certainly had sympathy for anybody fleeing the modern world, thought the brief encounter between ancient and modern – in so far as the Colonel could be said to personify modernization – of marginal interest to their mission. Certainly such timid and retiring people as the *Spirits* posed no threat to it. He slashed once with his kukri and the snake was dead. The Colonel returned to throw its headless body, still wriggling, at Souk's feet. "Okay. If we are staying here for a while, might as well make a fire and cook lunch."

Souk was on her feet in a flash, saying that it would be much better to take lunch once they arrived at the banks of the river. There were no further interruptions to the Colonel's pace of travel. The Colonel popped the wriggling, headless snake into one of the empty treasure bags. The journey was difficult but by the time they arrived at the banks of the Mekong, the Colonel had a bag full of edible mushrooms, some bamboo shoots, two frogs, a handful of termite larvae, some aromatic leaves and a fine snake to chop up and throw into his own jungle stew, patent pending.

Thanks to Norman's excellent map-making skills, they had come out precisely by the deep pool where the muddy waters should hide the long-sunk gunboat. The river to their right was wide and shallow, with sand bars breaking up the water into many small streams, and to their left, after the many rivulets merged into the deep pool of almost pond-like stillness, was the sound of water falling over jagged rocks in rapids that made the river impassable in the dry season. Having set a fire going, cut a length of bamboo below the node to form a cooking pot, and thrown in his ingredients for a sustaining and natural soup, the Colonel set to the task of clearing away the undergrowth and cutting enough small willowy trees to weave together a lean-to shelter which he covered with wild banana leaves – a temporary shelter, the Colonel reflected much like that of the *phi tong luang*.

After their long walk, everybody was hungry and enthusiastically tucked into the sticky-rice that Norman had carried with him, dipping small round balls of rice into the bamboo cooking pot, to flavour it with jungle soup – the Colonel's very own recipe that all agreed was marvelous, although the Colonel noted with some disappointment that the girls seemed to be more inclined to the can of corned beef that Norman produced from his pocket.

The girls stretched out for a siesta under the lean-to, comfortably cool on a bed of palm leaves and bracken that the Colonel had made for them. The Colonel felt a natural inclination to join them but fought it – time was of the essence. Norman and Soubanh assisted in fitting out the Colonel with aqualung, mask and divers gloves and shoes. The rope and recovery bags were loosely tied around his waist and the Colonel waded into the water, which very quickly rose up to his neck. The Colonel started breathing canned air and pulled the face mask over his eyes as he caught Pon's eyes and saw there briefly all the love and attachment that he had successfully avoided for years. He slipped quickly beneath the water. From the darkness of the surrounding forest, confused eyes witnessed the white man who had killed the snake cover his face with a mask, lash a large metal container to his back and voluntarily disappear under the water; they waited, but he did not surface.

As the Colonel was disappearing below the water, Chantavong, Welder, and eight fully armed policemen were just ten minutes flying time away, eating lunch at a small settlement, their helicopter a curiosity for the village children. For both Welder and the Colonel, it was a race against time in a land where time could stand still for centuries.

12

# Diving for Dreams

**"Nothing further in from Welder or the Colonel,** I suppose?"

"No, Godfrey. Nothing at all."

"We're left cliff hanging overnight, then?"

"Looks very much like it. I'll check the mail before turning in. Want me to call you if there is anything?"

"Please, Nige."

"What's this then? A new caring Godfrey? I remember you got quite annoyed when I called you with the last late night news."

"Yeh, well, things are different now, aren't they Nige? I feel kind of responsible somehow, sending the poor old Colonel out there all alone. He did ask to take along his two men, but we said 'no, you just have to deliver a letter, sorry, we don't have the funds'. And now he's wanted dead or alive."

"He's a gurka, Godfrey. Gurkas thrive on this sort of thing."

"An ex-gurka," Godfrey corrected. "Retired early among rumours of doing things with orang utangs and creating a female liberation insurrection in the Bollywood film industry."

"Been doing your research, have you Godfrey?"

"Just listening to corridor rumour."

Considering the waters were almost stagnant a few metres down, they were surprisingly cloudy. The Colonel very quickly sank into a quiet world of almost zero visibility. He clicked on the powerful torch that Norman had strapped onto the Colonel's forehead, but this gave him only a narrow view of the under-water world that stretched two or three metres straight ahead. And the bottom of the pool seemed further away than ever.

Welder looked at his watch as they took off from the village in search of the Colonel. The Colonel looked at his watch as he felt his way across and between the huge rocks at the bottom of the pool in search of the treasure ship; he had one hour. It was one o'clock in the afternoon.

Norman put the finishing touches to a makeshift but rigid bamboo tripod set into the ground and supporting a pulley wheel. Around the pulley curled loosely the rope lifeline to the Colonel, the line which would hopefully soon bring to the surface the lost national treasure of Laos. Soubanh, not one to waste his time, swung his fishing line far into the air, the cast falling in the still middle waters of the pool. The girls broke their siesta and left their shelter to join the waiting men.

The Colonel had feared the gunship might have capsized and ended up on the river floor upside down, denying him entry without some of Welder's under-water oxyacetylene torches to cut through the hull, or a major salvage operation to raise the whole boat. Fortunately, the Colonel's fears were unfounded and when, finally, the gunboat loomed into view, it looked like a picture postcard. In the middle and deepest part of the pool the waters cleared and his headlight was enough for the Colonel to make out the lines of the gunship and its gun turrets. The Colonel almost expected uniformed men to spill out from the doorway of the bridge, up anchor and sail away.

Hardly tarnished by the fresh waters of the Mekong, the 1930s

French gunship sat upright on the bottom of the river's deep pool, looking for all the world as if at any moment its engines would begin to turn and the captain would pull on the overhead cord and send steam scalding through a siren to announce its departure after an unscheduled stop of seven decades.

Opening the door to the bridge in the silence of the deep, the Colonel felt like an intruder. The Captain remained at his post. Threads of a once-pompous uniform hung like spider webs from the skeleton hugging the wooden steering wheel. The Captain's head, wedged between the top wooden spikes of the wheel, was turned towards the Colonel, the skull grinning as if in welcome. Most ludicrously, the Captain's hat still sat on his skull at a jaunty angle to impress the girls, the braid above its peak still reflecting its colours in the Colonel's electric lighting, the first light the Captain had seen for seventy years. Beside the wheel, a wall-mounted brass drinks holder contained an open bottle and two glasses. The Captain's last drink stood, a murky red colouring on the glass to show where wine had once been waiting the Captain's pleasure. No fears of drinking and driving, thought the Colonel, moved by the almost eternal spirituality of the scene and careful not to disturb it.

He went down an inside staircase and opened a door into a cabin. Two crumbling skeletons were entangled on a wide bed. The remains of a lady's evening gown and an officer's dress uniform lay, the Colonel thought, where they had been dropped or thrown by lovers in a last lustful tryst. For some reason that frightened him a little, the Colonel thought of Pon as he floated over the bed, inspecting the skeletons, unable to decide which was male and which female. Death the great leveler. Had they died in their sleep? Unlikely. Surely all hands should have been on deck in a storm? But, the Captain thought generously, these lovers must have been French. He imagined the end had come quickly, the boat filling with water, the couple unable to open the door and attempt escape, and the final, eternal, coupling as the water rose. He left them, said, "Excuse me", and closed the door on their silence.

Down more stairs, trailing behind him the rope looped around a pulley clipped on his belt, the Colonel came to a skeleton slumped in front of a closed metal door. He tried to move it carefully. It crumbled under his fingers. "Sorry," said the Colonel in his mind. "But I have to get through this door."

The handle came away in his hands. The Colonel touched the door and it swung open easily and quietly, as if waiting all this time for the Colonel to arrive. Inside, the Colonel was pleased to note that he had entered the storeroom. He would have liked to have time to open the sea trunks of the crew, but he went straight for three collapsing wooden boxes, each the size of a tea chest, the kind of boxes in which cargo, even precious cargo, would be packed. The wooden slats of the chests were dislocated and eaten away. The Colonel had only to move them apart and look inside.

"Is the Colonel all right?" Pon asked to nobody in particular, voicing her concern.

Soubanh looked at Norman. The Colonel had been gone over half an hour and the line remained slack. Before either of them could think of reassuring words, their train of thought was broken by the sound of a distant helicopter.


"Look, over there. There are some figures on the bank. Tell the pilot not to go too close. If it's the Colonel, we don't want him to know we are on to him. Give me the binoculars." Welder spoke to Chantavong as he looked out through the open door of the helicopter. "There are two men. One is Norman West, don't know the other. Any idea who he is, Thhanh Chantavong?"

Chantavong took the powerful military binoculars. "That's Soubanh, one of West's pilots. And there coming into the picture now are two girls: West's wife, Souk, and Pon, who I thought was with Winkle. No sign of the Colonel or of their helicopter."

Welder looked again at the group far away and below. "They are standing by a rope going into the water. I bet the Colonel is on the other end of the rope, under the water looking for the treasure."

"Can we land some men there?" Chantavong asked the pilot,

who replied that it was impossible unless he hovered over the water and they jumped in.

"If they do that," said Welder, "they are more likely to get caught by the Colonel than catch him. Besides, we might interrupt their treasure hunt before they find anything. Much better we just go straight on as if we have not seen anybody. Then we find their helicopter, land beside it and take them from behind."

"It's going straight past. They haven't seen us," said Norman, whose attention was suddenly taken by the rope on the pulley. "Something's happening. There's movement in the water." Norman pulled on the rope. Soubanh meanwhile landed a fine, large, Mekong fish that would give them all supper that evening. Pon hit it on the head and placed it high on the bank. "Hey," said Norman, "can I have some help here?"

Down in the deeps, the Colonel had finished unceremoniously pushing the national treasure into plastic bags which he hung on hooks set into the rope. He watched as, maneuvered by unseen hands in the world above, the bags disappeared into the darkness of the stairway and the rope circled around the pulley he had attached to the door frame. He emptied three cases of various artifacts in this fashion, mostly silver containers and the remnants of clothing, some smaller locked boxes which might hold other treasures or documents, and even a bunch of carved wooden flowers presented by a visiting Malay Sultan. Little of real value, the Colonel thought, half expecting to uncover a MacDonald's hamburger nicely wrapped in greaseproof paper. Up above, Norman disagreed as he excitedly opened each bag and put the hooks back on the descending rope, hoping for more; for Norman each item was an invaluable link with a past gone forever, a bridge to a world that existed before the world went mad.

The National Treasure had been inside wooden cases that time had already decayed, making it an easy job for the Colonel to take out each and every item and send it on its way. There was, in addition, a large and sturdy metal box that had been padlocked and bore the royal seal. The Colonel tried to feel its weight and could not shift it. He took out his kukri and tried to lever off the padlock, without success. The box was rusted tightly closed and to have persisted would have been to risk the blade of his beloved kukri.

With an eye on his watch, the Colonel covered the lock with a small plastic explosive charge, inserted a fuse, primed it by snapping off the end, and swam and grappled as far from the box as he could in the thirty seconds before the explosion almost emptied the cargo hold of water and slammed the Colonel against the hard metal bulwarks.

Above water, Pon heard the muffled explosion and saw the disturbance on the water's surface. Norman looked on, helpless and worried. He knew that gas pockets could survive under water for decades until ignited. He prayed silently for the safety of the Colonel. At his side, the rope jumped violently. Norman and Soubanh pulled it in as quickly as they could.

The rope was heavy and reluctant to leave the water. Norman strained under the effort, expecting at any second to see the Colonel's body hooked on the rope. Pon and Souk waded into the water and tried to help the two men in the task. Finally, a black plastic bag broke the surface. Norman grabbed it and it ripped open, spilling at his feet a one kilogramme bar of solid gold. All four stared at it but did not relax their efforts on the rope. Slowly, more bags came into sight.

The Colonel wanted to sing with joy as, walking like a man on the moon, he carried each gold bar to the door of the cargo hold and sent it on its way, each bag containing what constituted, in Laos, a small fortune. He worked as hard as he could. He would happily have taken all day over the task, but he did not have the luxury of time, could not allow himself the joy of running his hands and mind over so much gold, neatly packed and waiting for him. Finally, he sent the last bar on its way and, with the air in his tank exhausted, unbuckled the weights from his belt and kicked up to the bridge, saluting *en passant* the sentinel-Capitain, and, lungs bursting, raced for the surface.

"Two hundred!" Pon exclaimed, running hands over the stack of gold bars. "There are two hundred bars. That's two hundred kilos of gold. That's, let me see, that's, in dollars, at today's price, that's…" Pon's calculations were interrupted by the sight of the exhausted Colonel surfacing in the middle of the pool, gasping for air.

Norman and Pon waded in and helped the Colonel up onto dry land. He was still gasping but had a broad smile on his face. The same smile, Pon noted, that he had after making love to her. What a man, she thought, what a golden man, and so much gold. Beautiful old gold. Twenty-four carat gold. None of this eighteen-carat *falang* gold from Thailand. With this much gold, and with the Colonel, life could only change for the better.

Circling widely, far out of earshot of the happy gold-hunters, Chantavong spotted the camouflaged helicopter and instructed the pilot to put down beside it. "Can't do it. Not without cutting down some trees. They've put themselves right in the middle of the clearing. No space for us to land. Too dangerous."

"Do you have an axe?" asked Chantavong.

"Two," replied the pilot.

"Use a rope and lower two men with two axes onto the top of their helicopter. Clear enough trees for us to put down."

The Colonel knew that nothing attracts like gold, and a pile of gold bars would have the whole of Laos by their sides within the time it takes to say *I love you*.

"Okay," he said. "Tomorrow, we carry with us the National Treasure and one gold bar each girl and two bars each man. That's eight bars we take with us. The rest we put into plastic bags and bury in the forest right now. If we are caught, we all say that the eight bars plus the royal treasures are all we found on the boat." Reluctantly, all helped carry the gold and place it under a tall tree, in a hole the Colonel dug for it with his kukri. "We'll move it later, maybe by boat next month, if the rains increase the water in the river and allow passage of a small boat. Meanwhile, we must all swear an oath of absolute secrecy. Cross your heart and hope to die." Everybody swore.

"Shouldn't we place a big X on the spot?" Norman joked. "Who owns the gold anyway?"

The Colonel looked thoughtful but ventured no answer. Gold was weaving its spell. The national treasure belonged to Laos, no problem there. But the gold? Nobody even knew it was in the boat, so nobody would miss it. Who owned it? Was it the national treasury of the French-colonized Kingdom of Laos? Was it ill-gotten gains that belong to people long since dust? Were the Lao – or the French colonial masters – trying to move it before the arrival of the Japanese? To whom does it belong? The Royal Family exiled in Paris? The French? The communist Lao People's Democratic Republic? Or was it finders keepers? And who were the finders? Norman, who had located the ship? The five of them? Or, the Colonel alone?

The Colonel's eyes caught those of Pon. A magic thread seemed to tie them together. The Colonel broke contact with as much difficulty as he had dragged his eyes from the gold. Attachment was creeping into his life. Attachment would spin its threads and cocoon him. Time to do something about it. The Colonel walked off into the forest. After ten minutes, when the Colonel had had quite long enough for a pee or a poop, Pon followed him. She found him sitting not far from the buried gold, his legs tucked up under him, like a monk, his eyes closed, a low *om* vibrated from his lips. She left him alone.

The Colonel spent one hour cleaning his mind. Pon, in all the magnificence of her nakedness appeared clearly before him. She appeared fresh and innocent. But this was the girl who had been sleeping with the enemy for six months, and would probably still be doing so if Winkle had not given her away. Could he trust her? Of course, he could not. The Colonel dislodged her from his mind piece by beautiful piece. Those lovely little breasts and sweat nipples dissolved; her lovely face faded, her gorgeous legs and her perfect bum broke up before his eyes. Then all reformed, as sexy and as beautiful as ever: Pon, but a golden effigy of Pon. A solid gold Pon. That changed gradually into a golden skeleton, that first rusted, then melted under Welder's blowtorch until there was nothing left but a pool of liquid gold, which evaporated into thin air. Leaving Nothing.

The Colonel remained in that nothingness for an eternity. Until time, space and being had ceased to have existence or meaning. His breath slowed, his pulse became indiscernible. He floated without any reference, without any knowledge even that he was floating. When he was quite detached and empty, he allowed the noble values to fill the emptiness. Slowly and mindfully, he returned to his senses and to the temporary camp. Pon was there, sitting with Souk, gold bars in each of their laps. The Colonel, once more the noble bastion of virtue, saw them only as two piles of skeleton, skin and bone.

Pon turned her head. Her eyes met those of the Colonel. Cymbals crashed, bells rang, kukris cut rainbows in the sky, heavenly music played, Pon and the Colonel touched hands and rose a metre in the air, their eyes locked together, and the Colonel, in spite of his efforts to avoid it, fell in love. Oh well, the Colonel thought as he came down to earth, detachment can wait until tomorrow.

# 13

## Strange Allies

**Nigel's phone rang. 10.00 p.m. It was Godfrey.**

"Still nothing in, Nige? Think we should report it *upstairs*? Get some support sent in. After all, we're responsible for the Colonel being there. If something happens to him, there will be accusations of poor back up."

"There will certainly be that, Godfrey. And more. Library just got a bullet for, and I quote, *irresponsible deployment*. Don't want that in my record. But on the other hand, just because we haven't heard from a bloke for a few hours, or a day, could mean nothing at all. And if he's okay, we'd be accused of crying wolf and panicking. Better wait a bit. Never good to try to do anything middle of the night. Nothing in tomorrow morning, afternoon there, we'll ring the alarm bells."

As Nigel hung up the phone and turned back to his book, Welder and Chantavong were approaching the Colonel's camp, with four tough, heavily-armed policemen puffing along behind them. Welder looked at his watch. Four in the morning. The very best time, if it has to be done, for killing. The thought of a target dying in his sleep was less painful for all concerned, and certainly much safer and less messy.

Welder and Chantavong had finally settled their helicopter alongside that of the Colonel and Norman in mid-afternoon of the previous day. After what seemed an eternity, they had finally raised Sweetheart's helicopter on the radio. That machine was low on fuel and had gone to Luang Prabang for more. "Stay there!" said Chantavong angrily, knowing that there was anyway no place for them to put down and not wanting to wait. He gave their position as near as Welder could make it out according to the map and told them to come on the next morning.

The first man out of the helicopter walked straight into the Colonel's tripwires and was literally blown in half, reducing Chantavong's force to seven and sending those seven diving to the floor of the chopper. It was some time before they realised no attack was imminent and slowly disconnected the Colonel's system of booby traps.

They left one man behind to guard the helicopters and made off through the jungle with the remaining six armed and armoured police. They had no women to slow them down, but also had only a vague idea of the compass direction to follow and when they finally came to the river bank, it was only after losing themselves several times as the darkness descended. They covered twice the distance the Colonel's team had taken in the light and in spite of their police training, were twice as tired. They did not know it, but they were not far from the Colonel's temporary camp. It was one o'clock in the morning, and just staying awake was a major effort. They had been walking ten hours and had an unknown distance yet to go. Tired, wet and covered in leeches, the men were in mutinous mood as they ate their cold rations and drank water from the Mekong.

Not knowing whether they were upstream or downstream of the Colonel, they had no choice other than to split their force in two and follow the bank in the two opposite directions. Welder and Chantavong went together, each afraid that if they split up, the other would find the Colonel and get the treasure. They took three men with them and set off downstream, the other three moved upstream. There was no plan other than to find the Colonel and shoot him in the middle of the night, collect the treasure and return to the helicopter as soon as it was light.

This night, the Colonel had made a real camp fire. Dinner was fresh fish grilled over embers from the fire, along with frogs and mushrooms.

"Perhaps I shouldn't tell you this, but on the gunboat there was a nice stock of Gevrey-Chambertin 1935."

"You couldn't have managed one bottle?" said a disappointed Norman.

"Relax, Norman. It would have been undrinkable by now. But I did bring along from Vientiane a little something for medicinal purposes." The Colonel drew from his black bag a litre bottle of Black Label and poured measures into the five bamboo cups he had cut earlier in the day. Pon picked up a bamboo tube of boiled water and offered it, apologising for the lack of ice. But each mind was too full of gold to care. Shares had yet to be allocated but each mind was busy with its dreams that could now become realities. They were tired but happy with a joy inspired by stumbling across good fortune, rather than working to create good karma and reaping just returns.

The Colonel took Pon by the hand, led her under the lean-to shelter and made love to her. Pon looked up at the criss-cross of branches and leaves and thought of the day fighting through the mud, the horrors of the first leaches she had known in her life and waiting for the Colonel to surface from the depths. She was not a country girl and as she lay in the Colonel's arms on a carpet of banana leaves, she wondered that she could feel such excited happiness. "You know," she said to the Colonel. "I think it must be love."

The Colonel's thoughts were atypical of the man: less than noble and extremely jumbled. How could Pon switch from that filthy and value-less Winkle to a man of the Colonel's ilk? What did love mean to a person who, on the orders of her former lover, had joined with young Souk in giving the Colonel a Vientiane sandwich? And what did it mean to him? Love was a luxury he had denied himself for decades. Had he felt love back in the 17<sup>th</sup> century? Had he had children at that time? Were some of the people he had seen in this incestuous little country his descendants? Had he perhaps, in the best Hindu tradition, been with Pon in that past life? But in the best Hindu tradition, Pon would have waited, guarding her chastity, waited for fate to weave her destiny with that of the Colonel, and for the Colonel to take her virginity. There was a lot to disturb the Colonel. But mostly it was feelings he thought must be love, which he saw as a desire to possess and protect. And it was these feelings that rang little alarm bells of intuition in his mind.

"Pon," said the Colonel. "I too think it must be love. I did not expect to feel love, but I feel a very strong emotion and it must be love. The thought of being without you, or you being with another man, is just too much for my mind. There, I've said it. I think I love you. And because of love, I want to protect you. And because my protective instincts are aroused, my other instincts are on blade's edge. And the greatest of these instincts warns me of danger. Danger to all of us, but principally danger to me. Stay here, hidden from open view under this cover. Take Souk in with you and sleep. Don't worry. I shall be in the forest around the camp, and I shall see any danger and interrupt it before it can complete its mission." Then he kissed Pon, long and passionately. Then he followed his instinct and slipped out of the shelter and into the forest.

Welder, Chantavong and the three policemen followed the river bank. To the best of their ability, not possessing the Colonel's jungle craft, they moved in silence. But for a man of the Colonel's sharply-honed senses, they might as well have been crashing through the undergrowth on elephants and announcing their coming by loud-speaker. As they approached the campsite, they were completely unaware that their quarry was behind them and following.

This was what the Colonel did best. His mind was perfectly clear. Pon and the gold had been relegated to dormant pockets of inactive thought. He was hunter and hunted. He noted Welder with Chantavong and this troubled him a little. He had no argument with either man and found it hard to believe that Welder was hunting him for the $10,000 reward posted by Winkle. Perhaps their presence in the Sayaboury jungles had nothing to do with the Colonel. In which case, the Colonel had no justification in taking them out one by one as they stumbled through the forest. The group stopped and sat down for a smoke and the Colonel crept close enough to hear them talking.

"I am only interested in the Colonel," said Welder. "He must be killed immediately. There is no need to kill the others. And you, Thhanh Chantavong can have all the treasure they have found – if any."

"There will also be two girls with them," said Chantavong to his men. "One is Pon, who the Colonel stole from Winkle. The other is Souk, and you can expect Norman West to put up a fight for her. The girls are of no consequence. Play them as you wish."

So, they want me dead, the treasure in their pockets, and the girls to amuse themselves with. The Colonel had three justifications from the lips of Welder and Chantavong for killing all of them on the spot. He thought he stood a good chance of succeeding right there and then. The men stood smoking in a close group, their weapons propped on the ground at their feet. With the element of surprise, the Colonel could probably wield his kukri and cut down all of them before they realized what was happening. But probably, to the Colonel, was not good enough. His preferred method, when presented with choice and opportunity, was to be slow but sure.

The men flicked their cigarette butts into the river and continued their way in, as they thought of it, single-file silence.

The Colonel closed behind the last man in line. He waited patiently until the gap between the last man and the next lengthened slightly. He then tuned his hunter mode to the highest pitch and, acting naturally, sprung like a tiger, whipping the kukri through the air to connect with maximum impact on the unfortunate straggler's neck and send his head flying.

The sound of the dead man falling alerted his comrade in front of him, who turned to see what the problem was. He never found out. The razor-sharp kukri flashed again and the man fell before he could utter a sound, his vocal cords and artery cut, blood spurting from his neck, kicking on the forest ground like a stuck pig with its snout tied to stop the scream.

The Colonel could have continued in this way until only he and Welder were left. But their camp was close now and he had to shorten the odds quickly. He wiped his kukri blade on a dead man's shirtsleeves and picked up the man's AK 47 assault rifle. He pulled the trigger, rattled off a long burst at the backs of the men in front of him and saw one fall and the rest scatter before return fire caused him to take cover in the undergrowth. One policeman had been wounded by the burst of gunfire, but most importantly, the group, now effectively just Welder and Chantavong, were on the defensive and in disarray. In panic, they shot their guns wildly into the darkness and ran straight ahead of them, away from the danger behind and, by accident, straight into the camp.

Welder saw Norman and Soubanh asleep on the open ground and, still thinking the Colonel was somewhere in the camp, kicked down the makeshift shelter, his gun ready to shoot the man who even now was hurrying back to the camp. He stopped himself from firing as he saw Pon and Souk huddled together. He almost didn't recognize them with their clothes on. Chantavong clubbed Norman and Soubanh with his rifle butt and held the gun pointed at their heads.

When the Colonel entered the camp, gun leveled and ready to fire, he found Welder with his arm around Pon's neck, gun pushed into her temple, foot firmly pressed on Souk's neck.

"Put the weapon down, Colonel. Or I kill both girls." Welder spoke in English. Norman struggled to get to his feet but was again clubbed by Chantavong; Soubanh lay bleeding from the head.

The Colonel kept hold of his rifle. "Welder," he answered in Lao, so that Chantavong and the girls could understand the situation. "You know I won't shoot you for fear of hitting Pon. But if I drop my gun, you will certainly shoot me. I will only fire if you start firing. Then, even if you have never fired a gun before, you *might* kill me, but I would *certainly* kill you." All the time he was wondering if he dared risk a shot at Welder's head, deciding against it because the AK 47 was not made for such precision shooting. "This is known in the movies as a Mexican stand-off. Neither of us can be sure of winning – unless I am stupid enough to throw down my weapon. What I suggest is: you take the national treasure, which includes eight bars of pure gold, and disappear along with Thhanh Chantavong. After all, what purpose would my death serve? This way, you get the treasure. We get nothing, but we all keep our lives. Is it a deal?"

"It's a deal," said Chantavong before Welder had a chance to reply. Chantavong certainly had nothing to gain by the Colonel's death and would have a lot to explain. "Let the girl go, Welder," said Chantavong. You would never shoot her anyway."

And so it might have been. But fate had other ideas. As Chantavong spoke, three men who could move through the forest as quietly as the Colonel jumped the ex-gurka from behind, pinned his arms to his sides and clubbed him with the gun of the wounded policeman, who limped into the small clearing bleeding from leg and stomach wounds, looked at the situation in confusion and sank to his knees.

Welder held Pon by the hair and approached the Colonel. He could not believe his luck. He had no idea who the three men were or why they had intervened, but he could ask questions later. Now he had what he had come for, the Colonel's head. He had only to detach it from the Colonel's body.

The Colonel was tightly held and, groggy from the hard club to the head, easily forced to his knees. Welder considered taking the Colonel's own kukri from its sheath on the Colonel's leg and using it to nip off the Colonel's head, but, being totally unpracticed in the art of decapitation, decided to shoot him first between the eyes. He could then proceed to the beheading at leisure, with a plastic bag handy to hold the severed head. He pushed the nozzle of his assault rifle forward until its barrel rested on the bridge of the Colonel's nose. Even Welder, more at home with a welding torch than an AK 47, could not miss at literal point blank range.

The Colonel's head pounded from the blow delivered by the short, silent, men in loincloths, but his mind cleared enough to register that he was indeed in a difficult situation. He would have liked to know why Welder wanted to kill him, and why the *Spirits* were assisting Welder, but given the hopelessness of the situation, he concentrated on an immediate preparation for death and rebirth. He did not look at Pon, but detached himself from the situation by making his mind blank except for the face of Welder. By looking Welder straight in the eyes at the moment of death, the Colonel and Welder were fated to meet again in another life, when the Colonel would take his revenge.

---

# 14

# Head on a Plate

**"Godfrey, it's gone eleven o'clock at night.** Just one hour after you last called. I have checked the e-mail and there is nothing there."

"Yeh, okay, Nige. A bit annoyed, are you? Hang up if you like. I just feel, you know, kind of uneasy about the Colonel and this dead or alive business. Don't think I'll be able to sleep tonight. And if the Colonel does get topped, it could be ages before anybody tells us."

"Yes Godfrey," Nigel sighed. "But I thought we agreed to wait until morning and not to panic."

"Morning might be too late. After all, even if they decide to send in back up, it's likely to be some ponce from the Embassy in Bangkok."

"Godfrey! Some *ponce* from the Embassy! Indeed! It might well be some ponce from the FCO."

"Even worse. He'd probably wait until midnight for the next Bangkok flight, then take sixteen hours to arrive. Then go to Foreign Affairs in Vientiane and register concern."

"And what would you do, Godfrey? Want to go yourself?"

"I would if it would do any good. But it wouldn't and I would stick out like a sore thumb, wouldn't I Nige? Being black and all. No, we should send in somebody useful. Someone who knows the Colonel, knows this type of situation, you know, somebody who knows how to get results in a breakdown of order."

"You mean a regiment of Scots Guards?"

"Come off it, Nige. You know what I mean. The Colonel's own men, the ones he requested."

"Can't go sending in the gurkas just like that, Godfrey. Takes more than a phone call from bed. Sending troops – even just two of them – to a foreign country would probably require the Prime Minister's signature, if not a vote in Parliament. Plus, of course, an invitation from the country being invaded."

"It would, Nige, *if* they were in active service. But these chaps are retired, just like the Colonel, two people, who happen to have been gurkas, going to Laos for a holiday."

"Okay, Godfrey. Your Uncle Nigel is not that thick. No need to spell it out. I have their names and phone number right here. I'll call them immediately and explain the situation to them; suggest they might like to get on the next plane – I think there's one early morning. 'Though with the time difference, I doubt if it gets there in time for the afternoon flight to Vientiane. They would have to pay their own fare, although we could try to reimburse later if they keep the tickets. The Colonel gave them Welder's telephone number and address in case they were needed at short notice. Of course, nothing on paper, they would have to realize that if everything goes right, the FCO will pick up the costs. If everything goes wrong, the FCO knows nothing about it."

"Of course," said Godfrey.

"Now, hang up so I can get onto them. And Godfrey…"

"Yes, Nige?"

"Well done. Good thinking."

Winkle sat up in bed at the top of the *Blue Member*. His companion hid herself under the bedcover as Biggs and Stamford walked in. He looked at his watch and wiped his eyes. He was not an early bird.

"It's not yet daylight," he said. "This had better be good Biggsie."

"It is good, boss. Otherwise I would never have called you," said Biggs.

"Well, cough it up," ordered Winkle.

"The Colonel's dead," said Biggs.

Winkle sprang to life. All sleep left him. "You got him, Biggsie? How? When?"

"Not me, boss. Somebody who wants the reward. Brought in the Colonel's head in a rice sack. All warm and sticky."

"Bring the man up, Biggsie. With his prize of course. No, wait a minute. Let's do this right. Bring him up, but get a silver serving platter from the kitchen first. The Colonel's head presented on a silver platter. Then, at tonight's party, we'll put the platter in place of honour, in the middle of our banquet. You know I always like to find something new to entertain my guests. This will top them all. Afterwards we'll send it to Welder in an ice box. Welder can send it to London. Wow, this is going to be fun. Hope the Colonel enjoys it, haa, haa."

Biggs joined in the laughter of his boss and left to fetch the severed head. He returned within minutes, holding the elbow of an old Lao man who had difficulty seeing, who carried in front of him a silver tray covered with a lace-worked cloth.

"Over here man. Over here," Winkle said in his London-accented Lao.

The old man walked slowly over to where Winkle sat up in his bed. "I cut his head off myself, I did. With a chopper. When he was sleeping."

"Good man. And you will get your reward. Now, let's have a look at the Colonel's head."

The old man raised the white cloth and a blood drained face

looked straight at Winkle. Winkle, eyes bulging, stared at the head. Blood rapidly drained from his own face. "Where did you get this?" he asked the old man.

The old man proudly answered. "He came into my guest house last night with a girl. I recognized the man from the photo on the wanted announcement. I waited until the girl left early this morning and then took the chopper from the kitchen and opened his door. He was asleep, so I chopped off his head and brought it straight to you."

"And what, old man, is the name of your guest house?"

"Samsenthai Guest House, Sir."

"Well, old man," said Winkle with quiet anger. "You have murdered an innocent man. This is not the Colonel. Go, and take the head with you. And never come back."

"Can I keep the tray?"

"No, you fucking well can't keep the tray. Think yourself lucky to escape alive. And never try to deceive me again."

The old man put the head back in the rice bag and hobbled out.

"Biggsie," said Wilder, "I'm going back to sleep and will pretend this never happened. In the meantime, you contact every member of The Group and say to come tonight at 7.00 p.m. Dinner and entertainment as usual, but a very important announcement. And tell Rupert Sweetheart I expect all off-duty Sucksabit specials on permanent stand-by from now onwards. And double the guard on this building."

Welder felt the power of the Colonel's eyes even as his finger took up the slack on the trigger. God damn it, he thought, I don't want to kill the Colonel and hack off his head. I don't want to kill anybody. Why should I? He answered himself: because if you don't, Winkle or his boys will kill you and subject Kim to horrors you don't want to think about. He looked along the gun barrel into the Colonel's eyes. "I can't do it," he said, and lowered the gun.

The *Spirits* released the Colonel. "Snake," said one of them in

Lao. Just one word and they faded back into the jungle, Pon rushed to hug him, crying.

"I'm sorry," said Welder. "I really am sorry. I don't know what came over me."

"That's all right," said the Colonel, getting up off his knees. "Happens to all of us at some time."

"What about these two?" Chantavong asked, still waving the barrel of his gun at Norman and Soubanh.

"I have no argument with either," said Welder. "They are good men."

"And the gold? Do we still get the gold?"

"The eight kilos, yes. It's all yours, Thhanh Chantavong. I think, given the circumstances, Welder foregoes any share. Eight kilos of gold just for you. In exchange, I ask you and Welder to help us carry some black bags back to our helicopter, with no questions asked. And, of course, the rest of the National Treasure goes to Foreign Affairs initially, although I shall emphasise that Thhanh Chantavong helped immeasurably in its recovery."

Pon set about trying to stop the bleeding on the policeman. "You'll get a medal for this. And promotion," said Chantavong to the wounded man.

"I don't understand. What happened?" The policeman groaned.

"We were attacked by *Spirits*". Chantavong said. If there was anything he was good at, it was explaining. "They came up behind us and cut down two of our men, picked up their guns and started shooting at us, wounding you. Luckily, the Colonel, who we had come to arrest, wrongly suspecting him of the attack on Winkle's office – which it now looks like Winkle staged himself to destroy evidence that would support the request for his extradition – intervened and drove off the *Spirits*. Thus, we all owe our lives to the Colonel. Now do you understand?"

"Yes," said the wounded policeman, whose wounds proved less dangerous than at first feared and who was able to hobble around with the aid of a bamboo crutch that the Colonel fashioned for him in two minutes flat.

Welder explained to the Colonel exactly why he had tried to kill him. The Colonel listened carefully, and then looked Welder deeply in the eyes. "Winkle's threat still stands. You didn't kill me; would you be able to kill him?"

Welder had the image in his mind of little Kim being abused by Winkle. "I know I would kill him happily, if I get the chance."

"We can make the chance," said the Colonel. "Just don't look him in the eyes when you do it. I suppose we should shake hands?"

Welder extended his hand gratefully and the Colonel took it, putting on hold for the moment the question of who ran Winkle's drug empire. "Thank you, Colonel. You have taught me a lot today. You could have killed me."

"Yes, I could. But I didn't. A live ally is usually better than a dead enemy. I understand why you felt you had to kill me, and I understand why now you must remove Winkle. Neither you nor Kim can stay in Vientiane as long as Winkle is here – and since Kim has no papers or passport and cannot legally travel abroad, Winkle has to go. Now, I for one have been in the forest all night. So have you. Let's all of us sit and have some breakfast before that long walk back. While we eat, you can tell me how you managed to enlist the aid of the *Spirits*. That's the only thing I don't understand about events."

"I have no idea why they did what they did," Welder replied. "I had never seen them before in my life."

"I had, one of them at least. We were after the same snake. He got it, but was scared off by my presence. I killed it, and very tasty it was too. I suppose in a way I did steal his snake, but that's hardly reason enough to want to kill me."

"Perhaps I can explain," said Norman, "The *Spirit* did say 'snake' just before he disappeared, and that's the only word to come from any of their lips. I have read all the anthropological literature on the *Spirits* of this area – all very dated stuff, mind you, and full of French imagination and exaggeration. But it might offer some sort of explanation for their actions. There used to be far more *Spirits* than there

166

are now, far more forest of course. They moved around a lot, but one group would claim a certain territory and that group would live within that area, probably a vast area, providing plenty of game and vegetables to sustain the group. Each group had a *totem* animal that they would kill under no circumstances and would protect all they could. Such totemism ensured the survival of different species of animal – but that's the anthropologist speaking, not the *Spirits*. One group, for example, had the tiger as its totem – actually believed they were all descended from tigers. Another group was descended from elephants, another from a type of frog. I would guess the men we just saw belong to a group that has that particular snake you killed as a totemic ancestor. By killing it, you dishonoured their ancestors and threatened the entire tribal group."

The Colonel looked embarrassed. "I'm sure you're right Norman. Totemism is not as strange as it might sound to a Western mind. It's perhaps just one step from a primitive form of reincarnation. Of course, had I known, I would never have offended the group by killing that snake. Come to think of it, before he fled from my presence, he was holding the snake and almost playing with it. What you say makes sense, Norman, I now realise that *Spirit* I came across by accident had no intention of harming the snake. I regret that my actions might have placed us all in a dangerous situation."

"But the snake *was* delicious," said Pon, lightening the atmosphere as everybody laughed.

Any further analysis was interrupted by the sound of a helicopter following the river towards them. "It's Rupert Sweetheart looking for us," said Chantavong. "Anywhere they can put down here?"

"We can make somewhere," replied the Colonel. "If we can be sure Rupert and his merry men will not be hostile. After all, correct me if I am wrong, but I think their presence here is part of the man-hunt directed against me?"

"True, but I'm calling off the man-hunt as soon as we get to a radio or telephone. Don't worry, they will do as I tell them," said Chantavong. All present felt uneasy about trusting Chantavong one inch. But faced with an easy helicopter ride and passage for all the

gold on one hand and a long walk through the snake and leech infest-
ed marshes and angry *Spirits* on the other, the temptation to enlist
Sweetheart's assistance was great.

"And Thhan Chantavong, you will please tell them first to drop
an axe, two if they have two. Then, after we have cleared the trees
and they have landed, they get out and walk back to the other helicopters. We get in, together with your wounded man and the treasure – and *your* eight kilogrammes of gold. You use the helicopter
radio to call off the manhunt for me and redirect it against Winkle
and we fly back to Vientiane."

Thhan Chantavong agreed to everything and in exchange was
presented with eight kilos of pure gold. The Colonel thought he saw
tears forming in the eyes of Pon and Souk as they handed over their
share to the police chief. He made a mental note to reassure them,
out of Chantavong's earshot, that there remained plenty of buried
gold for everybody.

While the helicopter whirled noisily overhead, Chantavong went
into charades of chopping down trees. Eventually, two axes were
dropped from the helicopter, and the Colonel, Welder, Norman and
Soubanh took turns to cut down the trees near the river bank and
clear the undergrowth to prepare a landing site.

Finally, the hovering helicopter was waved in to land. As the
armed police tumbled out, closely followed by the huge frame of
Rupert Sweetheart, they were surprised to find their chief seemingly on the best of terms with the men they had come to capture or
kill, the Colonel and Norman West. They were even more surprised
when Chantavong gave them a compass and told them to start
walking towards the helicopters – knowing that finding such a small
target in the forest might take them days. Only Rupert was spared.
With hindsight, this was to prove a very big mistake indeed.

"Things have changed, Rupert," said the Colonel. "Chantavong
is calling off the man-hunt, or should I say, redirecting it. Winkle
will now be the target instead of the executioner. I need to know if
you are with us or still with Winkle. The difference is a ride home in
the helicopter or a long walk with your men. I'd like to know if your

Sucksabit-elite can be turned to use against Winkle or if there is going to be a useless waste of life there, if they try to defend him."

"As you might have sensed, Colonel, I've never been very happy with Winkle's activities. On the other hand, I've never had any proof of illegalities, unless we count fornication with under-age girls – but even there, they all seemed willing enough little whores. So, while I have never participated in his contemptible orgies – in the way for example that you have, Colonel – I would not have achieved anything more than losing my job had I opposed them openly. As for any involvement in gems and drugs, I have never been privy to the financial side of things and I think probably regular police are used for any drug movements. Maybe you should ask your friend there, Thhan Chantavong?

"As regards the loyalty of the inner guard of Sucksabit – those I have trained personally. I would like to think they owe some loyalty to me and to God – they are all hand-picked evangelical Christians and none participate in Winkle's sex events – but the fact is they have been trained principally as bodyguards to Winkle, and Winkle pays them well, with good conditions, so I cannot say they would all come across simply on my word. As for the rest of Sucksabit, they will follow whoever is in charge and paying their salaries – which at the moment means Winkle."

"Fair enough, Rupert," the Colonel concluded. "As long as I can count on your loyalty to the crown, or at least to your non-interference in any conflict, you are welcome to return with us to Vientiane, rather than forever wander around the swamps with your men."

"Colonel, you can count on whatever help I can give. I promise you that. And I don't give my word lightly."

In compliance with the Colonel's deal, Chantavong spoke into the chopper's radio transmitter to police waiting at Lao-West Helicopters airport office. At the request of Welder, who was afraid that Winkle might create mischief with Kim in his absence, Chantavong did not simply switch the hunt from the Colonel to Winkle, but stated that the search for the colonel had been happily resolved and that all police and militia could now stand down – that he was returning to Vientiane with the Colonel. Chantavong's statement left an ambiguity over the status of the Colonel that might yet rebound against the Colonel on arrival in Vientiane. The Colonel was willing to risk it, but placed the captured AK-47s into the helicopter as some kind of assurance.

The Colonel and Norman disappeared into the forest, dug up the gold, and carried it to the waiting helicopter. Chantavong watched them as they loaded the black plastic bags, but did not intervene or ask questions. The wounded man was now in good spirits and received pain killers from the helicopter's first-aid kit. Chantavong had ordered an ambulance to go to Welder's house, where it had been agreed to land the helicopter on the lawn. As a diplomatic residence, the house provided a level of safety for the gold and for the Colonel – and Welder, who had no way of knowing of Kim's abduction, was anxious to get back to his little girl as soon as possible.

When they finally took off, it was 14.00 hours. Welder was for immediate return, the rest set their priorities at food and drink and giving thanks. Thus an hour was spent in the small provincial capital of Sayaboury, eating noodles, drinking beer and, with the exception of the Evangelical Rupert Sweetheart, going to the local temple to *wai phra*, to honour the Buddha, give thanks for coming through alive with quite a haul and requesting help in what lay ahead. This they did by sinking to their knees in front of the Buddha image and in front of the temple's abbot and handing over an envelope with lots of money inside for the support of the temple and its monks. The abbot in return blessed them all by sprinkling water over their heads while monks chanted in the background. Afterwards, everybody except for Welder felt better.

"Do you know?" said the Colonel as they left the temple and rejoined Sweetheart. "I clean forgot to warn your men, Rupert, that there are some trip wires and explosives around our helicopter."

"They should look for them. Part of training," said Rupert, shrugging his shoulders. "If they fail to find them, that's a hard lesson."

When they came down in Welder's beautiful garden, it was four o'clock in the afternoon. The ambulance was waiting and took away the wounded policeman. The Australian neighbour glued herself to the window. "They're all back," said Mrs Australian Embassy. "Welder, that strange Colonel and Norman West, *and* their girls. And that looks like the Police Chief. And what are they carrying in those black bags? Looks very heavy. And why the ambulance? And why land on the lawn? My washing is out there." Welder's maid was also waiting, with an unwelcome message. Winkle and his heavies had come into the house and taken away Kim. Winkle had made the maid promise to state to Welder that he need not fear for Kim's safety, that nothing would happen to her. She would simply be kept as a guest at the *Blue Member* until Welder brought in the Colonel or the Colonel's head.

---

# 15

# The Colonel takes a bath

**"E-mail just in from Welder,"** said Nigel to Godfrey, who for once arrived on time at the FCO, but still behind Nigel, who always allowed that extra ten minutes. "Sounds like things are resolving themselves. The man-hunt for the Colonel has been called off. In fact the Colonel is at this moment holding a convivial council of war with the Police Chief, aimed at securing the release of a Lao hostage taken by Winkle and the capture of Winkle for crimes against the state and murder. Early this morning, Vientiane time, seems like an old man was picked up by the militia leaving Winkle's *Blue Member Club* with a severed head in a rice sack. Said Winkle had offered him $10,000 to cut the head."

"Sounds like I was a bit premature in sending in the gurkas. They caught the midnight flight to Bangkok, which had luckily been delayed one hour. They'll be in Bangkok by eighteen hundred local time, that's midday here, and, since the Ambassador is providing assistance at the airport, they should catch the six-thirty connection, arriving in Vientiane at seven-thirty p.m. Looks like they won't be needed. You were right Nigel, we should have waited until the cold light of morning."

"Don't be so sure, Godfrey. Better safe than sorry. And with Winkle on the loose and taking hostages, it sounds like things are far from being over."

Soon after landing, the Colonel, who had taken control of Operation Anti-Winkle, sent Rupert off to return to the *Blue Member* independently and make sure nothing happened to Kim, partly because he trusted him and wanted him back in place before the fireworks began, and partly because he did not trust him and did not want him around listening to his plans for dealing with Winkle. He had been looking forward to a good, hot shower and stretching out on a real bed with Pon relieving the stresses of killing and almost being killed in the jungle. Pon had been thinking the same way. But both felt they could not leave Kim in Winkle's hands after what Welder had told them about her earlier ordeal.

"Don't worry, Welder. We'll get Kim back. But no point in charging in without a plan, Winkle must have all his heavies concentrated on the *Blue Member* at this time. Thing is, Winkle probably doesn't know the situation at this moment, but he will very quickly find out, particularly with a helicopter landing in your back yard. We could send in the police but, with respect Thhanh Chantavong, I'm not sure they could not be bought off. Or even that they are a match for Sweetheart's specials among the Sucksabit guards, all trained personally by Sweetheart, ex-SAS, with the primary objective of protecting Winkle. Then there are over two hundred young and violent Englishmen, all with long criminal records in the UK or seeking refuge from justice in England. They would fight with desperation since their freedom and wealth depend on Winkle, who is in many ways their saviour. I think we will have to tackle this situation with something other than brute force."

"What do you suggest we do?" asked Welder, anxiety etched deeply into his face.

"I don't know," admitted the Colonel. "The abduction of Kim

greatly complicates any military intervention. I shall take a hot bath and meditate on the problem. In the meantime, Norman and Pon, try to get hold of the Acting Deputy Minister of Foreign Affairs and invite him over right now. Tell him we have the National Treasure and wish to hand it over to him. And while waiting, everybody get the plastic bags locked away in the steel-lined sanctuary room, lock the door and give me the only key. Set the National Treasure out nicely so that Thhanh Vatsana is immediately impressed on entry. And everybody try to take half-hour's rest, including you Welder. We shall all need it."

The Colonel disappeared into the bathroom and Pon followed him. Throughout the pulsating helicopter journey, every touch of their two bodies had created a chemical reaction that in the privacy of Welder's bathroom ignited into a spontaneous combustion of lust. The Colonel had his shower. Pon added a new dimension to a bar of soap. And all too quickly the Colonel exploded onto Pon's soapy body parts. "What about you?" the Colonel asked, always the gentleman, as Pon expertly twisted and milked him with one hand and, with the other hand engaged in a few equally expert twists of the shower head, simultaneously washing the Colonel's honey from her body and down Welder's plug hole.

"Yes, my turn now, my Colonel." And, still under the flow of hot water, Pon backed up to the Colonel's member, took his arms around her, placed his hands on her clitoris and began to giggle and groan loudly. Those in Welder's sitting room, not to mention the Australian neighbours, were left in no doubt as to the nature of the Colonel's meditation.

Having donned clean fresh clothing and run an electric shaver over his stubble, the Colonel returned to the group, which now included Thhanh Vatsana, Acting Deputy Minister of Foreign Affairs, looking as dapper as ever, and his cute assistant, looking like maybe she did more than just take notes at meetings.

"Hello, Colonel. Good to see you again," the Acting Deputy said pleasantly, stretching out a well-manicured hand. "I hear you had a good trip".

Christ, thought the Colonel – his mind still bulging with memories of swamps, skeletons in sunken gunboats, beheadings and an AK 47 barrel pressed against the bridge of his nose by his colleague in service to Queen and Country – he talks as if I've just come back from a dirty weekend at the beach. And no mention of the national manhunt for yours truly. This man would do well in the FCO. Welder's maid brought in iced Coca-Cola.

"Yes, thank you, Thhanh Vatsana. A very good trip. And, as you can see, we brought you back a souvenir. The National Treasure. Recovery was a joint effort between the United Kingdom – represented by Director of Lao-West Helicopters, Norman West, Head of British Trade Mr Welder, and myself, Adviser sent by the Foreign and Commonwealth Office – and the Government of Laos, represented by Thhanh Chantavong and the forces of law and order. We can perhaps arrange a suitably public official handover ceremony to the Ministry's Department of Antiquity at an early date. It would be nice if the British Ambassador can hand over personally to the President of the Republic. In the meantime, perhaps you would like us to lock these priceless treasures from the Lao past in Welder's steel-doored safe room."

"You have performed a great service to the people of the Lao People's Democratic Rebublic. And display of this treasure will be physical evidence of the long and substantial mutual cooperation between our two peoples and governments; cooperation that will one day lead to the exchange of embassies between our countries." As Vatsana spoke, his assistant produced a notebook like magic and noted every word.

"And Thhanh Vatsana, may I take this opportunity to enquire if the Government has had time to consider the UK's order for extradition of William Winkle?"

"Indeed it has, Colonel. And I'm pleased to say that the President will take a decision as soon as he receives a report of the police investigation of the subject. Which is no doubt being prepared at this moment, isn't that so, Thhanh Chantavong?"

"Yes, at this very moment," replied Chantavong. "It will be with the Minister of State Security tomorrow first thing."

"And for your investigations, have you taken Winkle into custody?" The Acting Deputy asked Chantavong.

"We are just about to do so, Acting Deputy Minister. As we speak, my men are preparing to detain Winkle."

"Good," said the Acting Deputy. "In that case, Colonel, I would not be surprised if the President makes a decision tomorrow. I rely on Thhan Chantavong."

Well, that's okay then, thought the Colonel. Now all we have to contend with, while waiting for Chantavong's police to detain the man who has been their principal pay-master for many years, is Winkle's private SAS-trained army, two hundred plus irate English football hooligans turned gangsters, Sucksabit, and those members of the governments and armies on both sides of the Mekong plotting an overthrow of the Lao power structure. Should be a doddle.

The sun was going down over the Thai side of the river; a huge golden ball sending strong rays across Welder's balcony and into Welder's sitting room. The sky was turning from blue to yellow and red. As the Acting Deputy Minister and his correct yet cuddlesome assistant made their goodbyes an aircraft sounded overhead. The Acting Deputy Minister looked at his watch as he shook the Colonel's hand and turned to leave, "The six-thirty from Bangkok. Right on time."

"There goes a happy man," said Norman. "He'll get big kudos for the retrieval of the National Treasure. And I daresay he is happy to have an excuse to push through the extradition. They must have already carved up who gets what of the Winkle Empire."

"It is tempting to say let things take their course," said the Colonel.

"Please, Colonel," Welder appealed. "If we don't act now to stop him, Winkle is going to get word of the changed situation. And he would certainly take out his revenge on Kim."

"No, we can't let that happen," said the Colonel. "I had the chance to think about things just now. Marvelous what a hot shower and an iced Coke will do, even better than a good cup of tea. Now, here's the plan."

"Why not have a little bit now? After all, Welder and that Colonel are not cuckoo, they are never going to show up. And here, look at this," Biggs unzipped and let out his huge member. Kim shrank further back into the armchair where she had been put by Winkle to watch the video tape made the last time she was in Winkle's power, and to wait, guarded by Biggs and Stamford. "Gorgeous little thing. Look at the screen. Love those little nipples. Must have a lovely tight little cunt. And I bet Welder's never given her a backsider yet. Has he lovey?" Biggs spoke in English, but Kim understood every word and was terrified that what she saw on the screen was all going to happen again, and worse. Biggs kneeled on an arm of the armchair with his glory at full mast in both hands and held it in front of Kim's frightened eyes. "After all, Winkle's had a taste of her already. Or, rather, she's had a taste of Winkle's winkle."

"Yeh, well Winkle is Winkle," said Stamford, himself bulging at the sight of the videoed Kimpen forced to take Winkle in her young mouth. And Winkle told us to guard her and not to touch her until he gives the word. Nothing I'd like better myself than to thrust it in there. Look at her frightened little eyes. I'm as turned on as you are. But if Winkle found out, no telling what he would do. He's a control freak, you know that. He'll certainly want first goes himself – particularly a virgin bum. He's giving a dinner for the big boys tonight – for all I know he may have scheduled this little darling as part of the entertainment, and he won't thank us for messing up his plans. I can wait until later."

In spite of his words, Stamford also opened up his trousers and eased out his swollen penis. "On the other hand, I can't see why we can't have a wank while waiting. That's not touching her, is it? And I don't see why we just have to look at the video of that lovely little body. No reason she can't take off her clothes, nice and slow, like she did before. You'll do that for us, won't you Kim girl? That's a very nice dress Welder bought you there. Buttons up the front. I like that. Just undo one button Kim love, one button at a time, start at the top, slowly, until they are all undone. We won't touch you, promise, just touch ourselves like this, like two little schoolboys watching you take things off through the cracks in the changing-room door, you be nice and slow like, while we play with ourselves like this. And as you're such a good little girl, we'll let you watch us big boys cum."

"We're waiting, Kimpen," said Biggs, getting impatient as Kim hesitated. On the TV screen, she saw herself taking Winkle's sex into her mouth and she remembered only too well how complying with one demand had led to another. "Come on now, you sexy little thing. Can't wait much longer or I'll cum all over you and the arm chair. Get them off now, or it goes in your mouth just like what Winkle's doing on the TV." Biggs moved in towards Kim's mouth and she began to unbutton her dress. "That's better. Now, leave the dress open, don't take it off, and pull it open so we can see your little titties. And look at me in the eyes, I like that when I cum. Biggs and Stamford were now fully engaged in, as the Lao say, flying their kites, jacking themselves silly. "Now, Kim, little darling, you stand up, let your dress fall down, that's a good girl, and look at me as you pull down your knickers, slowly now, that's it, just leave them at your knees, and turn around. Show Uncle Biggsie your little bum, that's it, jut it out a bit, yes, and turn your head, just your head to look at me. Don't worry, nobody's taking pictures this time. It'll be over before you know it. Won't hurt you at all, won't even touch you, and we won't tell Welder or Winkle, will we Stam, matey?" But Stam matey was beyond words. Too late now to reach for his pocket hanky.

Winkle came into the room in time to see Kimpen standing with her dress on the floor, her yellow snoopy knickers around her knees, his personal bodyguards with their hands frenetically jerking their extended members, and seminal discharge flying out and down and onto Winkle's deep-shag pile carpet.

At the front gate of the *Blue Member*, Norman pulled up in Welder's Land Rover without attempting to enter the compound. The

Colonel and Welder stepped down from the vehicle and made their way through the gates towards the fifty guards and heavies at the entrance. The Colonel carried a black bag but had left his kukri in Norman's care. "Good luck," said Norman quietly to himself, as he saw the reception party closing around the Colonel.

Before Winkle's angry face could explode, he received an urgent call and grunted into the phone. "*Very* lucky for both of you, Welder has arrived with the Colonel," said Winkle, his glee shining through the anger in his voice. "Get dressed, Kim. You're going home. The two of you come down with her – and make sure she is wearing her knickers. Front office."

Winkle almost danced his way into the front office. He had won. His power was uncontested. Now he had only to sew up the Colonel in the most profitable way.

"Hello, Colonel. Good to see you again." Winkle spoke the same words, with almost the same tone, that the Acting Deputy Minister had used to him. He could afford to be magnanimous at this point in the saga. "Have a good trip to – where was it? – Sayaboury."

"Yes, thank you, Winkle," said the Colonel. "Most profitable."

"Must have been. The guards tell me you brought me back a little present."

The Colonel handed over the black plastic bag. Winkle took out the kilo bar of gold and weighed it contemplatively in his hand. "Very nice," he said. "But it will cost much more than this to buy your life. Don't undervalue yourself, Colonel."

"What about 192 of them?" said the Colonel.

"That's nearer the mark, but why the odd number? Couldn't make up a nice round two hundred?"

"Eight went to Thhanh Chantavong, for his services."

"Of course. Where would we be without Thhanh Chantavong? I for one wouldn't know that you killed three of Chantavong's men and wounded a fourth, landed a helicopter in Welder's garden, had an erotic hot shower, was visited by the Acting Deputy Minister for

Foreign Affairs and seem to be very tongue in cheek with my old girl friend, Pon. Only thing is, I'm surprised that Chantavong accepted only eight bars – I mean, that's only 4%."

"He doesn't – or didn't – know about the other 192."

Winkle laughed. "Good. So, Chantavong thinks he's got a good deal and he's being taken for a ride. Should teach him something.

"But 192 bars is still not quite enough. After all you have been a good deal of trouble, Colonel. Why, one poor *falang* even lost his head over you this morning; case of mistaken identity apparently. Nothing else on offer, Colonel? After all, shouldn't be difficult for us to find your gold. And let's face it, you must have brought back something in all those black bags. Take me five minutes to get through Welder's steel-lined anti-terrorist bedroom doors – there's a full welder's set of instruments conveniently right on the premises, and I'm sure Welder would handle it for us, unless of course we decide to open the door a more conventional way, with the key. And who knows what I'll find behind that door. Then, there's Pon that you seem to be so fond of. And of course, there's still the fate of young Kim to consider."

Welder was preparing to launch himself at Winkle's throat, when Kimpen was ushered into the room by Biggs and Stamford, who took up positions threateningly behind the Colonel. Kim rushed to Welder's arm and hung on tightly.

"There is something else that might interest you," the Colonel said in the tones of finality that he might use in a market place bargaining.

"Yes? My goodness Colonel. You do like to play games. I'm having to drag everything out of you."

"There's the National Treasure of Laos."

"Bingo!" said Winkle. "Now Kim, Stamford will give you and Welder a lift home. Take two of the guards with you Stamford and bring back 192 one kilo bars of gold and the National Treasure. It will be in Welder's steel-lined sanctuary room. The Colonel will give you the key, won't you Colonel? Put the gold under my bed in my apartment and I want the Treasure set out on the party-room table for my guests to appreciate. Off you go now, Kim, with your Uncle Welder.

I've got something to talk to the Colonel about in private. Well, almost in private. You don't mind Biggsie being with us, Colonel? Just my little bit of security. He won't touch you, wouldn't touch anybody, unless I tell him to. Right Biggsie?"

16

---

# Princess Laksami

**On return from luncheon,** Nigel and Godfrey rushed to open the e-mail. "From Welder. I'll read it to you. 'The Colonel has voluntarily put himself in Winkle's hands in exchange for the Lao hostage, who is now in my care. Winkle seems to be willing to accept the National Treasure, which traditionally legitimizes the rulers of Laos, in exchange for the Colonel's freedom. At this point in time, however, the Colonel has not been released. Anyway, Winkle now has the National Treasure. Police are here with me at my home and willing to act against Winkle. But given a fifty-man private army protecting Winkle, the Colonel has a plan to secure Winkle's downfall and capture without the bloodshed that would certainly result from a direct attack on Winkle's bastion. Will revert as news comes in.' "

"So, everything's not as tidy as we thought this morning. No more a man-hunt for the Colonel, but he has placed himself in Winkle's hands. I wonder who this Lao hostage is? Some cute little thing, I bet."

"Godfrey! It might be the Prime Minister or somebody of equal importance. The Colonel does a noble act and you drag it down to 'some cute little thing'."

"Well, I bet it's not the Prime Minister. Welder would have said. And what about the back-up? No mention of them. Although I really don't see what difference two more ex-ghurkas will make when Winkle's got a sizeable SAS-trained bodyguard and over 200 Sucksabit guards obeying his every order."

"Why Godfrey! You seemed to think they could make a lot of difference last night."

"That was before the Colonel gave himself up into the evil clutches of Willie Winkle. What's he go and do that for? After all, it's a Lao matter, he could have left it to the police to sort out."

"Welder's already said that the Colonel is trying to minimize bloodshed. Again, another noble act. Wouldn't be surprised if he gets a medal out of this."

"Lot of good to him if he's dead," said Godfrey, who was concerned for the Colonel but wasn't at all into the nobility thing. "Let's hope his two mates arrive in time to spirit him out of Winkle's fortress."

"Well, Godfrey, if they haven't arrived by now, they'll have to wait for the next flight, which is tomorrow morning, by which time, of course, it might all be over."

Given the choice between being shot in the gut by Winkle, having his neck broken by Biggsie, or going to a dinner party, the Colonel, whose intuition had been developed and honed by a lifetime of experience making difficult decisions, chose the latter.

Thus it was that, at a time *when* Nigel and Godfrey were tucked up into their separate desks digesting the tiramisu, *when* eight of Rupert's elite guard were thrashing around among the snakes in leech-infested marshlands, *when* Rupert Sweetheart was raising his glass and eyebrows – which was just about all he ever raised, *when* Welder was consoling the ex-hostage now in his care the only way he knew how – with a video of Bugs Bunnie to watch and his swollen member to cuddle up to, *when* Norman was persuading his bride of two days not to go out for *som-tum* tonight, and *when* the devoted Pon was mourning the loss of all the gold to her old lover Winkle, the Colonel walked calmly and without demur into Winkle's inner sanctum and congenially shook hands with a dozen conspirators, while Winkle smilingly guided him gently by the elbow.

The scene was much the same as when the Colonel had first arrived. Young things wiggled naked between stroking and groping hands to serve champagne and caviar and took turns to gyrate on the table top, surrounded by the National Treasure nicely set out on red velvet.

Rupert Sweetheart was the first to shake the Colonel's hand. "I presume you have seen the light and Jesus has spoken to you. You have come to join us?" He said, leaving open whether the Colonel had come to join in the sexual follies of the *Blue Member*, Sweetheart's own decade-long sexual abstinence in the land of plenty, or the conspiracy to which all males in the room were party.

"Indeed, Rupert. And I might say if all had been explained to me from the beginning, we might have saved ourselves some trouble and heartache. But luckily Willie Winkle has now explained to me in a very clear manner that we all now have the opportunity to serve His Lord Jesus Christ, Her Majesty the Queen and international Democracy, and thereby England and, of course, the people of Laos."

"And what about that extradition stuff?" continued Rupert.

"A medal and a State Visit seem more appropriate," answered the Colonel, much to the pleasure of Winkle.

Winkle clapped his hands and immediate silence fell. He spoke in Lao but with a Shakespearean twang. "Ladies, dear ladies, off you all go to the bathroom and talk of girly matters. We men have manly things to discuss. Shortly you can return and make us happy once again." The girls were ushered *out* by Biggsie, who also ushered *in* a Doberman and a woman wearing a tiara *and* clothes, who looked, for a female of the human species, positively overdressed and at around thirty, positively ancient in the ambience of the *Blue*

*Member.* The Doberman padded directly to Rupert and sniffed the leg he loved. The Colonel scrutinized the woman; he had definitely seen her before.

"Friends," continued Winkle when all the girls were gone, the door was closed, silence reigned and the Doberman had pricked up his ears to the sticking point and was developing his natural attachment to Rupert's leg. "You see before you on the table the priceless long-lost National Treasure of Laos."

"Oooo," said the Conspirators in wonder.

"These emblems of kingship have been returned to Laos thanks to the efforts of the Colonel and tomorrow they will be returned to the legitimate ruler of Laos, the Crown Prince, who at this moment awaits in the sanctuary of a Bangkok kindergarten for word that the country has been secured. We have before us not only the crown jewels of the Kingdom of Laos but the very jewel in the crown herself, Princess Laksami. Gentlemen, I give you a toast. To Princess Laksami, mother of the crown prince. And to our future king, the Crown Prince."

Winkle raised his glass towards the dark-skinned lady who looked uncomfortable in traditional gold-threaded *sin* and untraditional tiara, as she set down a large picture of a very small boy among the National Treasure. A very large picture of a very small boy indeed. A very small boy who, to the Colonel at least, did not look very Lao. He had short, curly hair for a start, his skin was darker even than that of his mother and his nose, lips and eyes were Negroid rather than Asian.

"Three cheers for the Crown Prince and for his brave mother, in hiding all these years."

"Hurrah," said Rupert Sweetheart, feebly alone. "Hurrah," echoed the Colonel. The Lao and Thai present caught on and three resounding cries of *Saiyo-Chaiyo* rang out. The Colonel was perplexed. Where had he seen the princess before?

"Gentlemen," Winkle turned from Princess Laksami to the Colonel. "The current regime has been searching for the Colonel over the past few days. As you know, without success. The Colonel, who has an association with Laos and the kingship longer than any of us, returned to this country at no small risk to his life in order to recover the National Treasure. I am now delighted to inform you that the Colonel has accepted with immediate effect, the post of Minister of Defence in the new Kingdom of Laos. Gentlemen, another toast. The Minister of Defence."

Winkle raised his glass to the Colonel. So did Princess Laksami, and looked over its brim straight into her new minister's eyes. "The Minister of Defence," she said. The Colonel's memory stirred. Something else stirred. Princess Laksami wasn't unattractive and the Colonel liked them a bit on the dark side.

"I am even more delighted to tell you," continued Winkle, pausing for dramatic effect, "That the long awaited moment has arrived. Tomorrow morning at 9.00 a.m. you will each perform your allocated tasks and assume your agreed positions, supported by Sweetheart's elite troops of Sucksabit, which from now on shall be known as The Royal Guard. I shall personally arrest the so-called President of the Republic, while the Minister of Defence, assisted by a hand-picked selection of Rupert Sweetheart's crack troops and a dozen Doberman dogs will occupy Party Headquarters at Kilometre Six. By late afternoon, the Presidential Palace will be transformed back into the Royal Palace and crowds will line the road from the airport, to welcome back the Crown Prince and the Royal Family. We shall all be waiting at the airport to offer our allegiance to their majesties and escort them back to the Palace.

During the day, all traitors – those who do not willingly join us – will pay the ultimate price for their treachery and all red flags will be replaced by flags showing the royal symbols of the twelve-tiered white parasol, the eleven-headed elephant, the ten-towered pagoda, the nine royal urinals, the order of the eight stocking tops, seven naked goddesses, six copulating eunuchs, five cooing girls, four Dutch caps, three dicks in condoms, two French kisses, and a partridge in a pear tree."

"Saiyo, saiyo, saiyo."

"Of course, I seek no position for myself, but, since the Crown

186

Prince has yet to celebrate his fifth birthday, I shall offer my services to His Majesty as Adviser. Gentlemen, I give you a toast: the Kingdom of Laos."

Everybody drank to that except, the Colonel noted, the giant Rupert Sweetheart. While glasses were raised, the Colonel alone saw familiar shadows move upwards past a curtained window. The toast completed, Winkle added a P.S. to his speech. "You will of course all remain here as my guests this entire night. A fleet of armoured Land Rovers will be at your disposal in the morning, one each, with driver and four members of the Royal Guard. Meanwhile, there is food aplenty and bedrooms are available on this floor and the one above. Now, the girls may return."

Men rushed to shake Winkle's hand, before rushing to select the girl of choice as they were herded back in past Her Majesty. "You have a night's rest from Pon," Winkle said with a sly smile. "And Souk hasn't turned up. Looks like Norman's keeping a rein on her while he can. So who's it to be, Colonel? Plenty of choice, but the youngest always go first.

"Maybe I'll sit this one out," said the Colonel.

"Hallelujah," said Rupert. "You really have seen the light." The Doberman now had Rupert's leg in a bear-hug and was attempting to bore a hole in his upper calf. Rupert patted it on the head.

"We can always call for another Doberman, if you prefer, Colonel," said Winkle laughing.

"Maybe, after all, I won't sit this one out. What about the dark bit wearing clothes?"

"Princess Laksami!" Winkle said with pretended affront.

The Colonel's memory had returned fully. "Yes. I'll have Princess Laksami, please. Or Tik-Tok, if she's free. Twenty dollars a night I believe?"

"Shh," whispered Winkle. "Wouldn't you prefer something younger?"

"No," said the Colonel. "Got a hard on for Princess Laksami. She can keep the tiara on."

"I'll…I'll ask her," Winkle said.

"Don't bother. I'll ask her myself," said the Colonel, making his way through a roomful of little naked girls who held out sausages and chicken legs to tempt him towards their other charms, to the only female wearing clothes. People are going to think I have a fetish for women in clothes, thought the Colonel, as he took the dark hand, bent from the waist and kissed it.

"Princess Laksami. Would you allow me the honour of this fuck?"

"I can't hear the music," replied the Princess with a laugh.

"It's all in my heart," said the Colonel. "And you do look nice in a *sin*."

"Can't dance much in a *sin*," said the Princess. "Only Lao Lamwong. Restricts the movements you see. Only allows for something slow and rhythmical, forward, back and a bit sideways, would that be all right, Colonel?"

"I think that would be very all right, Princess."

"We must be discreet, Colonel. I think an upper room, don't you?"

The Colonel took her hand and led her through the door and up the stairs, to a nicely prepared room next to Winkle's private apartment. The Colonel, usually aware of every vibration of anger within the range of effective violence, completely missed the vehemence with which the eyes of Rupert Sweetheart followed their departure. "This is where I am staying, Colonel," said the Black Princess.

"Very nice," the Colonel said, as he closed the door behind them, ran his hands along her backside and carefully and slowly lifted up the *sin*. "Very nice indeed. You have beautiful legs, Princess Tik-Tok."

While Tik-Tok was giving the Colonel his second bath of the evening and spilling all the beans about her involvement in Winkle's royal coup, Pon quietly left Welder's house and stopped a tuk-tuk taxi to take her the short distance to the *Blue Member*. Her face was well known, so she easily walked straight in past the guards, who did nothing but salute her. Between her legs, the Colonel's kukri made quite a bulge, but if the guards noticed, they did not dare frisk somebody they still thought of as Winkle's girl.

Pon went straight to the upper party room, where all she saw was Rupert Sweetheart with a Doberman on his leg, a homosexual Lao evangelical pastor cuddling up to a Lao Minister and Chantavong being administered by the four remaining serving girls.

"Where's the Colonel?" she asked Rupert. The dog looked at her and growled *find your own man, bitch*.

"I don't know," said Rupert, trying to remember if this particular girl belonged to Winkle or the Colonel, "and I shall try not to care."

"Is he still alive?"

"Oh, yes," said Rupert. "Unfortunately, very much so."

"What's that supposed to mean?"

"I thought he had seen the light," Rupert explained, moving the dog onto the other leg. "I thought Jesus has spoken to him. But I was wrong."

"What the fuck are you talking about?" Pon looked around at the closed doors. "I suppose the rooms are full of Winkle's guests and girls as usual."

"Yes," Rupert said disapprovingly, rubbing the Doberman's neck hair the wrong way. "It's really quite disgusting. Won't be allowed under the Crown Prince."

"What on earth are you on about? Oh, never mind. I don't have time. Is the Colonel in one of these rooms?"

"No," said Rupert.

"Then where is he?"

"Winkle said nobody was to leave tonight. He went upstairs. I think in the guest room next to Winkle's. No doubt fornicating. Forcing the devil into the godly."

Pon wasted no time with this cuckoo. In seconds was up the stairs and banging on the door to Princess Laksami's room. Two hurried minutes and urgent bangings later, the Colonel answered, fully dressed. Pon went on tip toe and grabbed him around the neck, kissing him passionately and sucking his lip, until she opened her eyes and saw Tik-Tok demurring naked upon the bed.

"Don't mind me," said Princess Tik-Tok.

"But I do mind you," Pon retorted angrily, opening her bluejeans and taking out the Colonel's kukri from between her legs.

"It's a long story," said the Colonel in the tone of a man defending himself. When you're in love, everything is a long story. "That's Tik-Tok from the *Khop Chai*. Winkle has persuaded her – paid her – to act as Princess Laksami, and is passing off Tik-Tok's four year old son as the Crown Prince – with himself as Adviser to the Crown. Whether the deception works for awhile or not, who knows? But sooner or later somebody will see through the fancy clothing and make up and realize that Princess Laksami is Tik-Tok. Then she will be for it, and her son too. No doubt Winkle will have some fancy story – using substitutes to protect the real monarchy or such, until the country is really safe for their return."

"If she is pretending to be Princess Laksami, that's one thing. The other thing is: why is she naked on the bed, with you in the same locked room."

"She just had a bath," said the Colonel lamely.

"And you didn't touch her?" Pon unsheathed the kukri and waved it in the air.

The Colonel looked affronted.

"No, I suppose you didn't. After all, she's old enough to be…to be…to be…*your daughter*. So why are you in a locked room with a naked woman other than me?"

"Just talking," said the Colonel. "If Winkle ever gets as far as declaring her and her son members of the royal family, she will deny it and say Winkle forced her to act the Princess, threatening to kill her son if she backed out. Besides, I wanted to be in this room, next to Winkle, hoping that you would come with the kukri. He's with two girls at the moment. Later, when he's asleep, I'll get in and quietly put an end to the Royal Adviser."

"Okay, I believe you," said Pon.

"You do?" said the Colonel.

"Yes, why shouldn't I? And I haven't told you the best bit yet. Guess who called at Welder's soon after you had gone?"

Before the Colonel could guess, the door flew open and Rupert Sweetheart, six armed guards and four Dobermans burst in. The Colonel's hands were pinioned behind him and fists, boots and riffle butts struck without mercy. Two Dobermans flew through the air, grabbed the Colonel's legs between their paws and did their doggy thing to his helpless shins. As the Colonel went down, he saw Pon drop his kukri among Tik-Tok's cast-off clothing and with her foot flick the *sin* to cover it.

"That's enough, boys," said Rupert. "Don't kill our Minister of Defence. He simply needs a little reminder of our Lord's wishes."

# 17

# Revolting Rupert

**"Time to go home, Godfrey."**

"Still no word in from the Colonel?"

"I just checked. Nothing. Seems it's a one man show now. Either the Colonel captures or kills Winkle, or vice-versa. The police appear to be behind the Colonel, but they could be hedging their bets. The Foreign Affairs Acting Deputy also."

"So it's all up to the Colonel then, Nigel?"

"Yes, it is, Godfrey. I think it always has been. We just wait and see."

Welder and Kim and Norman and Souk were snuggled up in different beds being good to each other, when the glass front door of Welder's diplomatic home smashed open and six men wearing SAS-type face masks burst in.

"Aw, my gawd, Bruce. It's those neighbours again. They never stop do they? Now they're smashing up their own property. Can't you do something about it?"

"Like what?" said Bruce shortly, wanting only to get back to his dream where he has Welder's girl dancing naked in front of him waving her tiny knickers in his eyes.

"Well, you should know Bruce. You are the Consul after all."

"So's Welder, sort of. He's a Brit. I got no jurisdiction over Brits."

"You should complain to that Brit Ambassador in Bangkok. Disgusting the way they behave. Shouldn't be allowed in a diplomatic compound."

"It's not. But since Welder's got diplomatic immunity like the rest of us, it is."

"Not sure I know what you mean, Bruce. Either it's allowed or it's not allowed."

"Crikey, Sheila. How long you been living in dip quarters? You know as well as I do that unless Welder buggars the President, there's nothing you can do to change his behaviour apart from just not talking to him. And I'm sure that would have a great effect. Now, come away from that curtain and get back into bed."

"I can see right through their kitchen window. They never close the curtains, that lot. There are six men inside with masks over their heads, like the IRA. Why didn't the guards do something?"

"For Christ's sake, Sheila, give it a rest. What would six masked men be doing in Welder's?"

"Probably sex games with all those under-age girls. You should do something about it, Bruce."

"I am. I'm going back to sleep," Bruce buried his face in the pillow and willed himself back into his dream of sex games with Welder's under-aged girls.


Welder and Norman both awoke at the same time, in different rooms. Both were looking along the barrel of a short pistol resting between their eyes. At their sides, Kim and Souk lay naked, eyes wide, knives at their throats. "Get dressed," said one of the three masked men in each room. That at least was a positive note in a negative situation, everything being comparative. Kim and Souk got dressed and were dragged away. "Don't try to follow," the masked man said to Welder. "Don't interfere and nothing will happen to the girls. They are guarantees of your good conduct." With that Welder and Norman received a spray of gas in their eyes that blinded them and sent them into coughing fits, and Kim and Souk were dragged screaming from the house."

"Bruce! Bruce! The masked men are dragging away those girls."

"Pack it in, Sheila. I thought you wanted them gone? Probably their daddies and brothers come to rescue them."

"Then why are they being dragged screaming?"

"Are they wearing any clothes?"

"Yes. What's that got to do with anything?"

"Everything," said Bruce, sinking back into his dream.

"Tut, tut," tutted Sheila.


Welder and Norman rushed into their bathrooms and washed their eyes. Both were in an advanced state of anguish.

"Winkle!" said Welder.

"Winkle!" Agreed Norman.

"Time to rid ourselves of that man." Welder opened a locked cupboard and took out two pistols, four grenades and a box of dynamite that he had bought cheap on the Route 9 road construction project and kept handy, just in case he should ever feel the need to blow something really sky high. They hid the armaments around their bodies.

"You know, Winkle has all those fancy X-ray machines?" Norman asked.

"Yes, I know. But they won't stop me. Not this time. Not after what Winkle has already done to Kim. I'll kill them all if necessary."

The two men ran across the broken glass, down the steps and jumped into the Land Cruiser. Welder hit the horn until the guard opened the gate, revved hard and shot out onto Thadeua Road.

"Tut, tut," tutted Sheila. "Something should be done."

Welder tried to calm himself. Drove slowly and carefully and stopped at the gate of the *Blue Member*, opened the window and said pleasantly, "You know me, I was just here a couple of hours ago with Willie Winkle. Willie asked us to drop by."

"Winkle's not here, Mr Welder," said the guard. "He's spending the night at the other place."

"Investment Unlimited?"

"Right. Shall I phone there for you?"

"No need, thanks," said Welder and drove carefully away. At least he wanted to keep the element of surprise.

Arriving at the huge Investment Unlimited in the same quiet fashion, Welder was told that Winkle wasn't there. He was spending the night at *Blue member*. Welder drove past the gate.

"Okay, Norman, say if you want out. This is what I am going to do."

The Acting Deputy Foreign Minister left the President's house a happy man, arm in arm with the Deputy Minister of Justice. The President had just authorized the detention of Willie Winkle, pending negotiations with the UK over extradition procedures. The Acting Deputy Foreign Minister saw no need to delay the arrest and took out his hand phone.

Pol-Maj Chantavong was naked and in a large bed with four giggling girls, thinking life doesn't get much better than this. Then his cell phone rang. Couldn't ignore it, might be Winkle, or the Colonel. One had given him this sexual fantasy of a lifetime, the other eight kilogrammes of gold. What a great day it had been.

"This is Acting Deputy Foreign Minister Gop," said Acting Deputy Foreign Minister Gop, hearing giggles on the other end of the phone. "Where are you, Chantavong?"

"In my office, Thhanh Gop, interrogating suspects."

"Good," said Gop. "Then you have plenty of men at your fingertips?"

What Chantavong had at his fingertips he saw no reason to tell the Acting Deputy. Much easier, and safer, to lie. After all, this Acting Deputy would be dancing to a different tune tomorrow – if Winkle's plan succeeded. On the other hand, it might fail, so best take all precautions. "I gave orders that the men could step down, Sir. After all, they had been stretched for two days during the manhunt of the Colonel."

"And where is the Colonel now?"

"In bed, Sir," Chantavong said, thinking that this at least was probably the truth.

"Well make sure no harm comes to him. The President has agreed to Winkle's arrest and extradition, so get together a large body of men and arrest and detain Winkle in police cells – well-guarded ones."

"Right away, Sir." Whatever the President had agreed might be of no consequence tomorrow morning, but Chantavong knew how to play safe.

As the Acting Deputy rang off, Chantavong rang on to his own underlings and ordered them to get men together, all armed, and group at the front entrance to the *Blue Member Club*. The only orders he gave was that nobody was to pass in or out of the club. That should satisfy the Acting Deputy that I am acting. And if Winkle raised any questions, his men were there to protect those in the club and to assist in the next morning's activities. Pleased with himself, Chantavong sank down into the bed and wallowed in the portals of puberty.

One floor up, Winkle was also a happy bunny as he lay, literally sandwiched between the same two very young little identical twins that the Colonel had knocked out so effectively over at Investments Unlimited. He had clean forgotten to ask the Colonel how it was done. Well, there would be plenty of time now the Colonel was on his side. He liked to have people on his side. Particularly very young girls. One on each side. It appealed to his developed sense of symmetry. However, there were limits to symmetry. It might look nice, but it served no functional purpose to send both twins into a temporary paralysis at the same time. These twins were naturally tight, but the pseudo-necrophiliac experience had added a new dimension of heightened arousal, until he had got stuck, which was no fun at all. The fact that he had learnt later that the twins had been fully conscious but unable to move a muscle excited him even more and he longed to try it again. Next time he would proceed with caution. At the expense of sexual symmetry, he would use one twin as the 'control' and one as the experiment. Hmm, the thought made him extra excited. Should he call in the Colonel now? He was only next door. Winkle wondered if the Colonel had paralysed the Princess and was at this moment turning her over to have her black bottom.

No, Winkle wouldn't try anything new tonight. Tomorrow was going to be a big day. So he contented himself with conventional movements between the sandwich symmetry of two tight virginas, twenty little fingers, two pairs of lips, two tongues, ten toes, two bums, four earholes and a neat little collection of nostrils. Definitely, Winkle decided, twins gave an element of symmetrical perfection to the Vientiane Sandwich. The fact that they thought, acted and reacted as one produced absolute equality of sensation throughout his body. That would be enough for him today. After all, some days it paid to go conventional.

This day had netted him the Colonel as ally, 194 one kilo bars of gold, and the National Treasure. And his plans seemed very much set on go for the morrow. He had no complaints at all with today. Until, that is, the door burst open and in strode Rupert Sweetheart with an AK-47 in his hands and a Doberman on each leg. Say what you like about them, but Dobes definitely have a sense of symmetry every bit as developed as that of Winkle's twins and a doggedly conventional insistence on their own version of the Vientiane Sandwich.

Behind Rupert came the Colonel, arms still symmetrically pinioned at his side by two equally burly guards, legs still occupied by twin Dobermans that clung like limpets, enhancing the over-all symmetry of the coup within a coup as twenty uniformed guards fanned out in equal numbers to the left and to the right of Rupert, fully covering the huge bedroom, all guns trained on Winkle's dick, at that moment poised in mid-air between the pair of young twin lips locked around its head in the Vientiane Symmetrical Penis Kiss. Into this scene of almost perfectly symmetrical sex and violence, young Pon, even younger Souk, and the youngest Kim were led forward, to stand awkwardly before God's appointed judge. Kim was crying, wondering what protection a diplomatic home offered when Welder and Norman were held up in it at gun point and she and Souk were dragged away with the Australian neighbours and their own guards just looking on and tut-tutting as if the girls themselves were to blame.

Welder's head held no real plan, only the mental image of Kim being forced to go down on Winkle, and only his mind burning for revenge. His objective now was to kill Winkle and anybody who stood in his way, free his beloved Kim, and expunge the mental image that was driving him crazy.

Welder slowly backed the Land Rover into Investment International's gateway. The guards, knowing Welder as a colleague of big boss Winkle and thinking he was simply backing in to turn the car and go off to the Blue Member, sat and slouched with no concern. Norman and Welder opened their windows and dropped a live grenade into the two groups from each side of their vehicle. The Land Rover continued backwards with a sudden increase in speed, smashing through the glass doors and the X-ray machines as the grenades exploded at the gate and frantic alarm bells sounded in every room in the building. Guards inside the foyer rushed the vehicle and yanked open the doors. Welder and Norman shot them in the chest and head before they had time to level their AK-47s. "Out we go," shouted Welder as he tossed another grenade at a mixed group of guards and Winkle's shaven-headed London bully-boys, who were coming down the stairs at a run.

The two men knew they had very little time. Welder pulled open the back doors and dragged the box of dynamite out, letting it fall to the floor. Norman threw four smoke bombs that Welder had given him. The effect was instantaneous in the confined foyer. Thick smoke blacked out all vision. Norman and Welder held hands and ran up the stairs. Those they passed saw only two white men running from the disturbance and paid them no heed. The smoke funneled up the center of the stairwell from the atrium. The whole building was alive with men with guns, but nobody showed any interest in Welder and Norman, as they headed upwards to Winkle's apartment.

There was no guard at the apartment. The front door, ripped apart during the Colonel's recent sortie, had been only temporarily repaired with plywood, which Welder, fury and anxiety lending him strength, ripped down with his bare hands.

The two men climbed through the debris into Winkle's personal quarters. All was dark. The lights did not respond to the switch. Winkle's bedroom was empty. The safe remained as the Colonel had blown it. "He's not here," said Norman, stating the obvious.

"Bloody right. Must be at the *Blue Member* after all. We'd better try to get back to the car."

Their descent on the stairs created no more interest than their ascent. Even when they arrived at the scene of carnage in the foyer, they were just two of many whites milling around without knowing what to do, which way to run, from where the attack had come or was coming. Surprising even themselves, Welder and Norman went straight to the Land Rover's doors, opened them and climbed in without being challenged. Then suddenly, Stamford's face came through the thinning smoke and called for them to get out of the car. Immediately, guards leveled their guns towards the Land Rover. Welder turned the ignition, jammed his foot on the accelerator and smashed into Stamford.

Stamford went up into the air and landed hard on the bonnet, his huge face flattened against the windscreen, starring at Welder for seconds before the momentum of his movement and the acceleration of the Land Rover rolled his body up and over the roof. "At least I got one of the bastards," Welder said. But Norman was not listening. Window fully open, he was leaning out with the remaining grenade in hand. He bowled it gently and accurately underarm at the crate lying behind them. Bullets were tearing into the sides of the vehicle as the grenade exploded and a second later a huge blast from Welder's dynamite ripped through all those in the foyer. The blast seemed to pick up the Land Rover and propel it at great speed forwards through the gates. There was nobody to fire after them. Welder regained control and drove fast towards the *Blue Member*. Their mission remained, to save the girls and destroy Winkle.

Neither Welder nor Norman West had any idea of the large white figure that clung to their roof as they sped through the town.


"Fornicator!" said Rupert, as if this justified everything that was happening and would happen. Eyes looked at eyes, as each person in the room was unsure to whom Sweetheart was referring. Rupert had used the singular and the only person actually fornicating at that very moment, in that very room, was Winkle himself. So all eyes focused on Winkle, who, exhibitionist as he was, was unused to being the subject-interest of twenty AK-47 barrels and found it had a drooping effect on libido.

"Regard the fornicator," said Rupert, inching his way towards Winkle as the Dobes kept up their hammering of his lower legs. "Drooping in shame."

The Colonel had recovered enough to notice that the anti-fornicator, who seemed unable to drag his eyes from the very young twins sandwiching Winkle, had developed a large bulge between his legs that was not there earlier. He fixed eyes on Souk and moved his head to indicate she come close. "Souk," he whispered in her ear. "One hundred dollars if you go down on Sweetheart."

"Two hundred," said Souk.

"Done," said the Colonel.

"Fornicators, all," berated Rupert, moving into the plural. "Repent your ways before your Crown Prince Cometh and the Good Lord strikes you blind."

God, thought the Colonel, there are going to be a lot of blind people in Vientiane tomorrow. Souk moved in front of Rupert and sank to her knees, holding her hands up above her forehead as if in prayer.

"Good child. Repent and yee shall be saved," said Rupert. "Guards. Bring the Princess here, that she may witness the repentance and behold the new era void of fornicators."

Princess Tik-Tok, except for the tiara still as naked as nature intended was half-led, half-dragged into Winkle's room.

"Our dear Princess has herself this night been a victim of lust, or almost a victim, if I hadn't arrived in time to save her. A victim of a man who, above all others, should have offered his Princess the respect due to her as Mother to the Nation. I speak of our Minister of Defence, our ex-Gurka British Colonel." Rupert indicated the Colonel, as he himself fixed his eyes on the black bottom of Princess Tik-Tok and Souk expertly lowered the zip on his camouflage fatigues and moved discretely-expert fingers inside.

"Repent all of you and do penance, that you be saved." Souk eased Rupert's member out. For the first time in a decade Rupert felt himself harden and quiver. He moved his eyes from the black bottom and the twins of puberty and looked down at the eyes of Souk, which looked up and into his, as she closed her fingers and lips around Rupert's enormous organ and began to rock her head in time with the movements of the Dobermans on each side. "Ah," exhaled the Chief of Security. "You are doing penance for your past sins. Ah. Good girl. Look at me. That's it. We must all do penance. Pay for your sins. Rise up. Rise up. Good girl, Souk. Souk. Don't stop. Souk. Repentance is at hand."

The twins, taken by the evangelical rhetoric, spontaneously and conterminously latched the flagging member of Winkle and rose up from the bed to bring their naked childishness to Rupert and kneel before him on either side of Souk, each between Souk and a Doberman, and press their repentant lips in symmetry around each side of the base of Rupert's member, which, already impressively powerful, grew ever more almighty. The elite guards looked on half in envy, half in relief at finally understanding what redemption was all about. Clearly, apart from replacing one mad *falang* with another, there would be no great change between the rule of Winkle and the rule of Sweetheart.

The area around Rupert's groin was getting rather crowded for a celibate man. Rupert reached out his huge hands to his left and to his right and simultaneously they fell upon the breasts of Pon and Kim and fondled therein. Then, moving as if possessed by a will of their own, the hands tucked their fingers into the necks of the girl's tee-shirts and pulled. With an almighty rip the flimsy cloth was rendered, and breasts and navels were exposed to the multitude. The fingers of this man-giant continued on their downward path as if directed from a force outside of their master, hooked into bluejeans, popped buttons and tore apart zips, causing blue jeans and knickers to fall in tatters to tiny ankles, exposing one hairless and one wispily-fuzzed virgina.

"Repent," yelled Rupert. "Repent before your Saviour. Repent. Souk. Repent. Souk. Souk. Souk." The multitude took up the cry: Souk, Souk, Souk. Souk moved her head faster and faster, enjoying the attention. Then with an almighty yell of "Souk!", mixed with a rumbling groan built up over ten years of abstinence, Rupert let loose ten years of accumulated cum into the mouth of Souk. Souk pulled back, but the almighty explosion of a decade did not stop there, penance must be completed and as Rupert continued to groan, so the cum continued to flow and flow. Milk and honey covered completely the penitent faces of Souk and the twins. On cue, the Dobermans on Rupert's legs also climaxed into the camouflage. The Princess stared in disbelief then slowly put her hands together in a clap of appreciation for a grand show. Better than anything Winkle had ever put on for his guests. The guards let their automatic rifles hang from the slings around their neck and took up a slow handclap accompanying a chant of *re-pent, re-pent, re-pent...*

Pon, before anybody got the idea of repenting on her, took young Kim by the hand and slipped back to the guest room. She returned with the kukri, which she gave to the Colonel, whose guards were too busy handclapping and calling for repentance to notice. The

Colonel's immediate thought was to rid himself of the twin doggy appendages. But as he raised the kukri blade, Rupert gave a series of quick whistles and both dogs left the Colonel's legs and jumped onto the bed, where they continued with Winkle a job the twins had left unfinished.

The Colonel, kukri at the ready, ushered Pon, Kim and the Princess behind him. "Got a mobile?" he said. "We should call downstairs and invite up some of the girls. It looks like there's a lot of repentance about to take place here, and somebody should keep this lot busy."

Pon, her naked breasts and comely rump already the focus of many eyes, reached across and took the mobile phone from the pocket of the Sucksabit Chief, whose hands were too busy with the twins' repentance to notice or intervene. She called Chantavong and passed the phone to the Colonel.

"Thhan Chanatavong, how many girls are still there and in a moveable condition?" asked the Colonel.

"There's four here with me and several more eating noodles outside this room. Not counting a couple of young transvestites. Why? Who is this?"

"This is your Minister of Defence. Send all the girls to Winkle's bedroom immediately. They are needed for security purposes. Send the trannies too."

And as the girls came in naked and the transvestites came in wearing the shortest skirts known to the mind of man and no bras under their fully transparent shirts, to better emphasise their budding breasts, the Colonel, Pon, and Kim made a tactical withdrawal back to the guest room. Souk weighed up the pros and cons, hesitated, then joined them. Winkle lay helpless on the bed, his most private part now licked by slobbering Doberman tongues framed by Doberman fangs. "Wait for me," Princess Tik-Tok called and ran on tip-toe to the Colonel's side. Pon, unseen, slipped the neck cord of Rupert Sweetheart's mobile over her head, allowing the instrument to snuggle in the cleft between her small, round breasts.

Outside the police arrived on motor-cycles and in pick-up trucks and formed a tight cordon across the only way in and out. They were sure of only one thing. No one was going anywhere this night.

The phone rang between Pon's breasts. She handed it up to the Colonel. "It's Chantavong again. Just got news. Winkle's Investment Unlimited building has been blown up. Looks like Rupert Sweetheart wanted to cut off any possibility of assistance coming in to Winkle from that quarter."

---

# 18

# Penance and Perdition

**"Six p.m., Godfrey. Not like you to be working so late."**

"I was hoping some news might have come in from the Colonel."

"Then you did right to wait. The Colonel just called, while you were in the loo."

"Your going to tell me aren't you, Nigel? No waiting game. Tell me and it's my treat at the wine bar."

"Okay. But pay attention, Godfrey, because the situation sounds a mite confused. It's nearly six here. Nearly one tomorrow morning there. The Colonel was calling on a cell phone that Pon (whoever that is) has stolen from Rupert Sweetheart (whoever he is). This Sweetheart ripped open the T-shirts of Pon and Kim, whoever they are, exposing their breasts, then went on to tear off their bluejeans, exposing, presumably, everything. Rupert Sweetheart has apparently gone a bit crazy and is launching some sort of a fundamentalist-evangelical coup within a coup against Winkle. Winkle is in his bedroom, in bed with two Doberman dogs. Yes, Godfrey, dogs. Twenty guards loyal to this Rupert chap have AK-47s trained on Winkle, although they are at this moment not so much taking aim as taking off their uniforms and repenting all over naked young girls – sorry, Godfrey, no idea what the Colonel meant there."

"Wait a minute, Nige. Is the Colonel safe?"

"You tell me, Godfrey. He says he has managed a tactical withdrawal and is no longer a captive of either Winkle or Rupert. He has actually locked himself in Winkle's guest room with Princess Laksami – you'll like this Godfey – Laksami aka Tik-Tok is a half-black, half-Lao leftover love-child of the war…and currently, of course, naked. Anyway, Winkle had planned tomorrow to declare Tik-Tok's four year old bastard son the Crown Prince of Laos, and himself the Crown Prince's Adviser. The President, ministers, Politbureau and Central Committee members were to be ousted at 9.00 a.m. tomorrow and those not willing to join the coup eliminated and replaced by Winkle's allies. Sweetheart has led a coup against Winkle's coup which is really just a take-over of the same coup; he holds Winkle prisoner, plans to do precisely what Winkle had planned – but without Winkle. He would put Princess Tik-Tok on the throne and make himself her Adviser and probably lover. Both Winkle and Sweetheart would claim blood-line monarchy of the princess and possession of the National Treasure as the basic justification for the coup. But Winkle would use an anti-communist rationale to gain US support and, by the way, knock our attempts at extradition for six, while Sweetheart will stand on an Evangelical platform of return to biblical values – in a predominantly Buddhist country.

"The whole thing is really more complex than it seems, which is saying something. The Colonel says there really was, or is, a Princess Laksami, but, sorry Godfrey, the real one is not half black – although the Colonel does say she is reported as rather dark. What's more, Rupert Sweetheart, ex-SAS, is trainer of an elite bodyguard of some 50-odd handpicked Sucksabit supposed to be loyal to Winkle but actually loyal to their trainer, who has converted all of them to his own weird evangelism. Sweetheart plans to have the Princess declared

Black Princess: Defender of the Faith and launch into a nation-wide spiritual revolution of repentance, arresting all those involved in sexual activity except himself, who will have *droit de seigneur* over just about everybody remotely female.

"Pon, Souk and Kim are also with the Colonel in the locked room, in addition to the Princess. Souk is Norman West's fiancée. Norman West, you'll remember, is the treasure man. Kim is Welder's girlfriend. The Colonel says that Kim and Souk are safe with him. If you have been following this, Godfrey, you'll recall that all the females are naked – no exceptions to my knowledge – and just about all the males are armed with AK-47s or kukris. So I suppose safety is a relative concept. The real problem seems to be that the Colonel can't get out of the *Blue Member* – funny name that for a building – with all these naked women in tow and the guards divided between support for Winkle and Sweetheart. There's also a dog factor – seems this Rupert has a thing for Dobermans and has personally trained an unknown number to attack at his command. And just to put a cap on things, the President has just said that the police should arrest Winkle and hold him for extradition – so there are over two hundred regular armed police at the entrance to the building, ambiguously loyal to the current regime and refusing entry or exit to anybody and everybody. The Colonel says that given the current regime's positive attitude to the extradition request and the fact that both of the alternatives are clearly cuckoo, he plans to support the regime and prevent the coup or coups."

"From inside a locked room. In close proximity to four naked females. With, on the other side of the door, an SAS-trained elite, an unknown number of savage Dobes and a few hundred armed police of equivocal loyalties. Well, good luck, Colonel. That's all I can say."

"That is, indeed, all you can say, Godfrey. Either the Colonel gets himself out of this and the regime is saved. Or he goes down and there could be a lot of disturbance, particularly if the cousins poke their noses in. And who knows which way they'll jump? Perverted evangelism or corrupt anti-communism. Suppose they'll just go for the winner. Bit funny 'though, is it not Godfrey? Our ex-Gurka Colonel set on a course to defend a communist regime."

"What I find funny, Nigel, is that all this happened while I was having a pee."

The Colonel sat on the bed, surrounded by four lovely and naked girls wondering whether to suggest they get dressed, in whatever flimsy garments the Princess possessed, or to strip off himself and enjoy their company. He was well aware that their refuge was also their prison. He was also well aware that he was unlikely to be left in peace for long.

The noise from Winkle's bedroom quietened a little. There was a series of scratches on the other side of the door, like a gentle family dog asking to be let in, and a polite knocking on the heavy hardwood panels. The door handle turned on its lock.

"Colonel, are you in there?" came a friendly enquiry from the passage way. "This is only your friend Rupert. You can come out now. We have detained Winkle and he will be extradited as you wish, with the blessings of the Royal Government of National Repentance."

The Colonel motioned the girls to remain quiet. The world went silent.

"Colonel." Rupert almost whispered from the other side of the door. The Colonel ushered the girls quietly into the bathroom.

"Oh, little pig. Little pig." Rupert's voice remained constrained but now bore the barest trace of impatience. "Little pig, come out. It's repentance time. Come out little pig. Or I'll huff and I'll puff and I'll blow your house down."

As the Colonel closed himself in the bathroom with his harem, he could hear the big bad wolf huff and puff. Seconds later a shattering burst of AK-47 fire splintered the hardwood door into toothpicks. Rupert Sweetheart stepped through the hole. Apart from the AK-47 and two fresh Dobermans symmetrically-attached, the two-metre something giant was completely naked, making the Colonel, of all people, the only non-naked person in the room – a situation that could not last.

"Minister of Defence here. Get as many Sucksabit guards up to Winkle's flat soonest – with guns." The Colonel spoke quickly and quietly into Pon's breasts but before he could be sure the reception guards had really got the message, the mobile was lifted from its comely cradle by the huge hand of Rupert Sweetheart.

"My phone I believe," said the giant SAS man, as he tweaked in turn each of Pon's little nipples and hung the cord around his own neck, allowing the mobile phone to dangle down towards his rising erection. "Well now, Colonel. See this twinkle in my eye? Know what it means? I'll tell you. It means you've been caught in close proximity with four naked members of the opposite sex. This is a crime under the new regime. A crime times four in this case. The fact that one of these naked members of the opposite sex is a child, two look barely over the age of consent, which by the way is about to change from fifteen to fifty-seven, and one is heir to the throne, only adds to the gravity of the charge. God is telling me you have quite some public penance to perform." Rupert prodded the Colonel with the gun's barrel and pushed him out of the bathroom and into the guest room, which, while large, was too small for both Rupert's giant erection, the twenty-two born-again elite guards who followed their leader, two very horny Dobermans, one half-black love-child Princess left over from the war, and three beautifully provocative naked young ladies. Something would have to go – and it didn't look as if Rupert's erection was about to volunteer.

"Ah, my Princess, safe and sound and fulsome with repentance. And the goodly repentant Souk. And my little child Kim, sent by the Almighty for Rupert's special repentance package. And Pon, what to say? You have led the Colonel astray, my dear, and must be punished, oh dear. Now, back into Winkle's room. There's more space there and true repentance must be public. *Very* public. There are witnesses enough. But we will also film your repentance and air it on new national TV tomorrow. Then we will sell the film to Bangkok Balls and

Bosoms, the first of many national productions that will finance our revolution at the same time as bringing health back to the nation."

As Rupert's men closed on him, Pon kicked the kukri across to the Colonel. In less time than it takes to say apocalypse, the long knife was in the Colonel's hand and its blade was against Rupert's throat.

Immediately guns were leveled at the heads of the four girls. The classic Mexican stand off.

"What is it you want?" said Sweetheart.

"I think first we'll take back this," the Colonel's free hand fished the mobile phone from the Saviour's neck and threw it to Kim, telling her in English to call Welder and try to get some military muscle into the Blue Member. "Then, we all go slowly next door and see how Willy Winkle's getting on."

Willy Winkle was, as it happens, while remaining in the double-Doberman predicament, not giving up without a fight to turn the tables on the evangelical traitor who would pervert the course of his true revolution. As Saviour Sweetheart's Praetorian Guard assuaged its lust on the reinforcements of young unrepentants sent from below, the prone Winkle attempted to win back their loyalty.

"Did I ever deny you anything?" asked the immobile Winkle, stretched out on his bed not daring to move, only too aware that the slobbering Dobes could turn from tongues to teeth at any moment and strangely curious that his anxiety did nothing to reduce his erection, which seemed to increase in spite of the danger of supplementing its succulent sausage appeal to the dogs; Winkle could only presume that his member had remained intact so far because of the special training Sweetheart provided his dogs. He had no time to speculate on the relationship between the special training of Rupert's Dobermans and Rupert's declared decade of abstinence from the more conventional forms of carnal knowledge.

"Are these girls not some of the many that I provide for your pleasure?" Winkle continued his appeal to Sweetheart's special forces. "And has it not been Sweetheart who has denied you the right to enjoy them, as other Sucksabit guards enjoy the benefits of loyalty to Willie Winkle."

Those guards who did not have their mouths full had to agree among themselves that Winkle had a point.

"Sweetheart's revolution will banish all sex except for Sweetheart and the black-bottomed queen-bee princess. Your lives will be ones of eternal abstinence."

"No they won't." One guard raised his head from fragile thighs to argue. "Look at us now. We get what we want because Rupert Sweetheart gave it to us and he gives us not just a fuck, but a fuck with redemption built in. *You* never offered us redemption. Only the Saviour gives us fanny *and* clean souls. Only Saviour Sweetheart leads us forward on the great fuck to heaven."

"You may believe you will go on fucking your way to heaven," Winkle spoke as loudly as he dared, careful not to upset or over-excite the Dobermans. "But if Saviour Sweetheart rules, you may well be enjoying your last act of carnal knowledge right now. Sweetheart has some crazy idea that repentance is achieved through orgasm – and, for him, that is the only justification for sex. Once you are in a state of redemption, there will be no more sex for you. Not even handing out redemptions. That he'll keep for himself and the Princess. You will be simply soldier bees, working your knackers off to bring honey to the Saviour and his queen bee, and all their little descendents in the royal lineage. You'd be better off joining the Winkle Revolution, which carefully distinguishes between state and sex, leaving you free to enjoy the latter – indeed, providing every opportunity for you to do so."

"You can *say* that. You can *say* anything," piped in another naked Sucksabit soldier busy thrusting his way to heaven. "But how do we *know* it's true?"

Winkle knew he had only a limited time to convince these men and secure his escape. He would have to cut to the chase and appeal to that one instinct that is stronger than lust for pleasures of the flesh.

"Would a kilo of pure gold convince you I am speaking the truth?

One kilo each for the twenty men in this room. Just get these dogs off me, give me a gun and arrest Rupert Sweetheart."

"Okay," said a guard with his trousers down, his member up a young lady-boy's bum and another young man's member up his own bum. "Just as soon as I'm finished here. You know, I always thought there was something queer about that Rupert Sweetheart."

"Yes, do take your time," said Winkle tolerantly as if he had all day and as if the Dobes weren't starting to nibble his jolly roger, which, in spite of everything, had attained an erection of such proportions that Winkle had to admit to himself that fear was perhaps a greater aphrodisiac than pleasure. He would experiment on that one, after he'd completed the neo-necrophilia study, if he ever got out of this one.

True to his word, the guard pushed the young transvestite's face into the shag pile as he, the one behind, and even the young transvestite came together as a blessed trilogy. As they messily disentangled, the guard gave a series of whistles that brought the dogs bounding from Winkle's bed to lick the fresh cum from happily-ravaged arses. Those dogs were certainly well trained, nobody could deny Sweetheart that. The guard threw an AK-47 to Winkle and said dramatically. "I'm with you boss! Where did you say the gold was?"

"The gold is right here under the bed. But first, rouse the men to look to their arms instead of their dicks and we'll arrest Saviour Sweetheart."

A little humping and groaning later and Winkle's small naked army, almost half of the Sucksabit elite, had switched allegiance and was ready to go. To cement their loyalty, Winkle reached under the bed and pulled out a one kilo bar. "There's one of these for each of you. All in addition to the legitimate spoils of rape and revolution that will be yours tomorrow." A Doberman looked at Winkle quizzically as if wondering what was in it for him, then went back to licking the arses of the prone and buggared and the dripping cummings on the shag-pile carpet.

Sodom and begorrah had taken on a semblance of modest order, although nobody seemed to feel it worth while again getting dressed, after all there was still the black-bottomed princess and her three young chamber maids to come, and the twins were already begging for more. So Winkle's little army was partly at attention and partly flagging at half-mast as he reached for the handle of the bedroom door.

The Colonel moved backwards, towards the door from the other side, his kukri stationed across the throat of the Saviour. In front of him gun barrels pointed at the lovely heads of Pon and Kim and Souk. Only the Black Princess was spared direct threat – although a half-dozen erect penes hovered hopefully around her bottom. As the Colonel's back touched the wood of the door, he ordered, "Open it, Sweetheart!"

As Rupert's huge hand pushed down on the handle, Winkle's bony fingers did the same from the other side.

19

_____

# Enter the Gurkas

**The eight o'clock news** was dragging into the weather when Nigel picked up the phone to Godfrey.

"Just got a call from Welder, thought you'd like to know."

"Shoot, Nigel," said Godfrey, pushing the remote's mute button. "You know I'm all agog."

"Welder doesn't tell us much more than we already know, so we are not that far ahead in our understanding of the situation, although it does seem that things are coming to a head – several heads for that matter. Shortly after their girl friends were taken as hostages by Winkle's men, Welder and Norman West, believing them to be at Winkle's Investment Unlimited building, attacked that building, found that neither Winkle nor the girls were there, and somehow managed to blow it up, killing off most of those Englishmen we suspect of criminal activities and a fair bit of Sucksabit. They then went on to try the same thing at the *Blue Member* but were grabbed by men loyal to this Rupert Sweetheart chap, who apparently found one of Winkle's lieutenants unconscious on the roof of the British Trade Office Land Rover. They were told their detention is a precautionary measure, to deter any inclination they might have to interfere in tomorrow's revolution. They have been stripped naked, to discourage any escape attempts. They were taken up to the penthouse suite and held at gun point in Winkle's bedroom, where they were surprised to find Winkle in bed with two Dobermans who seemed to be sampling his private parts. Of course, we know all this from the Colonel's last call, but it's good to have confirmation. Anyway, Welder knows about Rupert Sweetheart but not that he's leading a coup within a coup, since Sweetheart has been out of the room the whole time. We know, don't we, that Sweetheart is in the room just next door, with the Colonel and assorted naked ladies, one of whom is Welder's girlfriend. Welder had just got a call from her on the mobile he keeps hanging around his neck – bad habit that, right next to the heart – and which nobody had taken away from him. She told him, just before his phone went dead, that the Colonel had Sweetheart with a knife at the throat and that Sweetheart's men have them all at gun point."

"Then who has Winkle?" Godfrey asked.

"At this precise moment, sounds like the dogs of war are having a tasting."

"Way to go! Well, Nige, I shan't be losing any sleep over that one."


Rupert Sweetheart and Willy Winkle found themselves face to face. Barely the width of a kukri blade separated them. And the sharp edge of that blade was just one centimeter from sending the Saviour back to his maker for a full brain refit.

"Bingo!" said Winkle, from the safety of a tight little pack of twenty AK-47s held by twenty naked men in various stages of erection.

The Saviour's swallowed curse of *fornicator* had nothing of Winkle's ring of triumph about it. With only five guns behind him and the minds controlling them more fixed on the bottoms before them than a shootout with their mates, and of course a razor sharp kukri at his throat, Rupert Sweetheart came close to admitting that he was hopelessly out-classed. Then he remembered that he had God on his side.

"Lay down your weapons!" he ordered his men inside the bedroom. "Lay them down or turn them on the Satan Winkle and the Satan Colonel and yee shall be saved."

"I think," said Winkle, "they might just prefer a bar of gold and the freedom and opportunity to fuck as they please. And there's a kilo of gold waiting for any of your men outside who cross the threshold right now."

The Saviour and the Colonel suddenly found themselves alone in the doorway as gold lust drew five more of Sucksabit's elite force into Winkle's bedroom. Kim and Souk rushed past them to try to release Welder and Norman, whose wrists had been handcuffed together above an exercise bar set high in the doorframe to the bathroom.

But the Lord moves in strange ways and just as Winkle was contemplating a nice repentance party for the Saviour, fifty Sucksabit men – wearing uniforms – rushed up the stairs and into the penthouse apartment. As luck would have it, they were all Sweetheart converts and, as yet, untouched by the degeneracy of golden promises. They saw their Saviour under threat and they saw the Colonel. And before you could say *Bingo*, the Colonel was stunned under a dozen rifle butts, Winkle was back in bed with the Dobermans, Kim and Souk were forced down into the shag in front of Welder and Norman, the twenty AK-47s inside the room clattered to the floor, fornicators raised themselves to their knees in prayer, and the tables were well and truly turned in the Saviour's favour.

"Bingo!" said the Saviour.

The Colonel lay groggy across the threshold of the bedroom as a seemingly endless supply of Sucksabit elite and three Doberman reinforcements bounded over his prone back. Through the mists of pain, he saw the huge and ugly nakedness of Sweetheart make its way to embrace Pon in a bear hug, ripping the cell-phone from her neck and pushing his erection into its place between her breasts.

The Saviour's fat fingers wrapped themselves into her long hair and pulled her head back. "Tit-job," he yelled as he released one hand from Pon's hair to force her hands onto her breasts, to squeeze them together and make a channel for his swollen member to piston its way up towards her mouth. He pushed her head down and yelled again, obviously eager to make up for ten years lost time, "Tit-job, blow-job."

The Colonel saw Sweetheart trying to force his way into Pon's mouth. He saw her resisting hopelessly, her head held in the giant's grip. He saw other men drop their guns and drop their trousers as they prepared to butt-weld Kim and Souk. He saw Welder and Norman turning in contorted anguish, trying hopelessly to break free from their chains and stop it all, or die trying. He saw Sweetheart again, forcing Pon to the carpet and flipping her over like a doll giving her buttocks a mighty whack, roaring, "Arse-job," and preparing to tear his way between her cheeks. And he saw the kukri lying there in front of his eyes. And he reached for it.

"Repent! Repent! Repent to your Saviour and beg forgiveness." Pon heard Sweetheart's words even as she felt his hot and sticky pole forcing its way into her tiny arse. From the corner of an eye, she saw little Kim about to suffer the same fate and heard Welder yelling in anguish and misery. She fought to free herself but that only made the giant more excited. She felt her face roughly pushed deep into the shag pile, stifling her screams, and she felt the searing pain of the giant's rear entry.

The Colonel's hand closed on the hilt of his kukri. He staggered to his feet and lunged forward on automatic pilot, swinging the long knife and yelling a battle cry to give himself the strength and resolution to reach his prey at the moment the long curved blade would bite into the giant's neck.

The giant, intent on getting a quart into a pint-size bottle, was blissfully unaware of his fate. Not so his canine guardians. They leapt from the relish of Winkle with no battle cry but with the same spring and force and determination as the Colonel. One set of teeth tore into the Colonel's arm, the other went straight for the Colonel's throat.

A gurka's leap and a kukri's swing, once set on its trajectory, cannot be easily deflected. But, neither can two Dobermans coming your way full frontal. Apart from everything else that's nasty about an attack from a pair of jaw-snapping Dobes is that the experience is enough to give anybody pause for thought, but, at the same time, does not allow even a split-second for thinking. The Colonel, of course, realized that survival relied on intuition, on a finely-tuned sense of intuitive combat action built-in over the centuries. There could never be a second chance.

Fortunately, the Colonel had – unique in the immediate environment – retained his clothing and wristwatch. It was into this watch that the first set of teeth bit home. The dog, thinking, in as far as Dobes are known to think at all, to have struck bone, twisted its jaws to wrench off the hand. The watch – one of the Colonel's special combat weapons – exploded, sending its full force outwards into the Doberman's teeth and head, the Colonel's wrist protected by a super-powerful heat shield whose petals blossomed out from the watch a millisecond before the force of the explosion blew the dog's head into little pieces that splattered the Saviour, still intently having his evil way with the lovely backside of the lovely Pon.

Even as the first dog's head was ripped from its body, the Colonel had adjusted the swing of the kukri's blade to meet the neck of the second animal, whose jaws closed on empty air as its head was neatly sliced from its shoulders and flew through the air to hit the giant smack in the face.

The giant rose with a roar, the delights of Pon's bottom placed on temporary hold as his almighty grip found the Colonel's wrist and wrestled the kukri from his fingers. The battered Colonel, meanwhile, had exhausted his hidden reserves of power in the leap to save Pon. He collapsed in a heap among the dogs, the giant and Pon's naked body.

"You killed my friends," yelled the giant, referring to the two Dobermans so recently dispatched and the three taken out at Investment Unlimited. In an instant, the Sucksabit Chief switched the object of his violence from the joy of popping the screaming Pon to the relish of revenge. He nipped the Colonel's kukri from his grip and swung it in an arc that would leave the Colonel's head neatly cloven from balding spot to jaw line.

Fortunately – for even a man like the Colonel needs the occasional injection of luck, although he prefers to think of it as the intervention of good karma – the beheading of the Dobermans, who had not had the time to brief their reinforcements on the situation, left the evil Winkle unguarded.

With so many AK-47s discarded among the shag and so many trousers around ankles, Winkle had only to reach out his hand to grab a weapon, point it vaguely in the direction of Rupert Sweetheart and pull the trigger on the automatic.

Sweetheart, and everybody else in a position to do so, dove for cover as bullets ricocheted wildly around the room. Pon reached for the Colonel and rolled with him under the bed. Winkle was shooting at anybody who had clothes on. The three newly-arrived Dobermans looked at each other quizzically, unsure who was the enemy and unwilling to act without orders. They saw their beloved Saviour falter and drop the kukri as scattered bullets tore through the palms of both hands and into his ankles. They saw the big chief Winkle standing on the bed, shooting with no obvious objectives. They rushed to lick the face of the fallen and bloodied Sweetheart and await his orders. The giant brought his lips close to the ears of the last three canine friends he had left in the world and whistled into their ears. Three canine minds translated the whistles into Doberman. "Get Winkle!" They sprang for the bed.

Discretion being by far the better part of valour, the reviving Colonel decided the space under the bed was as good as any other space in Winkle's room. It provided a certain protective cover from the bullets flying around and had the added attractions under it of Pon and neat rows of gold bars.

Meanwhile, Winkle's future Cabinet had been roused from their sleep or philandering by the noise of automatic fire on the floor above, the occasional thump of a heavy body and girly screams, none of which were unusual in themselves but exceptional in that they went far beyond the normal *Blue Member* pitch and volume to suggest that perhaps all was not quite as it should be upstairs. Some had already dressed and walked up to Winkle's bedroom to see what all the fuss was about. Winkle accidentally cut down the first three before he heard a familiar voice, coming from a familiar large, muscular and naked man who did not quite have the gigantesque features of Rupert Sweetheart but came closer to doing so than anyone else in the room. "Don't shoot boss."

"Biggsie!" Winkle yelled, more than a little delighted to see his muscle finally on the scene. His delight turned to confusion as Biggsie leveled his automatic rifle in Winkle's direction. Biggsie was a better shot than spray-em-all Winkle and he took out the flying Dobermans with a minimum of fire power and no collateral damage. However, the trajectory of three flying Dobermans, especially dead ones, is as difficult to influence as the course of a kukri in full swing, and the dogs posthumously homed in on target, hitting Winkle with the combined force of a Jaguar car traveling at two hundred kilometers an hour hitting a brick wall. Winkle, not wearing a safety net or air bag, was thrown clear off the bed and landed with the dogs on the massive fallen giant and the remains of dogs gone past.

As Winkle scrambled out, Sweetheart hugged his dear departed friends and cried. Years of training. Years of selfless devotion and loyalty; the kind you only get from a Doberman. All gone in a second. Dear friends wiped out by that unrepentant swine Biggsie. As the full alternative Cabinet filed in, their naked floosies bringing up their rear, Sweetheart, bloodied but not defeated, made a lunge for Biggsie and fastened his huge hands on the throat.

Another spectacle, thought the Black Princess, and about time too. Things looked like they were getting serious there for a moment. O why did men have to fight over her all the time? Well, if it had to be, she could understand it, she supposed, men were like that and she had that effect on them. But she didn't like all this gun business. So messy. Better to go at it like the two heavyweights were doing right then. She really wouldn't mind being the prize – and the loser could always take Souk or Pon or Kim or one of those less perfect specimens as consolation. She started to clap. There were no calls of *repent* now, but those still full-bodied enough to smack two palms together joined in. Kim renewed her futile efforts to free her Welder from his chains, Souk seemed more interested in the contest between the giants. After all, she reasoned, for once thinking things almost through, whoever wins the fight will control the scene, and that means controlling her and controlling Norman, so no point tearing at those chains, might as well enjoy the fight. So Souk stood beside the Black Princess and together their breasts and buttocks jiggled in unison to the slow handclap.

Nobody enjoyed the fight more than Winkle – principally because he was not in it. He sat like Nero on the edge of the bed, waiting to give the thumbs down. It was a slow drawn-out affair. Like Sumo wrestlers spending most of their time grabbing their opponents loincloth, except that neither contestant wore anything that might provide a handhold. The rules of the match were also far from certain and there were no prizes except survival. Both men fought sideways on, to limit the effects or opportunities for kicks to the publicly pubic area. The Saviour's hands, bloodied through the palms like a crucified Christ, went for Biggsie's throat, with the simple object of tearing off Biggsie's head. Biggsie, in spite of his huge size, was a shadow compared to the giant, and used his muscle wisely, hammering home blows from his army boots to the bullet wounds in the giant's ankle and foot.

The Cabinet in waiting dragged out of the bedroom two of their fallen martyrs and patched up a third who still had some life left in him. One of the Dobermans was still breathing and after receiving a litre of medicinal brandy, sat up and enjoyed the fight. The rest of the Cabinet stood around in their uniform grey suits that Winkle thought suitable for serious blokes. None had any idea of developments, but all could guess that Sweetheart was out of favour and therefore rooted for Biggsie. Nobody sought to free the suspended figures of Norman West and Welder and nobody thought to question the degree of nudity. This was, after all, Winkle's place. Nobody even noticed the Colonel's absence and nobody saw the Colonel and Pon and the gold under the bed, not even as the fight moved to the center of the room and the Colonel's hand reached out and retrieved the fallen kukri.

Biggsie's boots finally connected with Rupert's public privates and the giant folded, but retained his bloody hold on Biggsie's neck and pulled him down. For some minutes the two men rolled around the floor tearing at each other like women in a love match. Then their roll took them under the bed and all backs bent to follow their progress. The Colonel gave both men a series of sharp kukri jabs in the buttocks to move them out. Neither man dared free a hand to deal with the Colonel, so both men rolled out of range back into the public arena.

"The Colonel," said some bystanders. "The Minister of Defence," said others. "Under the bed. Hiding."

*Hiding*, thought the Colonel indignantly. Fate had granted him a natural defence from the gnashing teeth of enraged dogs and the random firings of a madman with an automatic rifle and he had demonstrated advanced military acumen by staying where he was. But now, the Colonel thought, the game was up and the bed could become a trap, whichever way the fight went. If there were to be more fighting, he preferred to be standing out in the open.

As the Colonel eased his head out from under the bed, he was able to witness the last act in the Sweetheart-Biggsie match. The Saviour's unremitting plan finally paid off and an almighty crack signaled that Biggsie had lost out. Final proof of victory was provided by the giant's hands twisting Biggsie's head around and around until with a fountain of blood, it was lifted from Biggsie's shoulders. Not much point in pushing for extradition of that one, thought the Colonel, as Biggsie's head was bowled the length of Winkle's bedroom, leaving a red track of its bumpy movements across the once proud shag, disappeared out the door into the corridor and was last heard of bumping down the stairs to the floor below.

A roar of victory went up as the giant picked up the headless body and threw it forcefully through Winkle's picture window, which shattered into the night. The Colonel decided not to be hasty. He slowly withdrew back under the bed to let his mind think things through. Winkle leveled his AK-47 towards the self-acclaimed Saviour and pulled the trigger. Nothing happened. He threw away the gun and picked up another. Same result: nothing happened. The giant picked Winkle up by the scrawny neck, flipped him over so he held his feet, wrapped a wire coat-hanger tightly around both ankles and hung him upside down on the exercise bar next to Norman and Welder. The three of them hung like carcasses covering the open doorway of the bathroom, meaning anybody wishing to wash off dicks or fannies had to part the naked trilogy like a beaded curtain before entering the bathroom.

The giant turned to face his audience. Blood ran freely down into the shag from the wounds in his palms and ankles. He held himself with the air of a Saviour just taken down from the cross. "Now, let's put some order into this show. Princess, come here." The Black Princess stood in all her naked pride and glory beside the victor. The giant took her hand.

"On your knees everybody and shed any arms and vestments. Eyes down and hands together in prayer for your immortal souls. Be naked before thy God. The Princess and I shall pass among you and administer repentance. Whosoever shall commune with us, let he or she praise God, for yee are saved and on the morrow will be the chosen ones, the Children of God. These are the words of God, spoken through me, his son."

The Colonel watched from under the bed, sure that the spirits of Kali and Vishnu had entered the giant.

"Take, eat, this is my body, this is my blood." The Saviour stopped before each female in turn, guided her hands down onto his enormous member and helped her take the member into her mouth. Ten years of abstinence had taught the Saviour to control his flow of semen every bit as well as the Colonel had learnt to do during his retreat in Tibet of three years, three months, three days, three hours, three minutes and three seconds. He allowed just a few drops of sacred semen onto each tongue, then moved on. Those men granted repentance by a light touch of the Saviour's hand on their heads drank of the Black Princess, holding out their tongues for her to straddle their mouths briefly and leave behind sanctified droplets of holy cum water. Those that Kali sought for her own, felt the gentle hand of the Saviour on their heads followed by a quick twist of their heads on their necks and a slow and final fall to the carpet.

Thus the acts of clemency and capital punishment proceeded like the liberations and beheadings at the great Hindu festival of Desaru, with apparently random selection of who was blessed to live and who was damned to die. The Colonel looked on with surprise that these young military men and their whores waited so patiently for their fate. But the Saviour spared more than he took, and he spared all of the girls, and he spared all the younger boys, and therein lay the hope to fuel their passivity. The key to heaven lay in the simple factor of age. Those who appeared over the twenty mark, of whom there were no females apart from the sacred Princess, went quietly to meet their maker. The younger girls and boys partook of the communion with their blessed Saviour or his black escort and felt themselves the selected ones, the true immortals, those who on the morrow would be the chosen few who would change the world.

From the exercise bar, Norman and Welder did not feel confident that they would be drinking of Princess Honey. For one thing, they were way beyond the cut-off age. Winkle, from his inverted view of the world, felt sure that he would again be the *piece de resistance* of Rupert Sweetheart's show.

From under the bed, the Colonel could see black shadows entering the hole that the giant had made in the glass through his dramatic disposal of Biggsie's body. Two black shadows wearing only loincloths, their bodies blackened for combat, sheathed kukris tied to their legs. From what seemed a great distance, the Colonel could hear the megaphoned voice of Thhan Chantavong.

"Throw down your weapons. You are surrounded and have no hope of escape. Come out walking slowly and naked. Hold your clothes in bundles above your head. You have thirty minutes. If you come out in that time, you will be taken to the bridge and allowed to cross into Thailand. After thirty minutes, all those remaining in the *Blue Member* will be blown to kingdom come."

The Saviour and Princess Tik-Tok continued their communion. No eyes looked up as the black shadows silently moved along the walls and approached their backs.

Souk and Kim had taken the twins into the middle of the naked and kneeling congregation, using the logic that the best place to hide a book was in a library. Miraculously, the shadow of death passed over them. All were skipped as the Saviour and the Black Princess continued to administer to tongues and snap necks in the name of the Almighty. Eventually, however, as it must for all born of woman, their time of judgment would come.

Saviour Rupert retained the hand of his partner and moved to the front of the congregation. He surveyed the fruits of his work. The taste of the Saviour and his Princess lingered on tongues that moved in silent prayers of thanks for the grace of God that passeth all understanding. The dead lay among the living as if in sleep. The Saviour allowed them another minute on their knees as he picked up a large bottle of Lao beer, nipped its lid off with a twist of his teeth and drank it down. Ah, thought the Saviour, needed some lead in the pencil. This judgment thing is thirsty work. Fun 'though. Only six left to go, not counting the three hanging around. We should have something special for the nine of them. Something the Chosen Children will enjoy and remember. The Saviour's purge was over. Those who survived would be his forever, even after death. There would be no going back to the old ways; no going back to the decadence of Winkle.

"Yee chosen Children of the Almighty. Now lift your eyes and gaze upon your father and your mother." Eyes timorously lifted. From their kneeling position, the giant white Saviour seemed to reach up to Heaven itself and his giant white member seemed to reach its protective shadow over all their heads. He stood with his virgin bride of the Immaculate Conception, right hand reaching down and across and into the virgina of the Black Princess. She stood, dark long legs emphasising her height, firm large breasts jutted forward over her children, right hand holding firmly the base of the Saviour's almighty erection. "You are now our children for as long as yee shall live." The mixture of *you*s and *yee*s fitted strangely into modern Lao and made the Colonel, watching the show from beneath the bed, with Pon pressed into him and trembling, and surrounded by a fortune in gold, wonder if he hadn't perhaps met the giant somewhere before, back in the seventeenth century.

"Souk and Kim and the twins come forward now and kneel before your parents and receive our blessings. And Pon – and you, Colonel – come out from under the bed and join them."

As the four younger girls moved forward and took up their positions of homage under the eye of the Almighty's member, Pon moved to join them.

# 20

---

# Bingo

**Nigel was again on the phone** to Godfrey. "It's getting on for dawn over there. No phone call or anything, but somebody has called my number and left the phone on. Sounds like a battle royal over there. Bursts of gun fire. Vicious dogs. A long drawn out fist fight which came to a sudden end in cheers and, before the battery went dead at that end, what sounded amazingly like a communion service."

"Something in there for everyone," said Godfrey. "I suppose there's nothing we can do?"

"Can't think of anything, Godfrey. Except prepare ourselves for the worst. No word from the Colonel, although he must have called my number – the fact that he never spoke is ominous in itself."

"You mean he's been cut down and the phone just continued to transmit?"

"Can't think of any other possibility. Sorry, Godfrey."

"Not your fault, Nige. Should be a lesson to us 'though. I suppose tomorrow morning we'll wake up to a different world, at least to a different little corner of it. Don't suppose it'll be called the Lao People's Democratic Republic anymore. Any idea what it'll be, Nige?"

"Given all the religious twaddle before the battery went, I would say the Office will be trying to make peace with the Lao Kingdom of Heaven on Earth."


Not surprisingly, since everybody was naked and he, himself, was inverted to boot, Winkle had nothing up his sleeve. It was of little consequence to Winkle whether his end came, if come it must, at the hand of Rupert Sweetheart or by being blasted apart by Chantavong's constabulary, although the latter might be quicker and less painful. He shared his own exercise bar with the figures of Norman West and Welder, both of whom would have happily stabbed him in the back right there and then, had they had free hands and a brace of sharp instruments.

The Colonel had gone to ground under the bed and seemed to be waiting only for Sweetheart's mighty fist to smash its way through the bed and crush the Colonel onto more gold than any of them had ever seen in one place before.

As his head filled with blood, Winkle felt truly hopeless. Then, bleary eyes peering into an inverted world, he saw the two blacked-up figures moving silently and almost invisibly around opposite walls towards Sweetheart's back. He had no idea who the men were, but in the circumstance in which he found himself, any straw of hope was worth clutching.

Winkle's mind was working overtime and upside down. How could he best profit from the situation? He could alert Sweetheart as to the presence of the interlopers. This *might* prompt a struggle that *might* be to his benefit, although it *might* also leave him hanging upside down on a twisted coat hanger, whoever won. Winkle's mind, even in its desperate situation, was busy working out the various devious alternatives as Kaziman Limbu crossed the open doorway of the bathroom, saw the three white men chained up like human sacrifices, and knitted his eyebrows. Just who were the good guys and who were the bad guys? Only Colonel-saab would know. But *where* was Colonel-saab?

Aided by the guiding hands of the Black Princess, the Saviour was passing benediction between each of the five young mouths in front of him. First the tiny twins, who took the giant's Holy Grail together in an embrace of sacred symmetry as the congregation looked on. Then Souk, who the Saviour enjoyed and had decided already would need to be kept on hold for regular private repentances post-revolution. Norman strained at his chains and screamed, "No!" Souk wrapped her hands around those of the Princess, brought the Saviour between her lips and enthusiastically pushed her throat down on the head that had graced fifty young mouths and dipped between many a pair of tight young buttocks that night. Then Pon, who closed her eyes and accepted the drops of semen on her tongue and shed a tear at this public betrayal of the Colonel; truly, there is no love without betrayal, no betrayal without love. Then Kim, saved until the end by the Saviour. Little Kim, not one hair on her body, and breasts that were no more than the slightest shadows around tiny, sweet nipples. Little Kim selected for the final honour of receiving the spirit of her Saviour to the full.

It was Kim who had posed the greatest problem for the Saviour, whether the final release of his entire pending load should flush between those darling, childish lips or finally crack those deliciously tempting buttocks and let the holy spirit flow into and through her. Oh, blessed is he that cometh in the name of the Lord.

"Kim, you do repent as do all here, of a free and knowing spirit. I shall accept your repentance on behalf of Our Lord in Heaven. The biggest repentance issues from the tiniest of spirits. Now take, eat, for this is My spirit, this is My blood and My body." Kim's head was backing away. The Princess was having difficulties in helping her Lord consummate this last repentance. She leant her lips down to Kim's ear and whispered.

"Don't be a brat. You must take what the Saviour offers you and swallow it all. Refuse and you are forever damned. Accept, and

Welder shall drink of me and you both shall be together forever more in the Kingdom of Heaven on Earth."

Welder was screaming to Kim to refuse. Death before dishonour. The Princess held Kim's head firmly and forced her dark thumbs into the sides of her mouth to open a route for the Saviour to enter. And the Saviour held his rod fast and firm and the Saviour did enter the Child of God, that she might enter the Kingdom of God. The resistance this little child posed served only to make the giant even harder and greater, a magnificent member full to the brim with dribbling puss. Sweetheart gave just three great thrusts and a mighty yell of release and Kim's throat filled with the Holy Spirit. Kim, head held in the vice-like grip of a Princess who had really warmed to her role, choked and her mouth overflowed. Finally, the giant backed out, dripping onto the shag. Kim then did the unthinkable.

She spat the Saviour's spirit out onto Winkle's pride and joy, his shag, spat and spat again, and wiped her mouth with the back of her hand. Truly from the mouths of babes, truth will out.

And the whole congregation saw it. The giant looked horrified. He should have taken the back passage after all. Pon also saw and she too spat onto the carpet. From under the bed, the Colonel gave a cheer. The cheer was taken up by Welder and Norman hanging from their chains. Souk, who had swallowed the little she had been given and almost asked for more, now belatedly spat on the carpet. The twins, giggling, joined in this new game and also spat. Then the whole congregation, or those in it left alive, spat and wretched and vomited and tried to rid themselves of the giant's benediction, which had so easily become a curse.

The giant placed his right hand on Kim's head. The Colonel perceived those huge fingers begin their crushing squeeze. A pity, thought the Saviour as he tightened his grip of steel and prepared for the simple, final turn of the head on its neck, she would have to die, and Pon too. All of them for that matter. Better to destroy Sodom than to leave it free to spread its evil ways.

The Colonel flew, kukri slicing through the air in an arc that could only end on target. The Saviour's right hand remained poised on Kim's head just a second, then dropped onto his massive member, poised there, palm up to god, for a brief second and finally dropped to the shag. The giant gazed down in disbelief, holding his handless arm high, blood spurting over the heads of the congregation; the congregation stumbling to its feet and among screams and confusion seeking to distance itself from the looming fight to the death.

"Colonel-saab!" called Kaziman and DB in unison and rushed towards their beloved leader. The giant perceived the new threat, grabbed the Colonel's kukri arm with his good left arm and threw him, kukri and all, into the chests of the approaching gurkas. Enraged beyond even his usual super strength and certainly far beyond reason, he began to use those about him as human clubs. With his one good huge hand, he grabbed Kim by both ankles and swung her into the air, bringing her down with a crack onto the fallen gurkas. Pon was lifted off the ground by her hair and thrown into DB as he tried to emerge from below the scrum. The twins were bowled one after the other into the winded Colonel. Only Kaziman managed to free himself from the tangle as the giant advanced on the human heap, swinging Souk by one leg around his head, building up momentum for a death blow to the Colonel.

Kaziman moved like the speed of light. His kukri flashed in the first rays of dawn. Putting all his force behind the blows, he cut through the chains and wires binding Welder, Norman and Winkle to the exercise bar. Winkle collapsed on his head and Norman and Welder stamped their bare feet into his face as they rushed to help Souk, who was now flying in circles approaching fifty miles an hour, knocking down anybody in her path like ninepins.

As the gurkas' kukris hung in the air, afraid of chopping at the mad giant for fear of hitting the whirling Souk, used by the giant as a human battle axe, it was, surprisingly, Winkle who saved the day. As he was sneaking off behind the congregation, seeking a way out of the carnage of sex and violence, his foot kicked a dropped AK-47. Third time lucky, he thought, as he picked up the weapon and pointed it vaguely in the direction of the giant.

This time the gun fired and a spray of low bullets miraculously missed the spinning Souk and everybody else and tore into Rupert Sweetheart's mid-quarters, mashing the redeemer's rod into mince meat and slowly severing his legs from his massive body. Norman plucked Souk from the air as the giant was literally cut down to size, then crashed to the ground.

The Saviour lay struggling on Calvary, refusing to admit God would forsake him in his noble cause, and waiting for his God, at the very least, to descend in a blaze of glorious light and, if not to make him whole again, to lift him up in glory to Heaven. The Princess Laksami went down on her knees and bent over his torso, her famous black backside raised high in the air. Tears filled her eyes. She looked down to where the miraculous member had been and she sobbed. The Colonel, Kaziman and DB stood, kukris poised, ready to put a final end to the giant. The Princess reached out for the Colonel's right hand and drew the razor sharp kukri across her throat, then slowly sagged onto her giant, face to face, eyes to eyes, blood running from both their mouths and mingling. The Colonel knew they would meet in a future world. He let them go.

Norman had gathered up his Souk and cradled her broken body in his arms. She would never walk unaided again. No more motorbikes, no more discos, no more midnight meetings behind Norman's back. At seventeen, her beauty had drained from her; she was doomed to a life of penance. But Norman would look after her. And he would have her fidelity; no trust required, nobody other than Norman would ever again look at her twice.

The Colonel surveyed the scene of carnage. The living had fled. Dead bodies from earlier gun battles, distorted in painful, untidy deaths, littered the prize shag. Others lay in neat rows where the Saviour had silently dispatched them for being too old. Among the congregation of the dead, the giant and his Black Princess lay with their small flock, in pools of congealing blood.

The living could scarcely believe it was over and they had been spared. They sought reassurance and comfort. Pon ran to hug the Colonel. Kim had survived with only a few bruises. She ran to the comforting arms of Welder, who had never been so proud of his little girl. The twins hugged each other. A silence took hold of the room as the angels passed overhead. A silence interrupted eventually by Winkle, who stood, AK-47 in hand, and said, weakly as if required to make one last pathetic attempt, "We can still win!"

"Come again?" said the Colonel. "Win what? Half your ministers are dead. Your police force seems to have fled, along with your girls. There are over two hundred armed police guarding the exit. And in about five minutes, they'll blow us and this building to smithereens. Unless we get out of it first."

"I said we can still win and we can. We can still defeat the evil communism and place the monarchy again on the throne."

"You might have noticed that the so-called Princess, alias good-time Tik-Tok from the Khop Chai, is on her way to another life. Who do you think will follow the four-year old son of a half-caste whore, deceased?"

"I've known worse leaders," said Winkle. "Anyway, the Americans will step in and help us. The Prince's mother, Laksami, died as a martyr fighting communism, as did all those here. There is video to prove it. Tomorrow, our remaining Sucksabit, none of them Sweetheart's specials, will march in normal Lao clothing to protest the lack of democracy. The Ministers, Prime Minister and President will be out of the way. And long before the army can trundle into town, the Kingdom of Laos will be recognized by the United States and France with huge promises of aid." As he was talking, Winkle, gun held out in front of him, moved around to stand by his bedside table.

"Aren't you forgetting something, Winkle?"

"I don't think so, Colonel." Without looking, Winkle keyed in a five-digit code on the console and the top slid open, revealing an array of switches.

"You are forgetting that the request for your extradition to England has been granted by the internationally recognized Government of the Lao People's Democratic Republic. You can never shoot the three of us, and if you shoot me, Kaziman and DB will take you back or take you out."

233

In the cold light of dawn, the fleeing members of the giant's congregation rushed the exit. Those who had any clothes held them above their heads.

"Slow down. Nothing to fear," said Chantavong. "Let my officers check you for weapons and take your names. Then you can go."

As Chantavong's officers were enjoying frisking the naked refugees for concealed weapons, and as Chantavong began to give the order to bazooka the top floors of the building, Winkle turned a key on the console's deck. Landmines preset in the speed bump across the line of the gateway exploded into the crowds of armed police and naked penitents. Round glass light fixtures on the gate posts burst and clouds of yellow gas swirled among those who had escaped the blast.

In his apartment, Winkle greeted the blast with a quiet, "Bingo!" He knew it was a way of gaining time, not a passage to liberty.

Chantavong was thrown by the blast into the shattered magnificence of the *Blue Member* entrance hall. His underlings rushed to help him onto his feet. He stood there, uniform singed and smoking, for fully one minute, trying to remember who he was and what came next. Then he remembered, and in the swirling yellow smoke of battle, drew himself up to the full stature of his authority, and continued with his interrupted orders.

Winkle remained out of kukri range and was the only one in the apartment with a gun in his hands. For the moment, those around him would not risk their lives or those of their girl friends in efforts to disarm or kill him, and he doubted that the police outside the building would be in any hurry or condition to storm it after seeing and feeling the effects of one bomb blast. Every one knows one bomb can hide another, and Winkle could still blow up each of the floors in his building at the flick of a switch.

The Colonel discreetly pushed Pon away from him, wanting Winkle's potential targets as independent from each other as possible. Winkle followed the movement. Norman West and Welder posed little threat, their arms full of their sobbing true loves. The two men in black grease paint seemed to be still trying to work out what was going on; after all, minutes ago, Winkle had been strung upside down in the bathroom entrance along with the other two. The two gurkas (retired) would look to the Colonel before initiating independent action. The Colonel stood quietly near the bed, thinking he had just to wait. With one hand holding the AK-47 leveled at Pon's nakedness, and the other manipulating a mobile phone he had taken from the console, Winkle spoke his orders quietly into the mouthpiece. "Stamford. Be ready to go." Welder and Norman West looked at each other. So Stamford had survived the Investment Unlimited explosion. Unwittingly, Welder had brought the only one of Winkle's men who knew how to fly a helicopter back to the *BlueMember* on the roof of the British Trade Office Land Rover.

The Colonel was indeed waiting. He did not doubt that any move from him would cause Winkle's finger to tighten on the trigger, and Pon would be the first to die. Kaziman and DB were also waiting, for some signal from the Colonel. It was an uneasy wait. The Colonel expected no rescue from Chantavong's men. If they stormed into the room guns blazing, probably they would shoot everyone in sight – with the possible exception of Winkle, the Colonel thought, remembering the gold bars under the bed. Winkle too appeared to be waiting for something to happen. This more than anything else keyed the Colonel to the highest pitch of readiness for sudden action. Both the Colonel and Winkle waited an opportunity to act. And then it came.

Bazooka shells ripped through the reinforced windows and the brickwork, sending shards of glass and lumps of brick flying through the apartment along with the shock waves of exploding shells and leading the waiting occupants to take whatever cover they could. This was the opportunity Winkle was waiting for and he sprang into action, lunged through the brick dust, gabbed Pon by the neck, fired a wild spray of bullets in the direction of the Colonel, and, dragging Pon behind him as a shield disappeared through the open doorway as more bazooka shells burst inside the room. The Colonel leapt after Winkle, and Kaziman and DB leapt after the Colonel, but even as Winkle escaped from the room, the gurkas were temporarily concussed by an exploding shell. The delay in pursuit was mere seconds, but as the finest fighting force in the world reached the door, an unexpected obstacle delayed them further. The door was locked from the other side. Winkle was nothing if not cunning.

As shells burst around them, Winkle dragged Pon up the last of the grand staircases onto the roof. There she struggled so violently, Winkle hit her hard across the face, almost knocking her from consciousness. He considered leaving her, her usefulness over. Perhaps, he thought, he would fling her from the roof top garden for the Colonel to find broken in the car park and cry over. But, on the other hand, she might still be of some use as a hostage, and there was no getting away from the fact that she was a really good fuck. So he dragged her into the helicopter with him. Stamford opened the throttle, the rotors screamed through the air, and the machine strained to be off.

It took the three gurkas a minute to chop their way through the heavy locked door, run the length of the passage and almost fly up the staircase onto the roof, as the shelling ceased and Chantavong's men came up behind them.

The Colonel broke onto the roof as the helicopter had already lifted itself slowly into the air and was a couple of metres over his head. The Colonel saw Pon struggling, he did not want to risk her life, but he could not let Winkle escape now.

Winkle suddenly reversed his hold and pushed Pon out; towards the Colonel. That should keep him busy for a few seconds more, then *bingo*, the helicopter would be beyond reach. But that was treating the Colonel as any ordinary man.

As Pon fell towards him through the air, the Colonel's actions became a blur. His hands whipped the special cigarette lighter from his shoulder pocket and snapped it in half, priming it for action in three seconds. One half, the smoke screen, he threw back at the pursuing police force, the other, the high-powered explosive, he expertly tossed up through the rotor blades to land on the helicopter roof. Even as he broke Pon's fall and was knocked sprawling, the Colonel rolled with her into a flower bed of tall plants. The helicopter had cleared the building when the exploding cigarette case ripped through its roof, sending small pieces of aircraft and smaller pieces of Stamford and Winkle onto the roof, where the Colonel covered Pon with his body. The larger bits of debris were broadcast around the sky in a spectacular explosion before crashing to the ground below.

The Acting Deputy Foreign Minister, Thhan Gop, reached down a hand to help the Colonel up.

"That's all right, thank you," said the Colonel. "I think I'll just lie here for awhile. Feel a little bit floored, if you know what I mean."

"Excellent job, Colonel. You got them all, and saved the People's Republic. When you have had time to clean up, the President wants to give you a medal. Your friends Norman West and Mr Welder too. And your two gurka colleagues, of course. Along with our own police chief, Thhan Chantavong."

Pon moved beneath the Colonel. Thhanh Gop saw a neat little breast protruding from under the Colonel's protective arm and discretely turned away. "When you're ready, of course. Mustn't hurry a possible concussion." With that, the Acting Deputy moved away and cleared the police from the rooftop.

As a great round sun pierced through the wafts of mingling smoke, cloud and morning mist, Pon looked up with adoration at the Colonel. "You saved my life, Colonel," she said in Lao. "Now you are responsible for it for as long as you live." Pon smiled captivatingly. She paused. She was searching her mind for an English word she had heard a lot lately. Her smile turned to a grin as it came to her. "Bingo!" she said.

The Colonel gulped. This was not in his terms of reference.

The phone rang by Godfrey's bedside. He eagerly reached for it.

"Message from the Colonel, Godfrey. Winkle on his way for extradition when he was blown up trying to escape. Do we want the bits? Rupert Sweetheart and just about everybody on our wanted list also gone to meet their maker. The President will present medals to the Colonel, Welder, Norman West, Kaziman and DB. Welder needs to know urgently if, as Her Majesty's Representative, he can accept. I think so, don't you Godfrey? After all, pretty exceptional circumstances and good PR. The Colonel also wants a four-week visitor's visa for three young ladies. Says details will follow within hours when the Lao Ministry has issued them diplomatic passports. They will accompany the Colonel, West and Welder for a holiday in the UK. One was severely injured in the attempted coup and needs an ambulance at Heathrow and immediate hospital care, followed by immediate marriage to Norman West. Also Welder needs special dispensation to marry the minor he'll be bringing over."

"Good old Colonel," said Godfrey. "I should think he'll get every-thing he wants, right Nige?"

"Well, ye-es. But there is something else."

"You mean the Colonel wants a special-dispensation marriage, too?"

"Don't think so, Godfrey. Least, he doesn't mention it. What he wants is a bit more difficult than that. Wants import clearance for 192 one-kilogramme gold bars, no questions asked."

"Well, I certainly won't be asking any questions. Will you, Nige?"

"There will be no need for questions, Godfrey. I have sent a mes-sage to the Colonel suggesting he encourage Welder to make sen-sible use of the stack of unused diplomatic bags tucked away in the trade office."

"So, that's that then, Nigel."

"Yes. Indeed, Godfrey, that is indeed that. I think we might al-low ourselves a little celebration tomorrow. After the press release. I think a little diplomatic crowing is in order. After all, the FCO, *you and me* Godfrey, black and white, Oxford and Hull, we all handled the affair pretty well considering. And we nipped that nasty little rebellion in the bud. No harm in giving ourselves a pat on the back occasionally. Good job, well done. Good old FCO. No?"

*What the reviewers had to say*
*about the first chronicled adventure of the Colonel.*

If you enjoyed this book, take a look at the Colonel's first published exploits (Times/Marshall Cavendish, October 2004, ISBN 981-232-790-8). Here are some of the reviews of *Red Fox Goose Green* by Robert Fox.

"*Red Fox Goose Green* gives a view of life that is deliciously tongue in cheek…Suspend disbelief and enter a world where nothing is quite what it seems – thank God!" Reverend Rupert R. Shephall, author of *God and the Devil*.

"An example of rococo humour of the Tom Sharpe variety, a mix of traditional English farce, with its innuendo, and the explicit absurdity of black hullabaloo." Tintin Torretto, International Book Reviews, *Forum*.

"Riddled with wry humour, language play, and lewd sexual innuendo, *Red Fox Goose Green* pokes fun at the English tradition of fox hunting. One of the most enjoyable aspects is the army of bizarre characters the Colonel runs into. There's the sex-crazed but God-fearing Vicar, the quiet and effeminate Rodg, the sultry and sexy Filipina Rita, the Rhodesian nudist Wahington…Perhaps the most interesting would be the Colonel himself, whose exploits are reminiscent of Don Quixote, but closer in ways to Peter Weller's Pink Panther – a clueless private detective who's a victim of his own "brilliance"…Robert Fox's writing style is one part Monty Python, two parts Terry Southern…on the rocks with a twist….Fox takes what amounts to jokes you might see illustrated on the wall of the men's room and describes them with intelligent and witty innuendos of the most indirect variety…An enjoyable, lightweight piece of fiction with plenty of delightfully perverted situations…this book is breezy fun for adults with their minds in the gutter."

Chris Otchy, Editor, *Metro Magazine*, September 2005.

"Finite knowledge of the foibles of English village life and the sort of perves that thrive there. A breezy, fun read that makes a change from the usual boring stuff that gets onto the bookshelves of WH Smiths… This book should be banned or awarded the Booker Prize for Humour. Very Adult humour…Thank God we have another Tom Sharpe. Very British, vulgarly delicious in every way."

Al Laurens (author of *Tropical Porridge*).

The author welcomes reader's comments, which will be posted on the website noted below. For information on other books by Robert Fox, excerpts and reviews, together with news of the Colonel's next chronicled exploits, click into:

www.bookfocusasia.com

Printed in the United States
105075LV00008B/77/A